FEELINGS OF FEAR

Recent Titles by Graham Masterton from Severn House

Rook Series

ROOK
THE TERROR
TOOTH AND CLAW
SNOWMAN

Anthologies

FACES OF FEAR
FEELINGS OF FEAR
FORTNIGHT OF FEAR
FLIGHTS OF FEAR

FEELINGS OF FEAR

Graham Masterton

This first world edition published in Great Britain 2000 by
SEVERN HOUSE PUBLISHERS LTD of
9–15 High Street, Sutton, Surrey SM1 1DF.
This first world edition published in the USA 2000 by
SEVERN HOUSE PUBLISHERS INC of
595 Madison Avenue, New York, N.Y. 10022.

British Library Cataloguing in Publication Data

Masterton, Graham, 1946-
   Feelings of fear
   1.   Horror tales, English
   I.   Title
   823.9'14 [F]

   ISBN 0-7278-5594-8

Some stories in this collection previously appeared in other
anthologies in a slightly different form, particularly *Manitou
Man: The Worlds of Graham Masterton*, a limited edition
published by The British Fantasy Society; *Hot Blood: The
Anthology of Erotic Horror* published by Pocket Books; and
White House Horrors published by Daw.

All situations in this publication are fictitious and any
resemblance to living persons is purely coincidental.

Typeset by Palimpsest Book Production Ltd.,
Polmont, Stirlingshire, Scotland.
Printed and bound in Great Britain by
MPG Books Ltd., Bodmin, Cornwall.

Contents

Foreword

F ear comes in many different guises. Many of us are afraid of the dark; some of us can't bear spiders; and there are those who panic in confined spaces.

The list of human anxieties is almost endless, from agoraphobia (fear of open spaces) to zoophobia (an irrational fear of animals).

In one recorded case in the 1940s, a man was so afraid of buttons that he had to wear clothes that fastened entirely with laces.

There is, however, a recognized way to overcome your fears, and that is to face up to them. Psychiatrists call it "systematic behavioral desensitization." So let those spiders crawl up your arms. Climb those darkened stairs, into the unlit attic. Don't hide your head under the bedcovers because you think that a devil is hunched on the other side of the bedroom – get out of bed and see it for what it really is, a bathrobe hanging over the back of a chair.

A patient who was terrified of pigeons was taken every afternoon by his therapist to Trafalgar Square, and after only a few weeks the reality of pigeons became more real to him than his phobic perception of them, and he was cured.

If you don't want to face your fears in the flesh, you can write them down, and try to analyze the way that you feel. Why is it that you're frightened of water? Or infection? Or by the thought of being shut up in a closet? Did something happen to you in your childhood that made you feel afraid? You'll be surprised how therapeutic it is to explain your phobias on paper, and read them back to yourself.

Or not. Because I have to admit that there are some fears that can never be overcome by self-help psychology – or even by rational explanation. There are some fears that have their roots in the darkest recesses of the human mind, and in the darker world of the super-natural.

These fears can never be exorcized, because they're real.

I believe that there are many parallel existences, as these days, many leading scientists do. I believe that somewhere, we are living out subtly different lives. Sometimes these parallel existences overlap our own, and we become uneasily aware of them – through strange coincidences, or oddly familiar names, or dreams, or strong sensations of *déjà-vu*.

Perhaps it's even possible to pass from one existence into another, simply by the choices we make, like a night-train switching from one track to another, or the errant adventurer in the fairy-story who decides to take the left fork toward the enchanted forest. Remember the uneasy travelers in H.P. Lovercraft stories, who took the wrong turning off the main road, and found themselves in a country of misshapen trees, and gambreled houses with sunken roofs, and inbred farmers staring at them suspiciously from barren fields?

You can try to face up to these fears if you like, but you may discover that you are drawn inextricably into a world where everything is recognizable but disturbingly unfamiliar.

You may find that you can never again escape your feelings of fear.

Out of Her Depth

It was a strange afternoon in May. The sky was thundery black but the sun still shone on the lime trees. Anne-Joëlle was walking through the Tuileries gardens, walking quickly because she was afraid that it would soon start to rain again, and she hadn't brought her coat or her umbrella. It was one of those days that had turned sour.

She had gone to an address in the Rue des Blancs Manteaux in response to an advertisement in *Le Figaro* for a job as an English translator. The advertisement had promised "Today, A Whole New World Awaits You!" When she arrived there, however, she found that the address in the advertisement did not exist: the building had been demolished and there was nothing but weeds and rubble. On the way back she had snapped the heel of her shoe on a broken paving-stone. Now she was hurrying through the Tuileries in her bare feet, the sandy-colored mud spattering her ankles. The breeze dropped and the gardens were filled with a terrible stillness. Even the traffic along the Quai des Tuileries seemed oddly muffled.

She suddenly realized that she was alone. There was nobody in the gardens except her. She walked more slowly, feeling the wet grit under her feet. Ahead of her lay a wide puddle which reflected the sky, as black and shiny as a marble gravestone. She walked straight into it, to clean her feet. At first it came up to her ankles, but as she walked further she found that she was wading in it, almost up to her knees. She tried to turn around and go back, but the puddle grew deeper and deeper, until she was up to her waist in it, her gray wool dress sodden and dark.

Anne-Joëlle cried out for help, but there was nobody there: only distant figures walking along the Rue de Rivoli. She took three more

1

steps forward and suddenly she was up to her neck, and then she was out of her depth. The water was freezing and she couldn't swim. Even if anybody had walked into the gardens, they would have seen only a woman's head, in the middle of a puddle, and one arm briefly waving.

Gasping, thrashing, Anne-Joëlle sank under the water, and under the water it was colder and darker than anything she had ever imagined. She sank down and down, her eyes wide open, her hair flowing behind her, still holding on to the last breath that she had taken before she disappeared under the surface. Six or seven bubbles broke on the surface of the puddle in the gardens, and then the water was still again.

Road Kill

He slept, and dreamed . . .

He remembered the blood, and the battles. The extraordinary clanking of swords, like cracked church bells, and the low hair-raising moan of men who were fighting to the death. He remembered how sharpened wooden stakes were thrust into the cringing bodies of weeping men, and how they were hoisted aloft, so that the stakes would slowly penetrate them deeper and deeper, and they would scream and thrash and wave their arms in anguish. He remembered how he had looked up at them, looked them in the eye, and smiled at their pain.

He remembered his own death, like the shutting of an owl's eye; and his own resurrection. The strange confusion of what he had become; and what he was. He remembered walking through the forests in torrential rain. He remembered arriving at a village. He remembered the women he had lusted after, and the blood he had tasted, and the wolves howling in the dark Carpathian mountains.

He remembered days and nights, passing as quickly as a flicker-book. Sun and rain and clouds and thunderstorms. He remembered kisses thick with passion. Breasts running with rivulets of blood. He remembered Brighton in the sunshine, and Warsaw in the fog. He remembered heavy, seductive perfumes, and women's thighs. Carriages, cars, railway-trains, aeroplanes. Conversations, arguments. Telegrams. Telephone calls.

It went on for ever, and sometimes he lost track of time. Sometimes he had written letters to some of his closest friends, only to realize halfway through that they must have been dead for two hundred years. He had hunched over his desk, in such a spasm of grief that he could scarcely breathe. He had stopped writing letters – and, even when he received them, which was very rarely, he didn't open them any more.

But every day a new day dawned, and every night the sun went down; and almost every night he pushed open the lid of his casket and rose from his bed of friable soil to feed on whoever he could find.

One night, early in October, he opened the cellar trap to find that the hallway was empty. All the furniture had gone. The hallstand with its hat-hooks and mirrors; the Chinese umbrella-stand beside the door. Even the carpets had gone. He stepped out on to the bare boards in his black, highly polished shoes, turning around and around as he did so. The pictures had gone. The landscapes of Sibiu and the Somesu Mic. Even the painting of Lucy, with her white, white dress and her white, white face.

He walked from room to room in rising disbelief. The entire house had been stripped. The dining-table and chairs were all gone, the sideboard gone, the velvet curtains taken down. Everything he owned – his chairs, his clocks, his books, his Dresden porcelain – even his clothes – everything was gone.

He couldn't understand it. For the first time in his existence he felt seriously unnerved. For the first time in his life he actually felt *vulnerable*.

It had been so much easier when he had been able to find servants – people who could handle the daytime running of the house. But in the past twenty years, servants had been increasingly difficult to find and even when he *had* found them, they had turned out to be demanding and unreliable and dishonest. As soon as they realized that he was never around during the day, they had taken time off whenever they felt like it, and they had pilfered some of his finest antique silver.

One night, in a pub, he had met a builder, a mournful Welshman called Parry, and he had managed to organize some repairs to the roof and a new front gate, but it had been years since he had been able to find a gardener, and the house was densely surrounded by thistles and plantains and grass that reached as high as the living-room window. He hated unkempt gardens, just as he hated unkempt graveyards, but as time passed he began to grow to enjoy the seclusion. The weeds not only screened him from the world outside, they deterred unwelcome visitors.

But now his seclusion had been devastatingly invaded, and he had lost everything he possessed. All the same, he gave thanks that the cellar trap had remained undetected. It matched the parquet floor so closely that it was almost impossible to detect. He was in constant fear that somebody would find his sleeping body during the hours of daylight – not a priest or any one of those scientists who had once hunted the Undead. Real death, when it came, would not be unwelcome. No, what he was afraid of was injury or mutilation. This part of the city, once fashionable, was now plagued by gangs of youths whose idea of an evening's entertainment was to throw petrol over sleeping tramps and set them alight; or to break their legs with concrete blocks. Death he could accept – but he couldn't bear the thought of living for ever while he was burned or crippled.

He went upstairs. The bedrooms were empty, too. He touched the shadowy mark on the wall where a portrait of Mina had hung. Then he threw back his head and let out a roar of rage that made the windows shake in their sashes, and started the neighborhood's dogs barking.

Shortly after eleven o'clock, he found a girl standing in a bus shelter, smoking a cigarette and chewing gum at the same time. She couldn't have been older than sixteen or seventeen and she still had that post-pubescent plumpness that he particularly relished. She had long blonde hair and she was wearing a black leather jacket and a short red dress.

He crossed the street. It was raining – a fine, prickling rain – and the road-surface reflected the streetlights and the shop-windows like the water in a dark harbor. He approached the girl directly and stood looking at her, his hand drawn up to his overcoat collar.

"You'll remember me the next time you see me, won't you, mate?" she challenged him.

"I'm sorry," he said. "You remind me so much of somebody I used to know."

"Oh, that's original. Next thing you'll be asking me if I come here often."

"I'm – I'm looking for some company, that's all," he told her. Even after all these years, he still found it went against the grain to approach women so bluntly.

"I don't know, mate. I've got to be home by twelve or my mum'll go spare."

"A quick drink, maybe?"

"I don't know. I don't want to miss my bus."

"I have plenty of money. We could have a good time." Inside, his sensibilities winced at what he was having to say.

The girl looked him up and down, still smoking, still chewing. "You look like a big strong bloke," she suggested. "We could always do it here. So long as you've got a johnny."

He looked around. The street was deserted, although an occasional car came past, its tires sizzling on the wet tarmac. "Well . . ." he said, uncertainly. "I was thinking of somewhere a little less public."

"It's up to you," she said. "My bus'll be here in five minutes."

He was just about to refuse her offer and turn away when she flicked her hair with her hand, revealing the left side of her neck. It was radiantly white, so white that he could see the blueness of her veins. He couldn't take his eyes off it.

"All right," he said, tightly. "We'll do it here."

"Twenty quid," she demanded, holding out her hand.

He opened his thin black wallet and gave her two ten pound notes. She took a last drag on her cigarette, flicked it into the street, and then she hoisted up her dress to her waist and tugged down her white Marks & Spencer panties. Somewhere in his mind he briefly glimpsed Lucy's voluminous petticoats, the finest white cotton trimmed with Nottingham lace, and the way in which she had so demurely clasped her thighs tightly together.

He kissed the girl on the forehead, breathing in the smell of cigarette smoke and shampoo. He kissed her eyelids and her cheeks. Then he tried to kiss her lips but she slapped him away. "What are you trying to do? Pinch my gum? I thought we were supposed to be having it off, not kissing."

He grasped her shoulders and stared directly into her eyes. He could tell by the expression on her face that she had suddenly begun to realize that this wasn't going to be one of her usual encounters, twenty quid for a quick one. "What?" she asked him. "What is it?"

"One kiss," he said. "Then no more. I promise."

"I don't like kissing. It gives you germs."

"This kiss you will enjoy more than any other kiss you have ever had."

"No, I don't want to." She reached down and tried to tug her panties back up.

"You're going to go back on our bargain?" he asked her.

"I told you. I don't like kissing. Not men like you. I only kiss blokes I'm in love with."

"Yet you don't mind having sex with me, here, in the street, somebody you don't even know?"

"That's different."

He let go of her, and lowered his arms. "Yes," he said, rather ruefully. "That's different. But there was a time when it was the greatest prize that a man could ever win from a woman."

She laughed, a silly little Minnie Mouse laugh. That was when he gripped her hair and hit her head against the back of the bus shelter, as hard as he could. The glass frame holding the timetable was smashed, and the timetable itself was splattered in blood.

As she sagged, he held her up to prevent her from dropping to the ground. Then he looked around again to make sure that the street was still empty. He hoisted her up, and carried her around the bus shelter and into the bushes behind it. He found himself half-climbing, half-sliding down a steep slope strewn with discarded newspapers and empty lager cans and plastic milk-crates. The girl lolled in his arms, her head hanging back, her eyes closed, but he could tell by the bubbles of froth that were coming from her mouth that she wasn't dead.

He took her down into a damp, dark gully, smelling of leaf-mould. He laid her down, and with shaking hands he unzipped her jacket and wrestled it off her. Then he tore open her dress, exposing her left breast. He knelt astride her, lowered his head, and with an audible crunch he sank his teeth into her neck, severing her carotid artery.

The first spurt went right over his shoulder, spattering his coat. The second hit his cheek and soaked his collar. But he opened his mouth wide, and he caught the next spurt directly on his tongue, and swallowed, and went on swallowing, with a choking, cackling sound, while the girl's heart obligingly pumped her blood directly down his throat.

7

*   *   *

Whether he was driven by rage for his lost possessions, or by disgust for the world in which he now found himself, or by sheer greed, he went on an orgy of blood-feeding that night. He slid into a suburban bedroom and drank a young wife dry while her husband slept beside her. He found a young homeless boy under a railway arch and left him white-faced and lifeless in his cardboard bash, staring up at the sodium-tainted sky. He hated the color of that sky, and he longed for the days when nights had been black instead of orange.

By the end of the night, he had left nine people dead. He was so gorged with blood that his stomach was swollen, and he had to stop in the doorway of Boots and vomit some of it up, adding to the splatter of regurgitated curry that was already there.

He returned to his empty house. He would have liked to have stayed up longer, walking around the rooms, but the sun was already edging its way over the garden fence, and the frost was glittering like caster sugar. He raised the cellar trap and disappeared below. He slept, and he dreamed . . .

He dreamed of battles, and the screaming of mutilated men. He dreamed of mountains, and forests as dark as nightmares. He thought he was back in his castle, but his castle was collapsing all around him. Chunks of stone fell from the battlements. Towers collapsed. Whole curtain-walls came roaring down, like landslides.

The earth shook, but he was so bloated with blood that he barely stirred. He whispered only one word, "*Lucy . . .*"

It took the best part of the day to demolish the house. The wrecking-ball swung and clumped and reduced the walls to rubble and toppled the tall Edwardian chimneys. By four o'clock the demolition crew were working by floodlight. A bulldozer ripped up the overgrown garden and roughly levelled the hardcore, and then a road-roller crushed the site completely flat.

During the next week, trucks trundled over the site, tipping tonnes of sand to form a sub-base, followed by even more tonnes of hydraulic cement concrete. This was followed by a thick layer of bituminous road pavement, and finally a top wearing course of hot asphalt.

Deep beneath the ground, he continued to sleep, unaware of his entombment. But he had digested most of his feast, and his sleep was twitchier now, and his eyes started to flicker.

The new link road between Leeds and Roundhay was finished in the middle of January, a week ahead of schedule. In the same week, his property was sold at auction in Dewsbury, and fetched well over £780,000. A Victorian portrait of a white-faced woman in a white dress was particularly admired, and later featured on the BBC's *Antiques Road Show*. Among other interesting items was a Chippendale secretaire. The new owner was an antiques dealer called Abrahams. When he looked through the drawers, he found scores of unopened letters, some from France, many from Romania and Poland, and some local. Some were dated as far back as 1926. Among the more recent correspondence were seven letters from the county council warning the occupier of a compulsory purchase order, so that a new road could be built to ease traffic congestion and eliminate an accident black spot.

He lay in his casket, wide awake now and ragingly hungry – unable to move, unable to rise, unable to die. He had screamed, but there was no point at all in screaming. All he could do was to wait in claustrophobic darkness for the traffic and the weather and the passing centuries to wear the road away.

Lolicia

He came home from the studio just before eleven in the evening, his chinos crumpled, his hair sticking up, and the back of his shirt stained with sweat. He slung his coat over the back of the living-room couch, came straight into the kitchen, kissed Susan on the cheek and then went straight to the freezer and took out a frosted bottle of Stolichnaya.

He poured himself a large glass and drank it as if it were water. Then he poured himself another, and drank half of that, too.

"Jesus, you don't know what a day I've had."

"Oh, yes?" Susan banged the pot sharply on the hob and he should have taken his cue from that.

"We didn't finish shooting the last scene till gone nine."

"You could have called," said Susan. "The clam sauce is ruined."

"Hey, I'm sorry. I had no idea it was going to go on so damned long. That scene when the girl gets strangled—"

"You still could have called."

"Listen, I've said I'm sorry. If the meal's ruined I'll take you out to eat. I'll take you anyplace you want to go."

"Jeff, I don't want to go out to eat. I've spent most of the afternoon making all of this. It was supposed to be special. I've made you *frittata*. I've made you *pinzimonio* salad. What do you want me to do with it? Throw it all away?"

Jeff came over and peered into the saucepan. "Looks all right to me. Kind of gummy, maybe. But so what. We could call it *spaghettini alla gummy vongole.*"

"That's it!" she said. She picked up the pan and turned it upside-down over the sink.

11

"For Christ's sake, Susan, what are you doing? Listen, that was a joke, okay? I'm sorry I'm late and I'm sorry I made a joke, but let's forget it, okay? Let's just have something to eat, okay? I could eat a horse. I could even eat a gummy *spaghettini*."

She dropped the pan with a clatter, and turned on him. "You have been late every single night for the past three months – that's when you've bothered to come home at all. Ever since you started this series I haven't seen you from one week's end to the next. You keep telling me you've come alive. 'Oh, Susan, I feel twenty years younger.' Haven't you thought for one minute what it's been doing to me? Haven't you thought for one minute how *boring* it's been?"

"Susan, listen sweetheart, apart from post-production the series is finished. It's wrapped. We can go away for a couple of weeks. Up to Napa, maybe. We'll visit your mother, we'll drink some wine. Well, maybe we'd better drink some wine *before* we visit your mother."

Susan pulled off her butcher's apron and threw it across the floor. "Jeff, I don't find you funny any more. You've turned into somebody I don't even know and I don't even like. Even when I've seen you, you've talked about nothing else but *Creatures* this and *Creatures* that and say, 'honey, I'm so worried about *Creatures*.' You're selfish and obsessive and totally one-dimensional."

Maybe it was sheer exhaustion after sixteen solid hours of shooting the last episode of *Creatures*. Maybe it was too much vodka on an empty stomach. Maybe it was simply the let-down of leaving the studio to whistles and cheers and coming back to someone who had no idea what he had managed to achieve. Whatever it was, he slapped her.

There was an extraordinary moment in which he felt as if he had stepped through a mirror. Out of one life and into another.

He said, "Shit, Susan. I'm sorry. I'm really sorry."

"You—" she began, and she tried to slap him back, but he dropped his martini glass and caught hold of her wrists. The glass shattered on the kitchen tiles. She tried to slap him again, but when she couldn't, she wrenched herself free from him and went straight to the front door.

He followed her, trying to catch her arm. "Susan! I'm sorry! I lost my temper, that's all! It's not your fault!"

She snatched her keys from the hook by the door. Her cheek was flaming red and her eyes were filled with tears.

"Listen, I'm really sorry, sweetheart! Don't go! You can come back here and hit me back, OK? I'm sorry!"

"You *bastard*," she said, with a terrible vehemence.

"Susan, for Christ's sake, don't go out! You shouldn't drive while you're feeling like this!"

"What, are you worried I might kill myself?"

She went out of the door and slammed it behind her. Again he followed her, but she was already halfway down the steps in front of the house.

"Susan! Listen to me!"

But she didn't listen. She climbed into her little black Honda sports car and backed down the driveway. By the time Jeff reached the street she had sped off out of sight.

Across the street, his neighbor, Bill Arnold, was standing in his bathrobe in his open doorway, staring at him.

"What the fuck are you looking at?" Jeff shouted at him.

He went inside and poured himself another large vodka. He looked around the kitchen – at the carefully prepared salad, at the freshly fried *spaghetti frittata*, at the beans still simmering on the stove. He smashed his fist down on the counter and the lid toppled off Susan's favorite cookie-jar – the one in the shape of W.C. Fields – and broke.

How the hell could he have hit her? He stared at his offending hand and he couldn't believe it.

They had argued before, frequently, and sometimes their arguments had led to slammed doors and nights on the couch. But he had never touched her, not once. If only he could run those few seconds back, and cut them out. If only they could be sitting down at the table, drinking a celebratory glass of Orvieto and eating the dinner that she had spent so much time preparing. He lifted the saucepan out of the sink and flushed away the splattered clam sauce. He felt so upset so that his hands were shaking.

He went through to the living-room and picked up the phone. It rang for a long time before anybody answered. "Hazel? Listen, this is Jeff.

I'm sorry to call you so late. No, nothing like that. Susan and me have just had a bit of a bust-up. Well, yes. It was all my fault. I was tired, I lost my temper. Well, look, I expect she'll come over to your place. About five minutes ago. Sure. But when she gets there, can you ask her to call me? Can you do that, please? And can you tell her how sorry I am? Well, I will, for sure, but it might help if she hears it from you, too."

Hazel was Susan's sister. She lived a half-hour away in Sherman Oaks. She and Susan had always been especially close, right to the point of choosing the same color dress to wear on the same day and finishing each other's sentences.

He put down the phone. Beside it stood a large framed photograph of himself and Susan that had been taken last summer on the beach at Cancun, in Mexico. Susan had her arms around his waist and she was laughing. Look at her, he thought. How could I have hit her?

They say that people always fall in love with themselves, and that was certainly true of Jeff and Susan. They were both tall, both very slim, and they had a chiseled look about their faces which occasionally led people to think that they were brother and sister. But while Jeff was dark-haired and brown-eyed, Susan had a mass of soft blonde curls and eyes as green as crushed emeralds. In the photograph she was wearing a peacock-blue one-piece swimsuit which showed off her figure – full-breasted, slim-waisted, with long, long legs.

He had been captivated by Susan the day he had first met her, when she was an extra in some surfing movie and he was assistant script-editor. Well, more like assistant to the assistant script-editor's assistant. But Susan had thought that he was somebody important, and so she had agreed to go out with him. He had practically emptied his bank account taking her to The Palm in West Hollywood. They had made love the same night; and again the next day; and by the time Susan realized that he wasn't much more than a glorified gofer, she liked him too much to care.

He sat alone with his head in his hands and thought that he should have remembered those days, when love was more important than ambition.

She didn't go to see Hazel. Instead she went to the Café del Rey on

Admiralty Way in Venice Beach for no other reason except that she and Jeff used to go there almost every week when they were first dating, and there was a bar where singles could eat or drink alone. She ordered a Chardonnay spritzer and sat looking out at the lights of the marina. She didn't know if her cheek was still red but she untied her hair and drew it across her face so that nobody could see.

The barman had a huge black quiff and looked like Frankie Avalon from one of those 1950s beach-party movies. "You want to eat?" he asked her. "We have ikura caviare with spicy miso vinaigrette. Or maybe you'd care for the black pepper hamachi carpaccio."

Susan shook her head. "I've had enough of food for one lifetime," she said.

"You look upset if you don't mind my saying so."

"Do I? I think my marriage just finished and I don't really know why."

"Come on. You know what Scarlett O'Hara said."

Susan pushed her glass across the counter. She felt bruised and miserable and she didn't really want to get drunk but she didn't know what else to do. In the corner a woman cellist with long swinging hair was playing an absurdly mournful version of "Yesterday". She felt like crying but she knew that if she started she wouldn't be able to stop, and what could be more embarrassing than a woman sitting on her own with a flaming red cheek and tears pouring into her drink?

The barman passed over her spritzer and said, "There you go. It's on the house."

She had taken only one sip before she became aware that a man was standing close to her elbow. He was huge, the size of a wall, and he was darkly suntanned, with improbably blond hair. He was wearing a white linen suit and a bright turquoise shirt.

"You looking for some company, ma'am?" he asked her.

Susan shook her head. "I'm sorry. Not right now."

"Well, that sure is a pity. Mr Amberson wants to know if you'd like to join him tonight."

"What?" asked Susan. She turned around on her stool. There – on the opposite side of the restaurant, flanked by two more enormous bodyguards – sat a short, stocky man in a wildly patterned Hawaiian shirt. His head was rather too large for his body, but he was handsome in a raddled, worn-out way, with devilish eyebrows and an equally devilish grin. He raised his glass to her and called out, "*Salut!*"

"Is that Jack Amberson the movie actor?" she asked.

"You'd better believe it, ma'am. And he'd really like to make your acquaintance. In fact, he insists."

"I don't know," said Susan. "I haven't had a good day. Will you tell him I'm very flattered, but no thanks."

The man bit his lip. "Listen, I can't tell him that."

"What do you mean, you can't tell him that?"

"Mr Amberson isn't the kind of man who takes no thanks for an answer, ma'am. Especially when it comes to his favorite."

"His favorite?"

"Tall blondes, ma'am. Just like you. Especially when they're taller than him."

"Well, I'm sorry," said Susan. She glanced back toward Jack Amberson's table. He was beckoning to her and mouthing the words, "C'mon over here."

She hesitated. It was so strange, seeing him sitting there in the flesh. She had seen him in so many movies that she felt as if she knew him already. He always played wolfish men with bad reputations, although he usually managed to convey a sense of little-boyish vulnerability, too. He mouthed "C'mon, come here," for a second time, and she thought to herself: why not? We're in a public restaurant, what harm can it do? Think of the story I'll have to tell Hazel tomorrow. She's absolutely crazy about Jack Amberson.

And besides, at least it shows that some men appreciate me for what I am.

She said, "All right, then," and slipped off her barstool. The big blond bodyguard led her by the elbow to Jack Amberson's table. He stood up, and grinned, and kissed her on the wrist. For a man who played laborers and cowhands and oil-rig workers, his hand was unexpectedly soft.

"Why don't you let me buy you a drink?" he asked her. "They do great frozen daiquiris here. Or maybe a tequila slammer?"

"A glass of wine will do fine, thanks."

Jack clapped his hands and called, "Champagne, please, barkeep! A bottle of your Dom Perignon, and some of those Parmesan nibbles!"

He turned conspiratorially to Susan and said, "I can't resist their Parmesan nibbles. I mean that's the way I'd like to die. Making love to a tall blonde woman and choking on a Parmesan nibble."

"Your friend here said you had a thing for tall blonde women."

Jack Amberson frowned at her as if he didn't understand what she meant. "My *friend*?" Then suddenly he turned to the big blond bodyguard and laughed. "Christopher isn't my *friend*! He's simply a hired lump of meat. Anyhow, I don't have any friends. Only enemies and lovers."

"But I'm neither of those things. Why did you want to talk to me?"

"In the hope that you might become one before you become the other."

"Well, you obviously have a pretty high opinion of yourself. I'm already married."

"I know you are. You're too badly dressed to be single."

"Thanks for the compliment. You sure know how to make a woman feel on top of the world."

Jack Amberson laid his hand on top of hers, and when she tried to draw it away he pressed it harder against the tablecloth so that she couldn't. His eyes looked like two gray mismatched stones, and he had the screen actor's trick of never blinking.

"You're also too beautiful to be single. Women as beautiful as you never stay unmarried for long. The men in their lives think that if they're married, that'll keep the wolf-pack at bay. In my experience, of course, that almost never happens. A beautiful woman is still a beautiful woman, even if she's wearing ten wedding-bands and a chastity belt with a Bramah lock."

Their champagne arrived, along with a large glass dish of Parmesan pastries. Jack Amberson crammed a huge handful into his mouth and sat smiling and munching and staring at Susan and never once blinking his eyes.

"I'll give you a toast," he said, when he had swallowed the last of the pastries. He raised his glass and clinked it with hers. "Here's to simultaneous orgasm."

She didn't know exactly when she decided to sleep with him. But after

17

he had turned the Dom Perignon bottle upside-down in the ice-bucket he said, "I've got plenty more champagne at home," and she knew that she was going to go back with him, and what it would mean if she did.

They left the restaurant shortly after one o'clock, surrounded by a human barricade. Two girls screamed and called out, "Jack! We love you!" but when they tried to approach him they were pushed forcefully away. A glossy black Lincoln slid up to the curb and they climbed inside, where it smelled of leather upholstery and very expensive perfume. Then the door was closed and they were swept behind darkly tinted windows into the night.

"What kind of a guy is your husband?" asked Jack.

"Jeff? He's a TV producer. Very hard-working. *Too* hard-working."

"Is that why he slapped you?"

Susan blushed and said, "How did you know that?"

"A beautiful married blonde sits alone in a bar at eleven o'clock at night with a red mark on her cheek and her mascara all blotchy – what conclusion do you draw?"

Susan hesitated for a moment. Then she said, "He was late home. His supper was ruined. I'd been working all afternoon to make it special."

"You should humiliate him. A guy like that needs to be humiliated."

"I don't want to humiliate him. I just want him to pay me more attention. Everything centers around *him*, and what he's doing. I could have been a good actress if he'd let me. Tony Scott said I was one of the most promising young personalities he'd seen for years."

Jack laid his hand on her knee. "And I agree with him. And that's all the more reason that you should make your husband feel small. Do you know what you should do?"

"Tell me."

"You should come to bed with me, and then, when you go back home, you should tell this Jeff of yours exactly what happened, in every microscopic detail. Tell him how big my schlong is. Tell him how you screamed when you came."

She said nothing. She had already decided that she wanted to go bed with him. But she knew that she would never tell anybody, ever – not even Hazel. She wasn't out to make Jeff feel bad. She was looking for reassurance that other men found her sexy and arousing and interesting, and that six years of marriage hadn't washed all of her personality out of her, like ink out of a handkerchief.

They turned into a steeply-sloping driveway in Bel Air. Automatic wrought-iron gates opened, and they drove inside. On top of the hill ahead of them, surrounded by flowering shrubs, stood a huge white Italianate house with a red-tiled roof. Lights shone from every window.

"Welcome to my humble abode," said Jack, and gave Susan's thigh the lightest of strokes.

He was waiting for her on the bed when she came out of the bathroom. He was wearing nothing but black silk pajama bottoms and a black bandana. He was watching one of his own movies on a television the size of a small building.

"I switched it on and there it was," he told her. "*The Cloud Riders.* It must be an omen."

She was wrapped in his black silk bathrobe. She approached the bed and knelt beside him, watching him. The bedroom was all white: white carpets, white drapes, white lilies in white vases on top of white-painted tables. A large original oil-painting hung on the wall opposite the bed – a white-skinned girl with bone-white hair. Her thighs were wide apart and the only color in the room was a single brushstroke of fuchsia pink.

Jack switched off the television's sound but not its picture. On the screen he was riding a horse across the spine of a mountain-range in Montana. On the bed he reached up with his left hand and unfastened the loose silk tie around Susan's waist. Then he sat up and slid the robe off her shoulders, so that she was completely naked.

Her skin was almost as pale as the girl in the painting, apart from the blue tracery of veins in her breasts and her nipples the color of fallen rose-petals in a rainswept garden. Her blonde curls shone in the lamplight.

Jack pulled her down beside him and kissed her. It had been so long since she had been kissed by another man that she found it deeply disturbing, but electrifying, too, and she could feel that she had almost immediately become wet. Jack turned her on to her back and knelt beside her, taking his erect penis out of his black silk pajamas. It was enormous, much bigger than Jeff's, with a swollen purplish head and a hole that gaped at her like a landed trout.

He took his penis in his hand and massaged it against her nipples, around and around, until they stiffened. Then he guided it into her armpits, and around her shoulders and her neck. Teasingly, he ran it across her lips, so quickly that she hardly had time to lick it. But then he lifted himself up higher, so that he was straddling her. He opened her mouth with both thumbs and forced his penis down her throat, so that she couldn't help gagging.

"How do you like that?" he said, looking down at her triumphantly. "Now you can tell Jeff that you almost choked on Jack Amberson's dick."

For some reason, his roughness excited her even more. When he tried to take his penis out of her mouth, she took hold of it and pushed it even further down her throat, even though it was so huge and hard that it almost suffocated her. When he tried to take it out, she sank her teeth into it, until he yelped in pain.

He grew even more aroused. He knelt over her face and rammed himself into her mouth, again and again. She took hold of his black silk pajamas and tore them open, tore them down to the knees. Then she gave his penis one last ferocious suck and started to bite and suck at his balls, almost as if she were determined to wrench them off. She bit his thighs and clawed with her fingernails at the cheeks of his ass, until they bled. Then she thrust two sharp index fingers into his anus.

"Goddamnit!" he shouted, and so she pushed her fingers in even harder.

He swore at her. He called her everything that he could think of. Cunt, whore, bitch. They were both out of control. He was enraged because no woman had ever dared to suck him and scratch him like that. She was frustrated and furious and drunk. Not only that, she was actually in bed with Jack Amberson the movie star but she wanted to show him that she was only there because she wanted to be, and not because he had decided he had to have her.

He forced her on to her back, spread her legs, and thrust himself into her. She kept on struggling and kicking and scratching, but although he was short he was very fit and very strong. He rammed into her again and again, cursing her with every stroke. She panted with excitement. She had never known a cock so big. She thought that she had never met a man she despised so much. She gripped his hair and pulled it so hard that some of it came out by the roots.

It was then that he lost his temper completely. But when Jack was really angry, he didn't shout and he never swore. His eyes unfocused and a terrible calm came over him.

He drew himself out of her and climbed off the bed, his penis still erect. He walked across to the mirror over the dressing-table and spent over a minute examining his scalp, patting it to make sure that he could cover up the bald patch that she had given him. Even then she didn't fully understand what she had done. She didn't realize that he was a star. The physical pain of having his hair torn out was nothing. What he cared about was his looks.

She lay back watching him. Slowly she drew the sheet up over herself. She could sense his fury and it began to frighten her.

"So that's what you like?" he asked her. His voice sounded like fingernails scratching a brick. "You like living on the edge."

"I'm sorry. I didn't mean to hurt you."

"Oh, you didn't hurt me. Nobody can hurt Jack Amberson, sweetheart. He just likes to know what game he's playing."

He walked over to the closet and opened it up. Inside were rows and rows of coats, Armani and Versace and Commes des Garcons, all arranged according to shade. But Jack pulled out a drawer below the coats and took out a black nylon cord and a black plastic bag.

He came back to the bed holding up the cord in one hand and the bag in the other. There was an expression on his face which made Susan shiver. Still calm, still slightly unfocused, as if he were looking right through her.

"I think I've made a mistake," she said.

"Whoa, no, darling. I don't think so. The fun has only just begun."

"Please, I'm sorry I hurt you. I was angry, that's all. I'm not used to drinking so much champagne."

But Jack leaned right over and said to her, "When you came into this bedroom, you had a choice. You could have been sweet. You could

21

have been pliant. You could have let me take you to the moon. But you chose something else, didn't you? You chose to make a little war out of it. Getting your revenge on men, were you? Or was it something else?"

"I'm leaving," said Susan, decisively, and climbed out of bed.

Jack immediately seized hold of her left arm and twisted it behind her back. Then he caught hold of her right arm, too. He pushed her face-down on the bed and clambered on top of her, pinning her down with his knee.

"Get off me!" she demanded, in a breathy scream.

"Whoa, no. You made your choice. This is what you wanted and this is what you're going to get."

With that, he lashed her wrists together with the black nylon cord, quickly and expertly, like a yachtsman. Then he took the black vinyl bag and pulled it over her head, twisting it into a knot around her neck. The cord was painfully tight. It bit into her skin and forced her arms so far back behind her that her shoulders ached. Inside the bag she was totally blind and it took only three or four panicky breaths before the vinyl was wet with moisture and clinging to her face.

"Take this off me! *Jack!* Take this off me! I can't breathe!"

"Your rules, sweetheart," said Jack. He kept her prone on the bed while he dragged open her thighs. She tried to wriggle, and let out a series of muffled shouts, but with every shout the vinyl bag was sucked closer to her face, until Jack could actually see her eyes and her nose and her mouth as she desperately tried to breathe.

"You're going to love this, baby," he told her. He pulled apart the cheeks of her bottom. Then he leaned forward and pushed himself into her, hurting her as much as he could, really hurting her.

The vinyl bag crackled rhythmically against her face as she sweated and struggled and fought for air. On top of her, his expression cold and calm, Jack Amberson quietly grunted in his throat as he tried to force himself into her further and further. It took him almost a minute before he was completely buried, and his black hairy balls hung between her cheeks like exotic but uneatable fruits.

Susan felt as if the whole world were collapsing all around her. She tried to suck in air but all she could suck in was wet vinyl. She could feel Jack's penis inside her, and the pain was intense. But she began rhythmically to push her hips down, and to squeeze her muscles. She was trying to survive. The quicker Jack reached a climax, the sooner he would take the bag off her head.

She pushed faster and faster. She tried not to breathe too deeply, but every now and then she gasped for oxygen, and the bag stuck to her face like a second skin. She felt that she was suffocating but at the same time the sexual feeling was overwhelming.

Jack shouted out, "Oh, shit!" and ejaculated deep inside her. Susan climaxed, too – an orgasm like nothing that she had ever experienced. It effervesced inside her, from her feet upward, and then a dark explosive force turned her whole existence inside out.

She thought for one moment that she had fallen out of the universe. She thought that she was someplace else, where the skies were eternally black, and the stars never shone.

Jack climbed unsteadily off the bed. He staggered two or three steps sideways, and then he sat down next to Susan and started to rip off the vinyl bag.

Her blonde curls were stuck together with sweat. Her lips were turquoise. Jack lifted one of her eyelids with his thumb and her eyes stared at nothing at all.

"Susan?" he said. He shook her, but her head lolled against the pillow like a puppet's. "Susan? Come on, Susan, don't start fucking me around here, Susan."

He shook her, and then he slapped her cheek, in exactly the same place that Jeff had slapped her. "Susan, this isn't fucking funny, all right?" He slapped her again, and then again.

He untied the black nylon rope that bound her wrists, and turned her over so that she was lying on her back. He pressed his ear against her bare breast but he couldn't hear her heart beating. He touched his fingertips against her carotid artery, the way that the Los Angeles Police Department advisor had shown him in *Deadly Heart*.

He was still sitting beside her when his Chinese manservant Heng came into the bedroom to ask him if he wanted his usual nightcap. There was blood between her legs, and he had dipped his finger in it and daubed a cross on his forehead.

"She's dead," said Jack. "She's fucking dead, and I don't even know who she is."

The trial lasted five weeks and two days. Jeff sat in the public gallery every single day and every single day was another step toward Calvary. He didn't shave. He barely washed. He sat through thirty-one hours of hearings with his head bowed, folding and unfolding the same piece of paper. It was a message from Susan: Don't forget the Roach Motel. The last message she had ever sent him.

They check in he thought. *But they don't check out.*

Jack Amberson was unanimously acquitted of manslaughter. The jury had been persuaded by his attorney that Mrs Susan Pearce had gone to his house voluntarily and enthusiastically taken part in a sexual act which she must have known to carry a high element of risk.

"Restricting breathing during intercourse is known to intensify sexual feelings," said Jack Amberson's principal defense counsel. "Mrs Pearce enjoyed those intensified feelings with Mr Amberson – of that, there is no doubt. But regrettably, she paid the price. My client deeply regrets what happened, but his conscience is clear."

Outside, on the courtroom steps, Jeff saw Jack Amberson surrounded by newspaper reporters and TV cameras. He elbowed his way through the crowd and snatched hold of Jack's sleeve.

"You bastard! You liar! My wife never did anything like that! You killed her! You murdered her!"

Jack gave him a look of deep, stagey sympathy. "I'm sorry for what happened, Mr Pearce. I really am. But it was something that your wife wanted to try . . . and, well, I tried to talk her out of it, but she insisted. You know yourself what a strong-willed woman she was."

"You killed her," said Jeff, quaking with loathing.

"Whoa, no. I didn't kill her. No way. You know who killed her?" – and here he leaned close so that the jostling press couldn't hear him. "She was killed by the husband who slapped her and sent her out into the night looking for somebody who cared about her. I'll tell you something, Mr Pearce: if anybody should have stood trial these past five weeks, it should have been *you*."

Jeff swung at him, but Jack turned away, as if he knew for certain that the blow would never connect. And it didn't, because Jack's blond-haired bodyguard hit Jeff so hard in the chest that Jeff lurched back down the steps, missed his footing, and fell all the way down to the sidewalk. He lay there in agony, two ribs cracked, the cuff of his pants torn open.

A Carmelite nun came up to him and said, "Are you all right, sir?"

Jeff said nothing, but regurgitated a half-chewed Denver omelet all over the sidewalk in front of her.

"Kill him?" said Lenny. "You can't be serious."

"How else am I going to see justice done?"

It was ten after eight in the morning at the Beverly Hills Hotel. Lenny had invited Jeff for a breakfast meeting to discuss publicity for the *Creature* series. He was horribly sharkish to look at: with upslanted sunglasses and dyed-black slicked-back hair, and he had a fondness for white unstructured suits that billowed around him when he walked, but he knew everybody who was anybody, and almost as many people who weren't anybody yet, but soon would be, and Jeff respected his opinion on almost anything concerned with the movie business. He had made only one error of judgement that Jeff could remember: he had raved about *Ishtar*.

Lenny said: "You have to understand that a man like Jack Amberson is almost bullet-proof when it comes to the law. What a lovable rogue, what a star, what an institution. You say that your Susan was murdered. But how many women would willingly die if the last thing they were doing on this earth was balling Jack Amberson? I heard some blue-rinsed woman outside the courtroom, and do you know what she said? 'What a way to go!'"

Jeff pushed aside his plate of fruit. "I warn you, Lenny. I'm going to kill that son-of-a-bitch and I don't care who knows it."

Lenny shook his head. "You'll never get near him. Not a hope."

"I managed to grab hold of him outside of the courtroom. If I'd had a gun—"

"If you'd had a gun, I wouldn't be having breakfast with you, I'd be dropping a handful of dirt on your casket. Jack Amberson's bodyguards all have permits to carry concealed weapons and they were all trained to blow off Bette Midler's earrings at fifty paces. Not that *that's* too difficult."

"There must be some way. Maybe I could pick him off at home."

Lenny said, "I'll pretend I didn't hear that, but he has security that makes most Bel-Air properties look like open house. You can't do it, Jeff. They took Amberson to court and they tried him and they found him not guilty. However bad you feel about it, maybe he's telling the truth."

"The *truth*? You're trying to tell me that Susan would agree to having her hands tied and a plastic bag put over her head, and then be forcibly sodomized? In all the time we were married we didn't do that, not once."

"Some women have needs that they don't like to tell their husbands about. Same way with men."

"Oh, come on, Lenny. Susan and I were close, we were close. We could tell each other anything."

"I don't know, Jeff. I don't want to criticize. It's not my place. But Susan called me a couple of months ago and told me that she was very upset about all the time you were spending away from home. She even asked me if you had another woman."

"Another woman? How the hell did she think I had time for that?"

"Because you didn't involve her, Jeff. You got carried away with what you were doing and you forgot to take Susan along with you."

"So you agree with Amberson? Susan died because of me?"

Lenny picked up his spoon and ate the chocolate flakes from the top of his cappucino. "I didn't say that, Jeff. All I said was, you shouldn't try to kill the guy, and I don't want you to die trying."

Jeff said, "I wouldn't mind that."

"What are you talking about? You wouldn't mind what?"

"I wouldn't mind dying, if I could be sure of killing him."

Lenny looked at him for a long while, and then he said, "Eat your eggs. You want to starve yourself to death before you die?"

He waited in the shrubs opposite the entrance to Jack Amberson's house for over three-and-a-half hours. He was wearing a black Adidas tracksuit and dark glasses, and a black woollen hat on his head. Inside his half-zipped top he was carrying a Colt .45 automatic that he had bought yesterday afternoon from Phil Forlenza, the movie armorer. He felt conspicuous and absurd, as if he was playing the killer in an episode of *New Columbo*. He was hot, and impatient, and the gun was much too heavy. But he was determined that Jack Amberson wasn't going to get away with suffocating Susan, even if she had wanted it.

He bitterly regretted the way that he had treated her. Jack Amberson had said that he was guilty and he believed that he was. But Jack Amberson should have taken care of her. Even if he had made love to her, he should have taken care of her.

Jeff was almost ready to call off his vigil and go home when a black Lincoln appeared around the bend in the road and pulled up outside Jack Amberson's gates. It happened so quickly that he didn't really know what to do. But as the gates began to swing open, he thought: *This is your chance. This is your only chance. And this is for Susan.*

He came out of the bushes and strode across the road. The sun was as bright and hot as an arc lamp. He took the automatic out of his track-suit top and cocked it. Then he circled around the back of the car, holding the gun in both hands. The windows were all blacked out, so that he couldn't see anybody inside. All the same, he fired four times into the offside back window. The noise was deafening and the Colt kicked back like a mule. The glass shattered, and he saw an arm flap up. Then – before he could fire again – the Lincoln screeched up the driveway toward the house and the wrought-iron gates began to close.

They clanged shut, and Jeff found himself standing alone in the roadway with his gun, unsure of what he had done.

He didn't sleep all night. He sat in his armchair drinking 7-Star Metaxa Brandy with the gun on the coffee table in front of him, and the television flickering with the sound turned down. He watched *High Noon* and – ironically – *Cloud Riders*, with Jack Amberson.

He was beginning to doze by the time the six a.m. news came on. He saw the picture of Jack Amberson even before he had time to turn up the volume.

"*. . . seriously hurt in a shooting incident outside of his three-million-dollar home in Bel-Air . . . but surgeons said that his injuries were not life-threatening . . . police meanwhile are looking for a masked gunman who attacked Mr Amberson with no apparent motive.*"

Jeff let his head fall slowly back. The sun was shining and the quail were warbling on the roof. Against the pale calico blinds, the shadow of a rose nodded and nodded, like a miniature death's-head on a stick. He hadn't been able to satisfy Susan. He hadn't been able to keep her. He hadn't even been able to avenge her.

He lifted the gun from the table, cocked the hammer, and pressed the muzzle against his forehead. It was surprisingly cold. There's only one way out of this, he thought. I have to die. Somebody else will have to punish Jack Amberson for Susan's death.

Jack Amberson walked into the Café del Rey and sat down at his favorite table. His four bodyguards sat next to him, much closer than they used to sit in the days before he was shot. He still looked the same, except that he was twitchier and nervier, and the left side of his face was indented. He had been lucky that Jeff's third bullet had passed through the skull of his blond-haired bodyguard before it had hit him in the cheek. All the same, it had penetrated his mouth and knocked away most of his upper teeth. Over two years later, he was still convalescing, and nobody knew if he would ever act again. Wes Craven had asked him if he would consider appearing in a new horror picture, but he had furiously refused. "What are you trying to say to me, Wes? I'm some kind of fucking freak?"

The young blonde waitress brought him a vodka martini with a twist and smiled at him, but ever since the shooting he regarded any woman's smiles with suspicion. He could never be sure if they really found him attractive or whether they pitied him. The way he felt at the moment, he would have been quite capable of killing any woman who showed him pity.

"Hey, how about her?" his bodyguard asked him. "Great gazongas, or what?"

Jack said, "You kidding me?"

"Of course not. She's a babe."

"About four feet tall, and an ass like Yogi Bear?"

"OK, I'm sorry. I forgot you like 'em tall."

Jack looked along the bar. There were two brunettes in clashing red suits, both of them as big as Xena the warrior goddess. There was a skinny ginger-headed girl in green. There was a blonde with huge thighs and a mole on her cheek, furiously smoking. And then – at the very end of the bar – there was a tall, quiet blonde in an ocean-blue silk dress, with half a glass of champagne in front of her.

Jack stared at her with his eyes narrowed. He couldn't make out if she was waiting for somebody of if she was just killing time. Her hair was curled into soft, loose waves that just reached her shoulders. Her profile was classic, with a fine straight nose and a well-defined chin, and lips that looked as if they had just been licked.

Her figure was sensational. Her breasts were enormous – high and firm – and the outline of her nipples was visible through the fine shiny silk. her stomach was flat, her hips were narrow, and her legs went on and on and on, like a love song.

"Tell her I want to buy her a drink," said Jack.

"Who, the redhead?"

"The blonde, you asshole. The cunt in the blue."

The bodyguard went over and talked in the woman's ear, his hands folded over his crotch and his head tilted slightly to one side. The woman looked over his shoulder toward Jack, frowned for a moment, and then shook her head. The bodyguard said something else. She shook her head again.

Jack lifted his drink and mouthed the words, "C'mon, darling. Come and join me." But the blonde shook her head again and picked up her pocketbook.

Jack did something that he had never done before. He got out of his seat and walked across to the bar and confronted the blonde himself. He smiled that old devilish smile and said, "I don't even know you, and already you've hurt my feelings."

"I didn't mean to," the blonde told him, in a soft, husky voice. "I just don't want your company, that's all."

"Well, don't you see how hurtful that is? Here I am, a famous Hollywood movie star, and you don't want my company? You know how small that makes me feel?" He held up his finger and thumb, only a half-inch apart. "That makes me feel *this* small."

The blonde stared at him with perfect blue eyes. "You can have almost any woman you want. How can I make you feel small?"

"Because I want *you*, sweetcakes, and the difference is that you don't want me."

"I didn't say that. I just told this goon of yours that I don't make a habit of going out with men I don't know. A very close friend of mine was killed once, dating a man she didn't know."

Jack's smile slipped slightly on one side. He hoped she wasn't making any kind of innuendo. If there was one thing he couldn't tolerate, it was people reminding him of what had happened with Susan. His pictures were still boycotted by some women's groups, and he had been dropped from several celebrity party lists. The last time he had seen Demi Moore, she had turned her back on him.

"Did you ever see *Painted Sun*?" he asked her. "Did you ever see *No Place Like Tomorrow*?"

"Tell me who hasn't."

"In that case, how can you say you don't know me? The Jack Amberson you've seen on the screen is the same man who's standing here talking to you now."

"You mean the way you act on the screen – that's not really acting?"

He shook his head. "That's right. And I'm not acting now when I tell you that you're the sweetest thing on two long legs that I've ever seen in my life."

The blonde couldn't help smiling. Jack popped his fingers at the bartender and said, "Pour this lady's drink away, will you, and bring a bottle of Dom Perignon over to my table. Only the best is good enough for you, my darling."

The bartender said, "That all right with you, lady?"

Jack gave him a look that would have killed a Galapagos turtle at twenty paces. Then he offered his arm to the blonde on the barstool and led her across the restaurant. She was certainly tall – almost three inches taller than he was, and that gave him a shiver of sexual excitement. There was nothing he enjoyed more than having a tall, strong-looking woman kneeling in front of him and doing whatever he wanted.

"So, what's your name?" he asked her, sitting close to her and immediately scooping his hand into the dish of Parmesan nibbles. "And what's a betty like you doing all alone on a night like this?"

"My name's Lolicia. I work for a little independent company called Reel Life Video. You know, 'reel' like in movie reel. I'm a personal assistant."

"Oh yes?" he said, with his mouth full. "And whose person do you assist?"

"Nobody famous, I'm afraid."

"I could do with some assistance myself. How do you like boats?"

"I don't know. I don't know anybody who has one."

"You do now. I was planning on sailing to Baja this weekend. Little sunbathing. Little fishing. Little bit of this and a little bit of that."

"It sounds wonderful."

"Well, it would be if you came along."

"You really want me to? You don't even know me."

He crammed more nibbles into his mouth and smacked the cheese off the palms of his hands. "Let me guess. You were brought up someplace small. Someplace in Iowa, judging by your accent. Cedar Rapids, maybe."

"Marshalltown, as a matter of fact."

"There you are. That's pretty close. You were always the prettiest girl in school. Cheerleader, prom queen, all that kind of stuff. At seventeen you were engaged to be married to your childhood sweetheart Chuck."

"Wayne, actually," Lolicia smiled at him.

"Ah, yes, Wayne. I should have guessed. Wayne had perfect teeth but Wayne had no brain. You wanted more. You wanted fame and acclaim. You wrote off to *Playboy* to be a centerfold but got turned down. So – still believing in your talent and your beauty – you packed your bags and came to LA looking for the big time."

"You're so *right*," Lolicia told him. "Even down to the *Playboy* bit."

Jack looked down at her swelling breasts. "Their loss, in my opinion."

They finished the bottle of Dom Perignon between them and then Jack steered Lolicia out of the restaurant and into his new white Mercedes with the blacked-out windows.

"Bulletproof," he said, tapping on the glass with his knuckles.

"Yes, I heard about that." She was sitting very close to him and her dress was riding up very high.

"Did they ever catch the guy that did it?"

31

"The LAPD couldn't catch the clap."

Lolicia put her arm through his and pressed her breasts against him. She was wearing a very strong, musky perfume that made him feel distinctly aroused.

"You know something," she said. "Your movies don't do you justice. You're so much more handsome in real life. You have so much more charisma."

Jack shrugged. "Sure. But a movie is like a team effort, you know? I deliberately soft-pedal my charisma so that I don't steal the picture from anybody else."

She licked and nibbled his ear.

"You shouldn't do that," he said. "It has a very instantaneous effect."

"Let's see, shall we?" Lolicia coaxed him. Before he could protest, she had tugged down his zipper and reached inside his off-white Armani pants. "Ooh, no shorts. You *do* have charisma."

She pried out his stiffening penis and slowly rubbed it up and down. Jack said, "Phew," and laid his head back against the headrest. Lolicia bent her head over his lap and took him into her mouth, licking him around and around.

"Jesus, Lolicia, you're something else. Nobody ever made me feel like this before. I mean *nobody*."

She sat up and kissed him. "That's because nobody ever knew what you really needed. But I do. I read all about what happened with that girl. I understand all about tying-up, and plastic bags, and a whole lot of other things that you never even dreamed about. Let me tell you something, Mr Famous Movie Star, you've never been the whole way before, have you?"

He looked at her with hooded eyes. "Depends what you mean by the whole way."

"Exactly that. Every deep-down desire you ever had. Every filthy fantasy. All that, and a whole lot more."

She dug her fingernails into his erect penis so that he winced. He looked into her eyes and for the first time in his life he was just a little bit frightened.

"You're something," he said. "Do you know that? You're something."

*　　*　　*

He was standing in front of his dressing-table mirror turning his face to the left and then to the right to see if his cheek was really as distorted as he thought it was. Lolicia walked softly up behind him and ran her hand into his red silk robe, taking hold of his penis as naturally as if she owned it. She gently masturbated him, circling her finger around and around the opening at the end of his penis until it was slippery with juice.

"What do you think?" he asked her.

She kissed the back of his neck. "What do I think about what?"

"My face, of course. I took a .40 caliber bullet right there. Right there, see it? Took half of my fucking teeth out."

"You look perfect to me."

He angled his head to the left. "You think so? You really don't think it makes me look like something out of a horror picture?"

"You look perfect."

He turned around. She was wearing nothing but a black lace bra and a tiny black thong.

"You're some woman, Lolicia," he breathed. He slid his hand into the front of her thong and slipped his index finger up inside her. "What do you say that you start taking me on that journey that goes all the way?"

"Lock the doors first," she told him.

"I've got two guys outside. Nobody's going to get in."

She kissed him. "Lock the doors. They might hear one of us screaming and get the wrong idea."

"Okay . . . whatever you say."

He went over and locked the doors. When he came back, Lolicia was standing by the bed, bare-breasted. Her nipples were stiffening and she had an expression on her face that gave Jack a strange watery feeling in his stomach. She almost looked as if she could eat him alive.

"You have some cord?" she asked him.

"Sure." He opened his closet door and produced two four-feet lengths of black nylon rope. "How about a plastic bag?"

"Sure. That too. I always make sure that I'm stocked up on household essentials, if you know what I mean."

"Yes, Jack. I know what you mean."

He approached her with the cord and the bag. He dropped his bathrobe so that he was naked, his penis pulsing with every heartbeat. "Face down on the bed," he told her. "Come on, face down."

"No, Jack. It's your turn first."

"*My* turn?"

She held him close so that her breasts were squashed against his hairy chest. She reached around and pulled the cord out of his hand. "You're amazing," he said, and his breath smelled strongly of Parmesan cheese.

She tied one of his wrists and then turned him around and tied the other. The knots were too tight, but they didn't restrict his circulation too severely and he found the tightness exciting. He was starting to pant and his chest was flushing crimson under his fan of black hair.

"Now then," said Lolicia. She took the black plastic bag away from him and lifted it over his head.

"We should have a signal," he said. "Just in case I feel like I'm suffocating."

She kissed him, very slowly and lasciviously. Her tongue probed around his reconstructed teeth. "If you feel you're in trouble," she said, "why don't you call out my name?"

"Your name? OK. I'll call out your name."

Lolicia drew the bag right over his head and twisted it so that it was bound tight around his neck. He took a deep breath in, and the bag crinkled and clung to his face.

She guided him to the edge of the bed and gently pushed him so that he was lying on his back. Then she lashed his ankles tightly together. She climbed on to the white silk bedcover beside him. The bag ballooned, shrank, ballooned, shrank, as Jack breathed in and out. Lolicia caressed his face through the wrinkled plastic. Then she ran her fingernails down his chest, and around his stomach. His penis was so hard that it was curving upward, like a red tusk. Lolicia took it in her hand and slowly stroked it, and inside the plastic bag Jack groaned with pleasure.

"I wonder if Susan enjoyed this so much," said Lolicia.

Jack said something muffled.

"Didn't you hear me? I wonder if Susan thought this was so exciting. I mean, it was something that she'd never done before."

Jack panted, "What? What the hell are you talking about?"

"I can't hear you very well, Jack, with that bag over your head." She kept on rubbing his penis but it was beginning to lose its rigidity. "I just wonder if she enjoyed being suffocated, like you're being suffocated. I just wonder if she enjoyed being hurt."

With that, she dug her fingernails deep into his testicles. He let out a stifled scream, and tried to twist himself free, but oddly enough his penis suddenly swelled harder, too.

"For Christ's sake!" he shouted. "I can't breathe! Take this fucking bag off my head!"

Lolicia smiled and kept on rubbing him.

"I can't breathe! I can't breathe! I'm dying in here!"

Lolicia tugged down her thong until it was halfway down her thighs, and climbed on top of him. She took hold of his penis and guided it into her. She rode up and down on him for a while, her back straight, her eyes closed, an extraordinary smile on her face.

"—*breathe! Can't—!*" Jack begged.

Lolicia leaned forward and kissed his mouth through the plastic. "We agreed on a signal, Jack, don't you remember? For all I know you're cheating."

Jack wheezed for breath, and then he managed to choke out, "Lolicia!"

"You're supposed to say my name, Jack," she said, very close to his ear.

"Lolicia!" he repeated. His chest was heaving now and he was beginning to shudder.

"Wrong name, Jack. My name's not Lolicia at all."

"—*breathe! Please—!*"

"No, Jack. Two years ago I was somebody quite different. But two years ago I discovered that there was no way that I was ever going to be able to get really close to you unless I changed my name. Oh, and changed my looks a little, too."

"—*please! I'll—*"

"I took a course of hormones, Jack, and you'd be amazed what a difference that makes. Then I went to a cosmetic surgeon, and you'd be even more amazed what they can do with silicone these days. I had my hair highlighted and I bought some nice blue contact lenses. Then last Labour Day I was ready to go to the urologist and leave the last reminder of my old life behind.

"It was worth it, Jack, believe me. It was worth the pain and it was worth the waiting and it was worth every dollar it cost me. I needed to watch you die in the same way that you watched Susan die."

Jack gave a last terrible rattle in his throat – and then he suddenly ejaculated. Lolicia remained on top of him for a while, to make sure that he had completely stopped breathing, and then she climbed off him.

"I'm sorry, Jack," she said, "but you didn't call my name."

She tore open the plastic bag with her fingernails to reveal his bright blue, sweaty face, his eyes still wide open and his tongue lolling out.

"You should have called out, 'Jeff!'"

Friend in Need

I had known Jan Boedewerf for over three months before I realized that his friend Hoete (of whom he spoke conversationally almost every day) was imaginary. To say that I was bewildered would be an understatement.

"Hoete and I went to see the Zandvliet Lock on Saturday," Jan enthused, on Monday morning. "Well, I persuaded him to go. He's not very interested in docks and locks. Afterwards we went to the Djawa Timur restaurant on the Klein Markt. He likes Indonesian food but he wouldn't eat anything. He spat out his rice! I don't know why he gets so angry."

On Tuesday, he said, "Hoete was still in a temper. Sometimes I think he wants to kill me."

"Really? Kill you?"

"Well, metaphorically speaking."

At first, there had been nothing to distinguish Jan Boedewerf from every other accountant at the Bank van België, of whom there were thirty-five. He arrived at work at Schelde Straat at eight a.m., parking his brown Volkswagen Passat in a numbered slot in the staff parking-lot. He wore a brown suit and a brown necktie and tan-colored shoes and carried a briefcase. He was always whistling between his teeth. He hung his coat up on a hanger marked with his name. He sat all morning in front of his computer, and at twelve p.m. he went out for lunch at Les Routiers on Cockerillkaai. Mussels, maybe a breaded veal cutlet, a glass of red wine. At one thirty p.m. he came back and worked until four thirty and then he went home.

He had short sandy hair and dandruff and brown-rimmed glasses and a round pale-freckled face. His weekend hobby was to visit the docks. He knew everything about the docks and the locks. The Kattendijk maritime dock had been built in 1860 and had a surface area of 139,000 square meters. The Boudewijn Lock was 360 meters long and had a high tide depth of 15.23 meters.

He was unmarried, and had never been married, as far as I could tell. Well – didn't altogether surprise me.

I don't usually have anything to do with accountants of any nationality, especially drones like Jan Boedewerf. To tell you the truth, I'm not much of a businessman, either. I'm an automobile man, not a money man. But Bill Kruse had been ill and we were desperately short-handed: so Randy Friedman sent me over to Antwerp a year ago to set up a new division of Fancy Cars Inc – "The Car You've Always Dreamed Of At A Price You Couldn't Imagine." We started nineteen years ago in a disused grain repository in Mobile, Alabama, bringing in specialist autmobiles, by which I mean Lamborghinis and Ferraris and suchlike. We went through a pretty sticky beginning, mainly due to the oil crisis, but after six or seven years and $137,000 in extra finance from Randy's grandpa we managed to climb gradually into profit. Then we wanted to expand into Europe, sending Porsches and light-bodied BMWs to America, and bringing Pontiac Firebirds and Chevrolet Corvettes into Belgium.

So that was where the Bank van België came in. Jan Boedewerf and I were supposed to work out a realistic finance package which would enable us to order eleven Maseratis and six Lamborghinis as well as two Bentley Azuras and a Rolls-Royce Silver Something.

To put it mildly, it was an uphill battle, in spite of the fact that Antwerp was one of the flattest places on earth. Jan was practical, straight-laced and completely literal-minded. We had to go through pages and pages of European Union directives and more small print than a Gideon Bible; and I knew that his bosses wouldn't tolerate anything less.

"Emissions?" Jan would say, picking up a sheet of paper and peering at me through those glass-brick lenses. "What about emissions? We have to have percentage guarantees."

"You're a banker, not a mechanic," I told him. "What do you care?"

"You can't sell a car if it smells," he retorted, which was just about the only faintly amusing thing I ever heard him say.

One morning in the second week of January it was so foggy that we could see nothing outside of our twelfth-story window but gray freezing fog, penetrated only by the black knobbly spires of Our Lady's Cathedral and Saint James's Church where Rubens was buried. I was tapping out a row of figures when Jan said, "Why don't you come to lunch today and meet my friend Hoete?"

"I don't think so, Jan. I want to finish up these forecasts first. We're running way over time."

"You're so eager to go back to Alabama?"

"Do you blame me, for Christ's sake? At least it's warm in Alabama."

"Still, we have almost completed everything, haven't we? And you will enjoy Hoete's company, I'm sure."

I sat back in my swivel chair and looked at him. "After everything you've said about him?"

Jan shrugged and made a silly face. Against my better judgement, I switched off my computer. We had almost pulled together a mutually agreeable finance package, and at our last meeting I got the impression that Bank van België were pretty much decided. They were going to go with us, I could sense it. All we needed was $2.75 million and Fancy Cars Inc was on its way to global domination. Today, Antwerp. Tomorrow . . . who knew? Aston Martins to Azerbajan? De Tomasos to Delhi?

"OK," I said. "Let's go meet this grouchy pal of yours."

We walked across the gray cobbles of Schelde Stratt in a fine wet drizzle and hailed a taxi to take us to the old part of Antwerp, to a restaurant called 't Spreeuwke in the Oude Koornmarkt. I was wearing gloves but it was so cold that I had to clap my hands together. That was the trouble with Antwerp: it lay so low that you hardly knew where the land ended and the Schelde River began. And there was always the feeling that ghosts were around, hurrying through the fog. Rubens, and the Rockox, and the Plantin-Moretus family.

'T Spreeuwke was warm and wood-paneled and almost all of the tables were crowded. The maitre-d' produced two enormous menus and led us through the restaurant to the very back, to a circular table beneath a circular window – a table set for three. The place was full of laughter and the pungent aroma of mussels. Jan said, "What will you have? A glass of beer?"

"OK. Sounds good to me."

He ordered in Flemish, and the waiter brought three glasses of pils, which he set out on the table in front of us.

"Jack," said Jan, raising his glass. "Allow me to introduce you to my friend Martin Hoete."

I lifted my glass, too, but I wasn't at all sure what he meant. "Cheers," I said, and clinked glasses with him.

Jan clinked his glass with the glass that had been laid at the empty place. "Cheers," he said. Then he waited – and when I did nothing, he nodded his head toward the glass and said, "You're not going to—?"

"What?" I asked him. I was totally baffled.

"You're not going to say cheers to Hoete?"

"I'm sorry?"

"No, no. It's my fault. I haven't introduced you. Martin – this is Jack Scott. Jack, this is Martin Hoete."

I stared at the empty bentwood chair. It really was very empty. Then I looked back at Jan. I was beginning to think that this was a practical joke, but Jan's expression was so deadly serious that my confidence began to waver. I had been the victim of practical jokes before, but there was always a give-away, always a smirk. Jan was pale-blue-eyed and totally unsmiling and there wasn't even a twitch of insincerity on his face.

"How do you do, Martin?" I found myself saying.

Jan suddenly beamed. "Martin says he's very well. Very well indeed. He has a strep throat so you'll have to forgive him. He's bought a new flat in Berchem and he's very happy with it. Well – if it wasn't for that woman."

"What woman?"

"His ex-wife, of course. Maria."

"What's the problem with Maria?"

"She keeps demanding more money. You know what ex-wives are like. Unfortunately Hoete has just lost his job with Best & Osterrieth."

"I'm sorry to hear that."

"Yes – well, it has driven him almost to despair, hasn't it, Hoete?

Sometimes he feels like cutting his throat. Sometimes he feels like cutting Maria's throat. What a slut she is. She went off with that Quinten Venkeler, from Atlas Shipping."

"I see."

I have to admit that I was close to making my excuses and leaving; but the maitre-d' arrived at that moment to take our order. Both Jan and I asked for mussels, as a starter. Hoete, apparently, wanted chicken soup.

"For his throat," Jan explained. "Would you care for some wine?"

We were presented with two huge steaming bowls of mussels, a heap of fresh-cut bread, and a bottle of cold Sancerre. The waiter set a plate of thin chicken broth in Martin Hoete's place; but even when I looked up and raised a querying eyebrow, he simply nodded to me, and said, *"Bon appetit, monsieur."*

"Hoete has been very hard done by," said Jan, with mussel-juice dripping from his chin. "He came here to work – didn't you, Martin? – thinking that his wife was going to be faithful to him. But as soon as his back was turned . . . well, she was flirting with every man she set eyes on. And of course, that Quinten Venkeler . . . he's always been a ladies' man. She fucked him on the very first night she met him, at an office party, on the forwarding manager's desk, no less. You can imagine why Hoete feels so angry."

I tried to look both sympathetic and reasonable. "Sure . . . but I don't think that violence is the answer, do you?"

The light from the circular window was amber. The discarded mussel-shells were the color of slate. When he spoke, Jan's mouth was a crimson gash in a face as pale as potatoes. I felt for a moment as if I had intruded into a sixteenth-century Flemish painting.

"What other answer is there? A woman takes a man's life away from him. What else can he do but take his revenge?"

I had finished my mussels and looked at the plate of chicken broth. "Hoete doesn't seem to be hungry," I remarked.

"Well, why don't you help yourself?" Jan suggested. He glanced toward the maitre-d'. "They always get upset in here if they think that you don't like the food."

I slid the chicken broth across the table toward me and picked up a

41

large silver spoon. I managed to drink almost half, and finished up by dunking my bread in it.

"Women have had it their own way for far too long," said Jan. "What do they think we are? We work every hour that God sends us, and then they spit in our faces."

"Have you ever had a serious relationship with a woman?" I asked him.

His plate of mussel shells were taken away and half a roast chicken was placed in front of him. He proceeded to tear off the leg and the wing, sucking his fingers to get rid of the grease. "I loved a woman just once. Really loved her, I mean. I think it happens only once in everybody's lifetime. Just like Maria and Hoete."

I was given a veal cutlet in dark brown breadcrumbs and thin fried potatoes. A large bowl of *waterzooi* was set in Hoete's place. Either the waiters and the maitre-d' were used to Jan's imaginary lunch companion, and humored him – if he was prepared to pay for it, what did it matter? – or else there really *was* somebody there, and I couldn't see them.

Over coffee, Jan took out a small pale cigar and offered me one. We both sat and smoked for a while in silence. Then Jan said, "Hoete wants to ask you a favor."

"Oh, yes?"

"Well, he wants to visit Maria this evening . . . have a chat with her. Try to make her see sense about this money thing."

"What does that have to do with me?"

"You're impartial, that's the point. Kind of a referee. If you could go along to make sure that nobody loses their temper. I know he'd appreciate it."

I looked again at the empty chair. "I don't really think so."

But Jan leaned across the table and took hold of my arm. He was so close that I could see his gold molars, right at the back. "There are times when you doubt your eyes, aren't there? There are times when you think that you might be going mad."

I shook my head. "Hoete doesn't exist, Jan. You're making him up. I don't know why. But what I *do* know is that I'm not going to go along with him tonight to see his ex-wife, because if I do, I'll be going on my own."

Jan stared at me for a long, long moment and then released my arm. "He doesn't exist? What do you mean, he doesn't exist? If he doesn't exist, then who ate his *waterzooi*?"

He pointed to the bowl in front of Hoete's empty chair. There was nothing in it but two or three chicken bones and a slice of carrot. I turned around, and even though the light was against me, and the restaurant was already clouded with cigarette-smoke, I saw a thin dark man in a snapbrim hat making his way toward the entrance.

"There was nobody here," I told Jan.

He gave me an odd, puckered smile. "Nobody is often the most dangerous person there is. If I were you, I would go to Maria's apartment tonight, just to make sure that he doesn't get up to any mischief."

With that, he pushed a black-and-white photograph across the table. A striking girl with high cheekbones and dark hair and a mouth that looked as if she just had finished kissing.

"This is her? This is Maria?"

Jan nodded. "She's something, isn't she?"

I turned the photograph over. On the back was scrawled *6 Ster Straat, De Keyserlei, 2100.* I took it and read it but I still wasn't happy.

"So where do *you* fit into all of this?" I asked him.

"Haven't you guessed?" he said, still smiling.

I didn't go back to the bank that afternoon. I called to say I was down with the grippe, and then I went back to my room at the Novotel on Luithagensteenweg. I emptied two miniature Johnnie Walkers into one glass and sat on the bed watching Asterix cartoons with the sound turned down, trying to get my mind straight.

I kept thinking of Maria's face and the more I thought about it the more it haunted me. She wasn't anything to do with me; so why was I so worried? Martin Hoete didn't exist, so she wasn't in any danger. But what if Jan believed that he was Martin Hoete? What if Jan were schizophrenic and "Martin Hoete" was his vengeful *alter ego*. Maybe that was why Jan had taken me to lunch and asked me to make sure that Maria wasn't alone at nine o'clock tonight. Maybe the good side of his personality was making plans to protect Maria from the bad side of his personality.

I tipped back the last of the Scotch. It was a quarter to nine, and it was dark and foggy outside, with the mournful hooting of steamers being towed up the Schelde to the docks. I went downstairs in the elevator and in the mirror I thought I looked pale and stressed. I guess I must have been working too hard lately. Too many late nights at the bank. Too much computer-time. I didn't have any real friends in Antwerp, only business friends, and most of my sightseeing I had done alone – standing in the gloom of Ruben's house or walking around the gloomy precincts of the zoo, while Polar bears paced relentlessly up and down.

In the hotel pharmacy I bought a copy of *Time* magazine and (as a second thought) an old-fashioned straight razor. Martin Hoete didn't exist but Jan was real enough, and if there was trouble between him and Maria it was just as well to go prepared. Not that I would ever *use* a razor on anybody, but it was something to wave around in case things turned ugly.

Then I took a taxi to De Keyserlei – the broad avenue that led to Antwerp Station – and asked to be dropped off at the end of Ster Straat.

Ster Straat was narrow and cobbled and lined with lime trees, a street of heavy gray apartment buildings that had somehow survived the war. Number 6 had a wide archway, with black metal gates, and a courtyard with a mosaic floor. I tried the gates and they swung open with a low, weary groan. I hesitated for a moment and then I stepped inside. There was a sharp smell of disinfectant and that ever-present pungency of Belgian drains. I walked across the mosaic with my footsteps echoing against the archway. A moped suddenly buzzed down the street behind me and startled me.

My heart was beating hard and I didn't really know why. Jan was eccentric, but he didn't frighten me. Hoete disturbed me, with all his threats of cutting throats, but then Hoete wasn't real, was he?

I reached the black-painted door that led up to the apartments. Beside it was a row of bell-push buttons marked in neat italic handwriting: *T & V Hovenier. D van Cauwelaert. M Paulus.* That "M" must have stood for Maria, because it was the only one. Apartment number 5.

I was tempted to push the bell and introduce myself, but then it suddenly occurred to me how ridiculous it would appear if I said that I was here to protect her from somebody who didn't exist. Instead, I decided to wait outside for a while, to see if anybody *did* show up.

The night grew damper and colder. I was beginning to think that I must be seriously mad to be pacing up and down this courtyard like one of the Polar bears in the zoo. Eleven o'clock passed, and then I heard the chimes ring out eleven fifteen and I thought that enough was enough. I would go back to my hotel and have a hot, deep bath and finish off the rest of the whiskey from my minibar.

I was about to leave when the gates groaned open, and a thin man in a dark coat came into the courtyard, clanging the gates shut behind him. He crossed to the door, taking out a bunch of keys as he did so.

"*Bonsoir,*" he said, as he opened up the door.

"*Bonsoir,*" I replied. He didn't look like Hoete – at least, he didn't look like the Hoete that I had imagined, when Jan had described him to me. A sharp nose, metal-rimmed glasses that glittered in the darkness. He went inside, but before he could shut the door I called out, "*S'il vous plaît, monsieur! J'ai oublié mon clef!*"

He held the door open for me and I followed him into the vestibule. There was a small table with a vase of dried flowers on it, and a reproduction of Rubens' *Toilet of Venus* – a big fleshy Venus with her back turned, watching me knowingly in a mirror held up by Cupid. The man opened the sliding door to a tiny elevator and we both crowded into it, shoulder to shoulder.

"*Quel étage?*" he asked me. He smelled of cigar tobacco and faded lavender cologne.

"*Deuxième.*"

We both got out at the second floor. He went straight across the corridor and opened up the door to Apartment 7. I gave him a jerky little wave goodnight, and then I walked further along to Apartment 5. I was only halfway there when the timing-switch clicked and I was plunged into darkness. There was a window at the end of the corridor but it was covered by heavy velvet drapes. Fortunately, there was a thin chink of light shining under the door of Number 5, so I was able to grope the rest of the way.

I stood outside, holding my breath. I could hear the television news in English and the sound of water-pipes rattling. Maybe Maria was taking a shower. Always a fatal thing to do when a murderer's after you, I thought wryly. Look at *Psycho*, and dozens of other stabbings-in-the-shower. I waited until I heard the chimes ring out eleven thirty. Then I thought: I've come so far, I might as well make myself known to her, even if my reason for being here *is* totally crazy.

I had my fist poised to knock when I heard the elevator whining. I stepped back, concealing myself behind the thick velvet drapes. They were choking, and they smelled of decades of dust, but I managed to hold my breath.

The corridor light clicked on and I saw a tall man step out of the elevator and walk immediately toward me. He was wearing a black coat and a wide-brimmed hat that concealed his face in shadow. He approached me with complete determination, almost as if he already knew that I was here. I slid my razor out of my copy of *Time* and opened the blade. If he tried to attack me, then he was going to be marked for the rest of his life.

He had almost reached the drapes when he stopped at the door of Number 5 and knocked. He waited for a while with his head bowed, and then he knocked again. After a moment the door was opened on a security chain, and I heard a woman's voice say, *"Qu'est-ce qu'il y a?"*

Without hesitation the man took hold of the door frame and kicked the door as hard as he could. The security chain was torn away and the door juddered wide open. I heard the woman gasp and then I heard a table toppled over and the sound of a lamp smashing.

I dragged myself out of the drapes and rushed into the apartment. The man had pushed the girl back on to a gold-upholstered sofa and he was trying to wrench away the bath towel around her waist. She wasn't screaming, but wrestling with him and letting out a concentrated whimper, as if she were mortally afraid of what he was going to do to her.

"Hoete!" I shouted at him, and slashed at his sleeve with my razor. But he twisted himself around and gripped my wrist so tightly that I couldn't break free, and then he pulled me sideways and got an armlock around my neck. I never knew a man so strong, and I used to be high-school boxing champion. He had me totally paralyzed,

half-throttling me with his left arm and gripping my right hand so hard that I couldn't even drop the razor.

He shoved me forward, toward the sofa, and forced my right hand from side to side in wide sweeping motions, so that Maria couldn't get up without being slashed.

"Hoete!" I choked. "Hoete, let go of me!"

But Hoete said nothing. He made me lunge my hand forward so that the razor drew a thin line of blood down Maria's left cheek. Then he cut her again, right across the bridge of the nose, so that her bone was laid bare. She moaned and tried to lift her arms in self-defense, but Hoete pulled my hand from side to side, slicing her forearms, slicing her fingers, cutting her shoulders through to the fat. The razor blade quilted the flesh on her face. It turned her lips into bloody ribbons and split open one eye.

I struggled widly, but Hoete had me in his grip like a marionette. He made me slice her breasts and cut into her stomach. He scored her thighs like joints of white pork. There was blood spraying everywhere, a maelstrom of blood, and it was dripping from both of our faces, as if we were out in the rain somewhere, dancing some intimate and terrible waltz.

Hoete suddenly stopped. It was obvious that Maria wasn't dead, but it was equally obvious that she would be facing years and years of surgery, and that she would never be the same striking woman that Jan had showed me in the photograph.

Hoete released his hold on me and I dropped the razor on to the carpet. I was surprised to find that the television was still on, its screen spattered with drops of brownish blood. The news anchorman was talking quite normally, as if he didn't know what had happened. I can't understand why Jan should say that he never talked to me about anybody called Martin Hoete. If you ask me, he's just trying to cover up for him. Well, yes, I know that Hoete was imaginary. That makes Jan's explanation even more insane, doesn't it? I mean you've considered the possibility that Jan and Hoete were one and the same person? That it was Jan who attacked Maria that night?

Did you talk to the maitre-d' at 't Spreeuwke? He remembers us together, yes? And he remembers that Jan ordered three beers and three starters and three entrées? He said that *I* wanted them? Why should I have wanted them? Jan ordered them for Hoete.

I can tell you something categorically. I have never been married and I certainly don't know where you found these divorce papers. Anybody can forge anything on computers these days. I came to Antwerp on my own and if a woman called Maria Scott happened to be sitting on the same plane, what does that prove? Scott isn't exactly an unusual name, after all.

It was Hoete who was married to Maria and I can understand why he was so angry with her. He turns his back for five minutes and she's off with some smooth character with a Mercedes and an apartment right in the center of town. And then she squeezed him for money. The sheer naked greed of it. If you ask me she deserved what she got. If you ask me she can count herself lucky that she wasn't killed.

My advice to you is, look for Martin Hoete. H-O-E-T-E, pronounced "Hurt Her". So he's imaginary, that didn't stop him cutting her up, did it? Nobody is often the most dangerous person there is, that's what Jan said, and he should know.

So, can I go now?

Heroine

He propped his bicycle up against the side of The Dog & Duck and went inside. The old oak-beamed pub was hot and noisy, and much more crowded than usual. Bombing operations had been stopped for two weeks to allow the aircrews to rest and the riggers to repair all of the damaged aircraft. Through the haze of cigarette-smoke, he could see McClung, his ball-turret gunner, and Marinetti, his navigator, playing darts on the other side of the bar, and one of his waist gunners getting intense with a ruddy-faced girl from Bassingbourn village.

He elbowed his way to the bar. As he did so, he jogged the arm of a girl in a rusty-colored tweed suit, and spilled her cider.

"Hey, watch it!" she said, turning around.

He held up both hands in surrender. "I'm sorry, that was clumsy of me. Let me buy you another."

"Oh, don't worry," she said, in her clipped BBC accent, brushing down her lapels with her handkerchief. "It wasn't much."

"Well, let me buy you another one anyhow. Just for the sake of the special relationship."

"I can't do that," she teased him. "We haven't been introduced."

He beckoned to Tom, the landlord, a podgy man with a ponderous way of talking who always reminded him of Oliver Hardy. "Tom, do you know this young lady?"

"This young lady here? Course I do. Anne Browne. Major Browne's youngest."

He took her hand. "Pleased to make your acquaintance, Miss Browne. My name's Clifford Eager II, but you can call me Cliff."

"I think Eager would be more appropriate, don't you?" she smiled.

Cliff ordered a pint of Flowers and another half of cider for Anne. He offered her a Lucky and lit it for her. "Major Browne's youngest, huh?" he asked her. "How many others are there?"

"Four, all told."

"All girls? And all as pretty as you?"

"Now then, Eager."

But the fact was, she was not only pretty, she was *very* pretty, she was showgirl pretty, and she obviously knew it, too. She had a pale, heart-shaped face, with wide gray-blue eyes the colour of sky when you see it reflected in a puddle. She had a short, pert nose. Her lips were full and painted glossy red, and they had a permanent seductive pout. Her hair was chestnut-brown, shiny and curly, and fastened with two barrettes. She was quite petite, no more than five feet four inches tall. Underneath her severe utility suit she wore a soft white sweater which couldn't conceal a bosom that was more than a little too large for a girl so slim.

"You want to sit down?" he asked her. They pushed their way through the jostling, laughing throng of customers until they found a small table in the corner, underneath a hunting print of the *View Hulloa!* In the public bar, a rowdy group of American pilots were singing "Tramp, tramp, tramp, the boys are marching" with increasingly ribald words.

"What's a respectable girl like you doing in a den of iniquity like this?" Cliff asked her.

"I'm meeting a friend. I'm going away tomorrow and she was going to lend me one of her dresses."

"You're going away? Anywhere interesting?"

"Torquay, that's all. I've got a job there, in an old people's home."

"I shall miss you."

"Good gracious, you don't even know me."

"That's why I'm going to miss you. I meet the best-looking girl in the whole of East Anglia and what happens? She leaves me and goes off to Torquay."

"Well, I expect you'll be busy again soon."

Cliff put his finger to his lips. "Ssh, mustn't talk about it. But, sure. They're giving us a break after Blitz Week. Then it's going to be back

to the old routine. Get up, fly to Germany, drop bombs, come back
again, wash your teeth, go to bed."

She drew sharply at her cigarette, her eyes watching him through
the smoke. He was handsome in a big, undisciplined way. He had a
broad face and strong cheekbones, and deepset, slightly hooded eyes.
He was wearing a leather flying-jacket with a lambswool collar. She
couldn't imagine him in a suit.

"Where do you come from?" she asked him. "Is it the South? You
have a very drawly kind of accent."

"I come from Memphis. Well, close to Memphis. A little place
called Ellendale. It has a store and a church and a movie-theater and
that's just about the sum total."

"I'll bet you can't wait to get back there."

"Soon as we've done what we came here to do."

She paused. Then, unexpectedly, she took hold of his hand. "Are
you afraid of dying?" she asked him. "I think I am."

He grinned at her. "Hey, you don't have to be afraid of dying.
You're going to be okay, down there looking after those old folks."

"Well, of course. I just wondered, that's all." But still she didn't
take her hand away.

Cliff waited for a moment, and then he said, "Listen – I'm *always*
afraid of dying, if you must know. I can never sleep, the night before
we fly, and I spend the whole time saying my prayers. When you're up
there, you don't have too much time to worry about it. You're too busy
getting yourself there and getting yourself back again, and trying not
to bump into the other airplanes all around you. But there was one time
when we were hit by flak over Emden, and we lost the whole of our
nose section. How we managed to fly that baby back to Bassingbourn
I shall never know. See this gray hair, right on the side here? I looked
in the mirror after that mission and there it was."

Anne crushed out her cigarette in the big Guinness ashtray. "If I ask
you something," she said, "will you answer yes or no, nothing else;
and if the answer's no, will you say no more about it, and pretend that
I didn't say a word?"

Cliff started to smile, but then he realized that whatever she was
going to say, she was utterly serious about it. "All right," he agreed.
"I think I can manage that."

"Tonight, will you sleep with me?"

He opened his mouth and then he closed it again. He looked around to see if anybody else had heard her, but they obviously hadn't. They were singing "Run, Rabbit, Run" and stamping their feet. He looked back at Anne and she still had the same intense expression on her face, and she was grasping his hand so tightly that her nails were digging into his skin.

"Are you sure that's what you want to do?" he asked her.

She nodded.

"Don't you have a boyfriend or anything? What's he going to say?"

"Nothing. We're only chums."

"Well, I don't know, Anne, you're a beautiful girl, but—"

"You're too religious, is that it? You're a Southern Baptist or something?"

"Anne, I don't know what to say."

"All you have to say is yes or no. Is that too difficult?"

Cliff took a deep breath. Then he said, "OK, then. Yes. I may be stupid but I'm not that stupid."

Tom had three rooms upstairs at the Dog & Duck. Two of them were occupied: one by a man who was traveling in laxatives and the other by a wiry, elderly couple on a hiking holiday. Cliff had seen them in the saloon bar, poring over pre-war Ordnance Survey maps and arguing with each other in tense, sibilant hisses. "No, we *can't* go through Little Eversden, it'll take us *miles* out of our way."

The third room was the smallest, overlooking the pub's back yard, where all the barrels were stacked, and the dog was kenneled. It was wallpapered with faded brown flowers, and furnished with a cheap varnished chest-of-drawers and a single bed that was covered with a pink, exhausted quilt, with a tea-stain on it in the shape of Ireland. On the wall above the bed hung a print of a First World War soldier saying goodbye to his wounded horse – "Goodbye, Old Pal."

"Cheerful," said Cliff, nodding toward the picture.

Anne gave a nervous little laugh. She sat on the edge of the bed with her hands folded and looked up at him with an expression that he couldn't read at all. It wasn't demure, but on the other hand it wasn't the expression he would have expected to see on the face of a girl who had just invited a total stranger to bed.

"I hope you don't think that I've ever done this before," she said. Her hair shone in the light from the bedside lamp. It had a pretense parchment shade, scorched on one side, with a picture of a galleon on it.

"I don't know what I think," said Cliff. "All I know is that you're a very pretty girl and I'm a very lucky guy."

He took off his steel-bracelet wristwatch and laid it on top of the nightstand.

"It's funny that, isn't it?" said Anne. "The first thing that people do before they make love is take their watches off . . . as if time doesn't matter any more."

Cliff took off his flying-jacket and hung it on the hook on the back of the door. "Do you want to switch the light off?" he asked her.

"No," she mouthed.

He sat down on the bed next to her. "I feel kind of strange," he admitted. "We haven't even kissed yet."

"Well, then, let's kiss."

He put his arm around her and drew her closer. He looked directly into her eyes, as if it would help him to understand her, but all he could see was the blue-gray rainwater color of her irises, and his own reflection. He kissed her very softly on the lips, scarcely brushed her, but that was enough. They kissed again, much more urgently this time, and her tongue found its way into his mouth and licked at his palate and his tongue. He kissed her cheeks and her nose and her eyes and her neck, and he felt his penis begin to rise inside his shorts.

He took hold of her fluffy white sweater and lifted it over her head. For a moment, with her arms raised and her eyes covered, she looked as if she were in a position of bondage. But then she emerged, her face flushed and smiling. "Here . . . stand up," he said, and lifted her on to her feet. Without her high heels, she came up no further than his second shirt button.

He unbuttoned her red tweed skirt and tugged down the zipper. Then he slid the thin straps of her satin slip off her shoulders, so that it slithered to the floor. She held him around the neck and kissed him again, dressed in nothing but her brassiere, her satin step-ins, her garter-belt and her sheer tan nylons. Her brassiere was slightly too small for her, so that her breasts bulged out on either side. In her deep, soft cleavage nestled a silver medal on a fine silver chain.

Cliff's hands were broad and big-fingered, and he had difficulty unfastening her brassiere, especially since it was too tight. "Shoot – this is worse than trying to unwrap chewing-gum with your flying gloves on." Anne laughed, and kissed him on the nose, and reached behind with both hands and unfastened it for him. Her bare breasts came out of the cups like two warm white milk puddings, with wide areolas of the palest pink. He cupped one breast with his hand and gently circled the ball of his thumb around her nipple, so that it stiffened and knurled.

He trailed the fingers of his other hand all the way down the curve of her back, and around the cheeks of her bottom. She shivered, and came in closer. When his fingers stroked her between the thighs, he found that her step-ins were already slippery and wet. He took hold of the thin elastic and drew them down her thighs. Then he picked her up in his arms and laid her down on the quilt. Her breasts spread sideways, and he took them in his hands and kissed them, sucking her nipples and flicking them with the tip of his tongue. While he did so, she reached down and started to unbutton his shirt.

"You're beautiful," she said, in the same way that he had said it to her.

He stripped off his shirt, dragged off his socks and unbuckled his belt. In a few seconds he was completely naked, kneeling between her glossy nylon-sheathed knees. His body was white-skinned but very muscular, with a crucifix of dark hair between his nipples. There was a white scar on his left shoulder where he had been hit by shrapnel over Emden. His stomach was so flat that it made his stiffened penis look even bigger than it was, with its purple helmet and its thick, veined shaft.

She reached out and gently touched it with her pink-painted fingernails. Cliff couldn't take his eyes off her, and quivered when she drew her nail all the way down the underside of his erection and lightly scratched his tightly wrinkled testes. A single drop of clear sparkling fluid appeared at the opening of his penis, and she collected it with one of her fingers as if she were collecting dew from a mushroom, and tasted it.

As she did so, she opened her thighs, and amid the dark fur of her pubic hair her vaginal lips opened with a soft but audible click, revealing a crimson opening that was brimming with juice.

And then he thought: *Holy shit – no rubber.*

She took hold of his shoulders and drew him toward her. For a moment he hesitated, and she felt his hesitation. "What's wrong?" she whispered. "Don't tell me you don't want to do it."

"Listen – I don't have any rubbers. Well, I do, but they're back at the base. Maybe I could go down and ask one of the guys if he—"

She smiled and shook her head. At the same time she grasped his penis and luxuriously rubbed it up and down. "I don't want you to use a rubber. I want to feel your naked cock inside me."

"But come on now . . . what if you get pregnant?"

"Then all the better. That will give me one more reason to stay alive."

With her other hand, she reached between her legs and parted her wavelike lips even wider, and guided his penis so that the head of it was nestling between them. He looked down at her and he thought that he was probably as close to heaven as he ever would be. Then she dug her fingernails into his buttocks and pulled him into her, and he wasn't even close, he was there.

They made love all night and she didn't want to stop. The stained-oak headboard knocked against the wallpaper so persistently that Tom came and told them to move the bed away from the wall. "You can shag all you like but the rest of us doesn't want to hear it."

When Cliff was exhausted, Anne knelt between his legs to suck and lick at his softened penis. She succeeded in cramming him all into her mouth at once, balls and everything. Then she sat astride his face so that his own semen dripped out of her vagina and on to his forehead. "I anoint you," she said.

Toward dawn she fell asleep against his back, with one of her fingers deeply inserted into his anus. He slept, too, and because of the blackout curtains neither of them realized it was morning until they heard the thunderous banging of beer-kegs being dropped into the yard outside. They sat up simultaneously and stared at each other.

"Jesus, it's eight-thirty. I have a briefing at nine."

"And I've got a train to catch."

They climbed out of bed, and Cliff pulled the curtains open. It was a bright, sunny morning, and he had to lift his hand to shield his eyes. His face was puffy and pale and his back and thighs were covered in red scratches. Anne's lips were swollen and there were chafe-marks on the white flesh just above her stocking-tops, from Cliff's stubble.

She came up to him and put her arms around him. Her breasts swung and her nipples grazed his stomach. "If I never meet you ever again, I want to say thank you," she said.

"Oh, come on, we'll meet again," he chided her, and then realized what he had said. "Don't know where, don't know when . . ."

"Well, perhaps," she said.

"What do you mean 'perhaps'? Give me your address in Torquay. I have three days' furlough coming up soon. I could visit you."

"I don't know the address yet. It's called Sunnybank but I don't know which road."

"You're not going to vanish and not give me any way of getting in touch with you? Not after last night?"

"I wasn't looking for any kind of attachment."

"Oh, really? I thought we were pretty attached. Most of the time, anyhow."

She kissed him and curled herself into him in a way that no girl had ever done to him before, almost as if she wanted to be part of him. "Eager . . . that wasn't the reason I wanted to do it."

"So, what reason?"

"Please, Eager. Don't ask me. I don't want either of us ever to find out."

They stood so close together by the window, and outside the huge white cumulus clouds sailed through the morning air, fully-rigged to cross the North Sea to Holland, and to Germany, and even beyond. Cliff watched them and couldn't bear to think that he and Anne were going to be parted, and that he might never touch her again, not even once. During the night, their intimacy had become complete, as if they had crawled through each other's bodies like potholers down some dark, wet sluice. They had done almost everything that two lovers are capable of doing, and more.

Eventually, however, Anne touched his lips with her fingertips and said, "I have to go. There's a train from Royston at nine fifteen." "Do you have time for breakfast?" Cliff asked her. "When he can get the bacon, Tom does a great bacon and eggs – and when he can get the eggs."

She shook her head. "Honestly, I'll be late."

"Then do you mind if I do?"

He picked her up in his arms and carried her back to the bed. He laid her on the twisted sheets and opened her legs. Then he licked her, very slowly and sensually, all around her clitoris. He probed the tip of his tongue into her urethra and finally plunged it as deeply as he could into her vagina. She lay motionless while he did it, one hand resting very lightly on his shoulder, staring at the ceiling.

They parted outside the pub. Although the day was bright there was a stiff wind blowing, and her scarf flapped.

"Cheerio then," she said.

"Cheerio."

She took hold of his hand and momentarily covered it with hers. When she took it away again, he found that he was holding the silver medallion that she had worn around her neck. On the other side of the road, a gaggle of geese were honking loudly as a postwoman cycled past. "What's this for?" asked Cliff.

"Well," she shrugged, "keepsake."

He held it up and it flashed in the sunlight. "What is it?"

"St Catherine. She's my guardian saint."

"Wasn't she broken on a wheel or something?"

"That's right. But no matter how much she suffered, she never denied her faith. She was a heroine."

A bus appeared in the distance, a toytown bus, cream and white. It came closer and closer across the wide, flat countryside, and all the time Anne said nothing, but smiled as if she were going into Royston for an hour or two to do some shopping, instead of disappearing out of Cliff's life for ever.

It was only after she had boarded the bus, and he saw her sitting at the back, with her hand half-covering her mouth, that he realized that tears were streaming down her face.

*   *   *

For the remaining four days of the rest and recuperation period that had followed Blitz Week, Cliff immersed himself in planning, organizing, and flying practise. He worked almost as hard as he had when the Eighth Air Force had been bombing deep into Germany every single day. His ground crew took to calling him Cliff Hanger, because he was always hanging around the hangars.

He was doing everything he could to keep himself busy, and not to think about Anne. But he couldn't get her out of his mind: the way she had felt when she was lying in his arms, the way she tasted, the way she laughed. What haunted him most of all her was the way in which she had been so demanding and yet so lacking in guile. She had only been going to Torquay, to nurse a whole lot of old folk, and surely there were plenty of men in Torquay. Why had she acted as if she had wanted to live through a whole lifetime of sexual experience in just one night?

Everywhere he went he carried her St Catherine medallion. It dangled from the switches above his head when the 379th Bombardment Group resumed bombing the shipyards at Kiel, the Heinkel aircraft factory at Warnemunde, and the Focke-Wulf factory at Oschersleben, only ninety miles southwest of Berlin. He didn't know whether it brought him good luck, but after eleven daylight missions to the Ruhr, the worst damage that his Fort had sustained was a flak-riddled starboard elevator.

In October, the weather closed in, and for days on end the East Anglian countryside was swept with rain and muffled with dirty, low-flying cloud. Three missions were attempted, and each time most of them were called back, because the cloud over Germany was even worse – sometimes rising up from ground zero to 30,000 feet. They managed another light raid on Oschersleben, but they spent most of their time waiting for the weather to clear, with rain dripping off the plexiglass noses of their grounded Forts.

One dark Thursday lunchtime, Cliff finished his twice-weekly letters to his mother and his brother Paul, handed them over to the censor, and then cycled to The Dog & Duck for something to eat. The cloud was so low that he was actually cycling through it, actually breathing it in. The countryside all around him was almost invisible, so that he felt as if he were cycling through a bone-chilling dream. The grass on the roadside was a vivid, unnatural green.

He reached the pub and left his bicycle where he always did, propped against the wall. He walked in and the saloon bar was almost empty, except for a ruddy-cheeked old farmer who grew potatoes and curly kale hereabouts, and a foxy-faced British squaddie who was smoking roll-ups as if he had only fifteen minutes left to live.

Tom came up to the bar and asked him "What'll it be?" as if he were asking Stan Laurel about his prospects with his sister-in-law.

"Pint of Flowers, please, Tom. And what have you got to eat?"

"Cottage pie. More cottage than pie, though." He meant that there was far more potato than meat.

"How about a cheese sandwich?"

He sat at the bar drinking his beer and eating his mousetrap sandwich, listening to *Music While You Work* on the wireless, turned up just loud enough to be irritating and not loud enough to be enjoyable.

He had almost finished when the door at the back of the pub swung open, and he saw somebody standing in the stairwell. The day was so dark that all he could see was a silhouette, lined by grayish light, but there was something about the figure's hair that gave him a cold sliding feeling all the way down his back.

"Anne?" he said. "Anne, is that you?"

The figure remained where it was for a moment or two, and then turned without a word and climbed up the stairs. The wireless was playing, "Sally, Sally, pride of our alley . . . and more than the whole world to me . . ." Cliff climbed off his barstool and made his way to the back of the pub. Tom didn't pay him any attention: the access to the toilets were through the same door. Cliff reached the foot of the stairs just in time to hear the latch of one of the upstairs bedroom doors closing. He hesitated, listening, and he was sure that he could hear someone walking across the creaky floorboards of the back bedroom, and sitting on the bed with a bronchial groaning of bedsprings. He grasped the banister and mounted the stairs two at a time, as quietly as he could, until he reached the landing.

He listened again, but all he could hear was the wireless; and in the distance, the harsh, lonely droning of a B-17's engine being tested.

He approached the back bedroom door and tapped on it. "Anne?"

he called. After all, if it wasn't Anne, all he had to do was apologize. But supposing she didn't answer?

"Anne, it's Cliff."

He waited almost a minute more. He was about to go back downstairs, but then he thought: damn it, what am I scared of? He opened the latch and pushed the door halfway open, giving a loud, false cough as he did so. "Hullo, there? Anybody there?"

Although the curtains were drawn back, the room was almost impenetrably gloomy. All Cliff could see through the window was fog. It looked just the same as it had before, with its dull brown wallpaper and its cheap varnished bureau. "Goodbye, Old Pal" was still hanging on the wall above the bed. And *on* the bed lay Anne, completely naked, with her hands held behind her head.

"Anne?" he said, closing the door and sitting down next to her. "Why didn't you answer me? I nearly gave it up."

She gave him a faint, tired smile. "I knew you'd come," she told him. She took one of her hands out from behind her head as if his appearance had freed it for her. He leaned forward and kissed her, and she ran her fingers into his hair. "I knew you wouldn't let me down."

He reached for the bedside lamp with its galleon shade, but Anne held his wrist and said, "Don't . . . not this time. I'm not really looking my best." And she was right. As Cliff's eyes grew gradually accustomed to the gloom, he could see that she was desperately pale. The only color she had were two plum-colored circles under her eyes, and two hectic spots of crimson on her cheekbones. They looked m like bruises than rouge.

"Honey, what's been happening to you?" Cliff asked her. "Are you all right? You look like somebody beat up on you."

She lifted her head to kiss him again, and as she did so she winced in obvious pain. "I'm all right, really I am. I'm just pleased to see you."

"I want to know who did this. It wasn't that old boyfriend of yours, was it? The one you were 'just chums' with? I'll have his ass in a sling."

"Sh – sh – sh!" Anne quietened him, a finger pressed to her lips. "It was an accident, that's all. A car, in the blackout. It was all my own fault. I don't want you to be angry, darling. I just want you to stay here and make love to me."

Cliff glanced toward the door. "I don't know . . . have you told Tom that you're here?"

"It doesn't matter. All you have to do is lock the door."

Cliff kissed her again, and then again. "Do you know what?" he said. "I think you're amazing. And this time I happen to have some rubbers with me."

"You don't have to bother about those."

"Well, if you're sure . . ."

He stripped off his flying jacket and his gray cable-knit sweater. It was so cold in the bedroom that his breath smoked, and he wondered how Anne could stand to lie there on the quilt with nothing on at all. He pulled off his pants and already his cock was rising. "Come on, let's get under the covers."

"I want to look at you first."

He knelt on the bed between her legs. She ran her fingers around his shoulders and down his chest. She sat up, wincing again, and kissed his nipples. She bit them, too, and he said "Ouch!"

"Why don't you do that to me?" she asked him. Those rainwater eyes were unusually dark, the pupils widely dilated.

"You mean, *bite* you?"

She held up her left breast in her hand, offering it to him. He looked at her for a moment, very unsure of what she really wanted him to do. Then he tentatively kissed her nipple, and sat up straight again, smiling. In return, however, she gripped his penis so hard that her nails dug right into it.

"Hey, ouch, Jesus," he said, trying to pull away, but she gripped him even harder.

"Why don't you bite me?" she repeated. "You're not frightened, are you? I'm only a stupid tart with no morals at all! What does it matter if you bite me? What does it matter what you do to me?"

Still Cliff hesitated, but then Anne took hold of his balls and caught the skin with her fingernails, pulling it upward. It hurt, but in a strange way he was beginning to find it exciting, too, and his penis swelled even harder. He bent forward and took her nipple between his lips. He could feel it stiffen against his tongue. She clutched his balls even more painfully, so he nipped her nipple between his front teeth.

"Harder," she demanded. "You can bite it right off if you want."

He bit it harder, and she gasped, and lifted her hips.

"Hey, look. I'm sorry, I didn't mean to do it so doggone hard."

"*Harder*," she panted. "For God's sake, darling, do it harder!"

He took a deep breath, and then bit her nipple so hard that he tasted blood. She let out a high, strangled yelp, and bucked up and down on the bed so that the springs scrunched. Cliff bit her again and again, first one breast and then the other, biting them until he could almost feel his incisors closing together, and then chewing them with his molars. All the time she gasped and shivered, and there was a thin slide of blood coming out of the side of her mouth where she had bitten her tongue.

Cliff lifted his head and said, "Anne – Anne, listen to me – I can't hurt you any more. I'm just not—"

But Anne opened her legs wide and said, "Fuck me, Eager. Fuck me just as hard as you can."

"Anne, I—"

"Fuck me, you bastard, if you care for me at all!"

He took his penis in his fist and guided it into her wide-open vulva. He had never known a girl so wet. Her upper thighs were smothered in juice and even the quilt was soaking. He thrust himself into her as hard as he could, but even that didn't seem to be enough for her. She rolled him over and sat on top of him, straight upright, so that he penetrated her as deeply as he could physically could. With every thrust he could feel the neck of her womb touching the head of his cock, and with every thrust she shuddered and wept.

She reached behind her and tried to force two or three sharp-fingernailed fingers into his anus, and it was then that his muscles tightened and he climaxed, far too soon but he couldn't help it.

Anne literally hissed with rage and disappointment. "You bastard! You complete bastard! How could you do that to me?" She pummeled his shoulders with her fists and then started to tear at his chest-hair.

"For Christ's sake, Anne—"

But she climbed off him, and worked her way up until she was kneeling over his face. "Now bite me some more. Bite me *there*."

"Anne, forget it, honey. I'm not going to do it. I'm not that kind of guy."

In a sudden and explosive rage, she seized hold of his hair and sat down on his mouth with all of her weight, so that her vulva was forced right into his mouth. She dragged her hips from side to side so that her lips were scraped against his teeth, and her pubic bone bruised his nose. All he could taste was salt blood and starchy semen.

This time, he took hold of her wrists, gripped them tight, and bodily twisted her away. She hit her head against the wall, but he rolled off the bed and stood up, panting for breath.

"What the hell—?" he asked her. He wiped his mouth with the back of his hand.

She stayed where she was, with her back turned to him, shivering, saying nothing.

"Come on, Anne, what the hell is this all about? I can't hurt you. I love you, if you must know. You can't expect me to – Jesus, I don't know."

"You love me?" she asked, without looking around. "You really love me?"

"What do you think, goddamit?"

With her fingertip, she traced the pattern of one of the brown flowers on the wallpaper. "If you really love me, then you'll do what I ask you to do."

Cliff stood on the threadbare rug beside the bed, wondering what to do. In the end he felt so cold that he pulled on his clothes. "Listen," he repeated, "I love you."

Still she said nothing. He looked at his watched and realized that he should have been back on base over twenty minutes ago. He bent over and kissed her shoulder but she didn't respond. Her fingertip kept on tracing the pattern of the flower, over and over, as if she were trying to memorize it.

"Major Browne?" he asked, one hand clamped against his ear to suppress the deafening droning of a taxiing Fort.

"That's correct. How can I help you?"

"I'm not too sure. My name's Captain Cliff Eager, I'm stationed at Bassingbourn."

"American, by the sound of it."

"Yes, sir. That's right. Well, the truth of it is, I met your daughter Anne just before she left for Torquay."

"Oh you did, did you?"

"Yes, sir. We sort of struck up a friendship. But I saw her this afternoon, and I have to tell you that she didn't look too good. I'm worried about her."

There was a lengthy pause. Then, "You say you saw her this afternoon?"

"Yes, sir. Anything wrong with that?"

"Well, nothing. Except that she's still in Torquay."

"She couldn't have come back to see you? I mean, maybe she's on her way now."

"Impossible, I'm afraid. Her contract won't allow it. You must have made a mistake."

"A mistake? What kind of mistake?"

"Well, you know, mistaken identity. One young English rose looks very much like another, don't you know?"

"You're trying to tell me that I didn't meet Anne, I met some other girl who just happened to look like her?"

"It's the only feasible explanation, old man."

"Major Browne, I hate to contradict you, and I hate to shock you, too, but Anne and I were more than just good chums. And we were more than just good chums this afternoon."

Another pause. Then, "Look here, Captain Eagle or whatever your name is, what you are describing is not only impossible but scurrilous. I seriously recommend that you forget all about Anne and get back to the business that your government sent you here for. Otherwise I shall have to have strong words with your commanding officer."

"But, you listen here, major—"

"No, captain, you listen to me. Anne has gone to Torquay, and she has not yet returned. And if you know what's good for you, you'll believe that, too. For her good, if not for your own."

Cliff hung up, and sat for a long time staring at the telephone as if it were going to ring, and it would be Anne.

A week and a half later, it did, and it was.

Cliff had just returned from a mission over Brunswick and Halberstadt, and he and his crew were so tired that they were hallucinating. Everything had gone wrong. Unexpected easterly winds had slowed them down on their way to the target, and the three-stream bomber force had failed to rendezvous with their fighter escorts as they crossed the Dutch border. Altogether the US Eighth Air Force had lost sixty-five aircraft that night, 650 men, and Cliff had lost so many friends that he couldn't even count them.

When the phone rang and he heard her saying, "Eager? Eager, is that you?" he couldn't believe it at first.

"Anne? Is that really you? Where are you calling from?"

"The Dog & Duck, where else? Aren't you coming to see me?"

"Your father said you were still in Torquay."

"Well, let's put it this way. I am, and I'm not."

"You sound tired," he told her.

"Well, my darling, I haven't been getting much sleep. The people here keep me awake most of the time. They're very demanding."

Cliff smeared his eyes with his hand. He was still trembling from six hours of battling with the Fort's controls. "Listen . . . how long are you going to be there? I just finished debriefing. I need to take a shower. I've been flying all day and I stink like a polecat's armpit."

"Don't worry about a shower. I need to see you now."

"Anne, honey – can't it wait until tomorrow morning?"

"I need to see you now. I *have* to see you now. If you don't come to see me now, I'll never forgive you."

"Listen," he said, "why don't we—" but he heard the click as Anne put down her receiver, and then the endless purring of the dialing tone.

"Oh, shoot," he said.

At that moment McClung came past, and said, "Problems, captain?"

He had a sudden apocalyptic vision of all the Forts he had seen that afternoon, plunging through the clouds with blazing young men on board them. He wondered what they were thinking about as they fell to earth, 23,000 feet below? Did they pray? Did they think of their mothers? Or did they calmly accept that their lives were over?

And McClung was asking if *he* had problems?

It was already dark by the time he reached The Dog & Duck – windy, and very cold, but dry. It was a real bomber's sky, eight-tenths cloud, with just enough breaks to see the stars. Across the road, in Poulter's Farm, a dog was barking.

There was a darts fixture taking place and the pub was crowded. He asked for a Scotch, paid for it, and tipped it back in one. Tom said, "All back safe?" but Cliff shook his head. There was a roar from the crowd as somebody scored a double top.

When Tom had his back turned, Cliff went through to the back of the pub and climbed the stairs. It was so dark that he barked his shin on the top step. He cautiously made his way to the back room door, and opened it. He had never realized before how much it creaked.

Inside, the blackout curtains were drawn tight and he couldn't see anything at all.

"Anne?" he said. "Can't you switch on the light?"

"Not yet," she replied. Her voice sounded oddly clogged, as if she had a bad sore throat. "Come in, darling. I'm here on the bed."

He groped his way into the room and closed the door behind him.

"Lock it," said Anne. "Now come over here, and sit on the bed."

Cliff did as he was told. Immediately, she sat up and put her arms around him, and kissed him. She was naked and she was very cold, as if she had been lying there uncovered for hours.

"You're freezing," he said. "Come on, get under the blankets. You'll catch your death."

But she ignored him, and kept on kissing him and kissing him. It was while she was kissing him that he realized how swollen and puffy her lips were. He fumbled for the bedside lamp.

"No!" she said. "Please don't! You won't understand!"

But he did, and when the light abruptly flooded the room, he couldn't believe what he saw. Anne's body was covered in weals and bruises. Both of her eyes were swollen up, so that they looked like scarlet plums. Her lips had been split and the sides of her mouth were crusted in scabs. Whole hanks of her hair had been pulled out, revealing patches of raw scalp. There were criss-cross marks across her thighs, and it looked as if her pubic hair had been actually burned.

"For Christ's sake," said Cliff. He was shaking with shock. "Who did this to you? What the hell bastard could have—"

She reached out and gripped both of his wrists. "Please, Eager, I'm begging you. Don't be angry."

"How can I not be angry? Look at you! I'm going to call the police!"

She gripped him even more tightly. "*No*," she pleaded. "Please, Eager, no."

"Then what am I supposed to do? Sit back and allow this lunatic, whoever he is, to beat you to death?"

"Just be loving, Eager, that's all I ask. Just tell me you need me."

Cliff took a pack of Luckys out of his shirt pocket, shook two out and lit them both with wildly wobbling hands. He passed one to Anne and took a deep, long drag on the other. "You need a doctor," he told her. "For Christ's sake, you need two doctors. One for your body and one for your brain. How can you let anybody *do* this to you?"

She stroked his cheek. "I love it, when we're together," she whispered. "It's all I have to live for."

"This has to stop," he insisted.

"Yes," she said, trying to smile. "And I promise you, Eager, it will."

"Promise?"

"There's only one more thing I want you to do for me."

"I'm not biting you again. Forget it."

She took hold of the hand in which he held his lighted cigarette. "I want you to write your name across my breasts. Then I want you to stub it out inside me. You *must*."

He pulled his hand away. "Are you kidding me, Anne? What the hell's wrong with you? Come on, I can't take any more of this! You're going to have to see a doctor, and then I'm going to call for a cop!"

"Please, Eager," she begged him. "Please, Eager. I can't bear it unless it's you."

But he stood up, and when she tried to cling on to him, he pried her fingers away, and she was in too much pain to be able to follow him. Her head fell back on the pillow and he dragged the quilt around her to keep her warm. "I won't be long," he told her. "I'm just going to call for a doctor."

She watched him go to the door. Her swollen eyes were crowded with tears. "Please," she whispered, her voice strangled with misery. "Please don't, Eager. Please."

He hesitated for a moment, then he went out and closed the door behind him.

The doctor puffed up the stairs like a GWR locomotive, every puff smelling of whisky. He wore a bowler hat and a pinstriped trousers and carried a brown Gladstone bag.

"I don't know who did this," Cliff told him, opening the door. "I just want you to understand that it wasn't me."

The doctor didn't say anything, but looked at him piggy-eyed.

"All right, then," said Cliff, and switched on the light.

The room was empty. The bed was empty. The quilt was smooth and undisturbed. Cliff laid his hand on the pillow and even the pillow was cold.

"I hope this isn't some kind of a joke," said the doctor, taking off his hat. "I was listening to ITMA."

Cliff lifted the quilt but even the sheet underneath was chilly. Nobody had been here, not tonight. He stared at the doctor and he didn't know what to say.

"She's not here, then, your lady friend?" the doctor asked him.

Cliff said something, but what he said was drowned out by the droning of a fully laden Fort taking off south-westward into the prevailing wind.

He let himself into the house and called out, "Babsy! I'm back!"

In the living-room, little Pete was sitting cross-legged in front of the television, solemnly watching *Howdy Doody*. "Hi, son! Howdy-doo to you!"

He hung up his hat on the hallstand, brushed back his close-cropped hair with both hands, and walked through to the kitchen, where the late-afternoon sun was shining. Babsy was rolling out pastry on the kitchen counter, her blonde hair tied up in a scarf. But she wasn't alone. A lean, tall white-haired man in an inappropriately wintry suit was sitting at the breakfast table, with a stack of papers in front of him. He stood up as Cliff came in, and Cliff looked at Babsy in surprise.

"You didn't say we were expecting visitors."

"You weren't, captain," said the white-haired man, in a rather faded

British accent. "I'm afraid to say that I arrived unannounced. Your good lady was kind enough to allow me to wait for you."

Cliff walked around the counter, put his arm around Babsy and gave her a kiss. "Is something wrong?" he wanted to know.

The white-haired man shook his head. "Quite the opposite. You might just say that I'm laying a ghost to rest. My name is Gerald Browne – Major Gerald Browne. You and I once talked on the telephone, several years ago."

Cliff said, in disbelief, "You're *Anne's* father?"

"Perhaps this is something you'd rather talk about in private."

"No, no – I—" Cliff began, but Babsy laid a hand on his arm and said, "Why don't you take Major Browne into the yard? I have to give little Pete his supper now, anyhow."

They went out into the small back yard and sat on the white-painted swing. It was a treacly Memphis evening and the sky was gold. Cliff offered Major Browne a Lucky but Major Browne declined.

"Anne told you that she was going to Torquay, but in reality she was doing nothing of the sort. She was being flown into France to make contact with the Resistance and to set up a communications system."

"She was *what*? Anne? But she was only just a kid!"

"I think you forget, Captain Eager, that in those days you were all just 'kids'. Anne was an SOE wireless operator, very highly trained."

"But I saw her, after she left. She came back and I saw her twice."

Major Browne's eyes brimmed with sadness. They were rainwater eyes, just like Anne's. "Well, captain, I didn't believe you then, but now I think I do. Although she was very brave, Anne was terrified of being captured and executed. She felt that she hadn't lived her life to the full. She hadn't even had a lover. That was why – well, when you met her for the first time that evening, she was so forward. She felt she had to cram a lifetime of experience into just a few hours."

"How do you know that?"

"Because six weeks ago, the French authorities returned her diary to me, the diary which she kept both before and after she was caught and imprisoned by the Gestapo. Your name comes up again and again. When they tortured her, she always tried to imagine that it was you torturing her, instead of them. She felt that she could bear the pain if it was inflicted with passion, and with love. And she did bear pain – much more than you or I could ever imagine.

"It was thinking of you that helped her to endure her suffering. In her mind, she says, she wasn't in Amiens prison, but in your arms. And, by the way, she never gave away any of her codes or any of her comrades, not till the last."

Cliff found that he had to wipe his eyes. "I saw her. I held her. I don't understand it. The last time she came – she was so badly hurt, I couldn't stand it. I left her and went to call for a doctor. When I came back . . . the bed was empty. She was gone. I thought she'd just—"

"Do you remember what date that was?"

"For sure. It was the day we lost sixty-five Flying Fortresses over Germany, all in one day. October 16, 1943."

Major Browne nodded. "That was the same day that Anne was tortured for the last time by the Gestapo. According to the French, they did unspeakable things to her with cigarettes, and burned a swastika on her chest. When she still refused to speak, they shot her."

Major Browne handed Cliff the small brown diary with its stained, creased cover. "Here, captain, I think this is yours, more than anybody's."

That night, while Babsy quietly breathed, Cliff stood by the bedroom window staring out at the moonlight. Between finger and thumb he twirled the St Catherine medallion that Anne had given him. St Catherine, broken on the wheel.

He was about to go back to bed when he was aware of a figure standing in the deep shadows on the far side of the room. Or maybe it wasn't a figure. Maybe it was nothing more than Babsy's wrap, hanging on the back of the door.

"Is anybody there?" he said, very softly.

Then, "Anne, is that you?"

Saving Grace

"Well, you did your best," said his grandfather, opening the Rover's boot-lid and dropping Jack's kitbag into it. "They were bigger than you, most of them. Don't know what their games master's been feeding them on. Six Shredded Wheat every morning, if you ask me."

Jack climbed into the car. As he did so, three of his team-mates passed him by and shouted out, "Butterfingers! You couldn't catch a cold!"

"He did his best!" his grandfather called back. "Maybe you shouldn't have let the other forwards get through to the goalmouth so many times!"

"Grandad," Jack protested. He was going to get even more teasing now. Can't stand up for yourself, Matthews? Have to get a hundred-year-old man to do it for you?

His grandfather slammed his door and started the engine. "It's true, though, isn't it? You were practically defending that goal on your own."

They drove between the foggy playing fields toward the school's entrance gates. Several Johnson House boys jeered and cheered as they passed by. Jack felt cold and miserable and exhausted, and now that his ears were warming up they were tingling so much that they hurt.

Barrons School had lost to Johnson House 3–2 – not the worst defeat in the school's 109-year history – but if they lost just one more match they would be out of the schools area championship for the first time ever. Normally Jack wouldn't have played for the first XI at all, but Peter Dunning, their usual goalie, had twisted his ankle. He had told matron that he was playing squash, but the truth

71

was that he had fallen off the roof of the bicycle-shed pretending to be Batman.

"How about some tea?" Jack's grandfather asked him. "We could go to that café where they do those meringues."

The café was warm, with flowery wallpaper and copper kettles hanging from its dark oak beams. Jack had a Coke and two meringues while his grandfather had a cup of tea and three squashed fly biscuits. His grandfather didn't come to see him very often, because he hadn't been very well lately, something to do with his heart, but Jack liked it when he did because he always gave him a giant-sized Toblerone bar and five pounds. And apart from that, he looked so much like his father, if his father had ever grown a white moustache.

Jack's father had been killed last year in a road accident in Kenya, where he had been helping to build a dam. Jack still missed him more than he could say.

"The thing is," said his grandfather, "you're either a natural footballer or you're not. Your dad wasn't natural footballer, not at all. Bambi-legs, that's what the other boys used to call him. Mind you, your great-uncle Bertie, he was brilliant, by all accounts. He used to play for Whetstone United before he was called up."

"Great-uncle Bertie? I've never heard of him."

"He was your great-grandfather's older brother. And the reason you've never heard of him is because the family never spoke his name. They disowned him. Turned his picture to the wall, so to speak."

"Why, what happened?"

"Great-uncle Bertie was in the trenches in France, during the First World War. I don't know whether you've been told anything about it at school. Perhaps you haven't yet. But on Christmas Day, all the shooting stopped. The Germans started to sing carols and light up little lanterns. After a while, the British soldiers joined in, and then both sides climbed out of their trenches and met up in the middle, in the place they used to call No Man's Land. They talked to each other and shared cigarettes. They even played football. It was your great-uncle Bertie who organized the football match.

"The officers were furious. This was supposed to be a war, not a game. So the order went out from the War Office that there was to be no more making friends with the enemy, ever. This made your great-uncle Bertie very upset. He'd seen for himself that the German soldiers were nothing more than young lads, just like he was – and he didn't want to kill them any more than he wanted them to kill him. He made the mistake of writing a letter to his local paper back home, saying that the war ought to be decided peacefully – by games of football, instead of bullets.

"Of course the editor of the local paper didn't print it. Everybody was very patriotic in those days, and to say that our soldiers shouldn't fight – well, that was regarded as treason. Instead he sent the letter to great-uncle Bertie's commanding officer. Uncle Bertie got into serious trouble. They took away his corporal's stripes and they gave him all the most disgusting and dangerous jobs to do, like going out at night to cut the enemy's barbed-wire; or dragging in bodies from No Man's Land; or digging out the latrines. But he was a survivor, your great-uncle Bertie, and he managed to stay alive until the following Christmas, 1915.

"On Christmas morning, though, without any warning, he climbed out of his trench and began to walk toward the enemy lines. The ground was covered in snow. He was carrying a white flag on a stick and he was singing a carol, 'O Little Town Of Bethlehem'. Nobody from the German trenches fired at him.

"The officer in charge of his platoon shouted at him to come back, but great-uncle Bertie didn't even look round. That was when the officer ordered one of great-uncle Bertie's friends to shoot him. The man refused so the officer took his rifle and shot great-uncle Bertie himself. Killed him instantly.

"All this was in a letter which great-uncle Bertie's friend sent to his parents. The friend said something like, 'Even though Bertram was attempting to desert, he was my chum and I could not bring myself to obey the order to shoot him.' I think the friend himself was killed about two months later."

"So that was why nobody ever talked about great-uncle Bertie again?" said Jack.

His grandfather nodded. "They were so ashamed that he had tried to go over to the German side that they cut every single picture of him out of the family albums, and threw away all of his football cups and all of his possessions. Everything."

Jack finished his meringue and wiped his mouth with the back of his hand. "Have you still got the letter?" he asked.

"It's at home. We'll stop off on the way back to school and I'll give it to you."

It had been folded and refolded so many times that it was almost falling apart. A single sheet of soft brownish paper with faded brown ink on it. It was embossed with the name of Browns Hotel, in Dover Street, London, so it must have been written while great-uncle Bertie's friend was on leave. He probably wouldn't have been able to get it past the Army censors if he had tried to send it from France. It was dated December 31, 1915.

Jack lay on his bed in the dormitory reading the letter again and again. He could almost picture great-uncle Bertie climbing the ladder out of his trench and walking across the snow-blanketed landscape, his white flag lifted and his breath steaming as he sang.

There was something so strange about what he had done. Why did he go across to the German side? Surely it wasn't to join them, because life in the German trenches must have been just as dangerous and horrible as it was in the British trenches. And even with his white flag, he had run a very high risk of being shot by a sniper.

And there was something else, too – something that his grandfather hadn't mentioned. The letter said that he had sung one line of the carol, and then omitted the next line, all the way through. Now, why had he done that?

Jack was still reading when Thomson and Patel and two or three more of the First XI noisily pushed their way into the dormitory. Thomson was the captain and Jack always tried to stay out of his way, because he was always shoving, punching and bullying.

He sat down heavily on the end of Jack's bed. "We've decided to put you on trial for losing us the game against Johnson House and for being a pathetic little creep."

"A *girl* could have stopped that last ball," added Patel.

"I just couldn't reach it," said Jack.

"Well, we could see that, and that's why the court has decided to have mercy on you. Because you're such a pathetic little creep, we're going to build you up. We're going to give you breakfast in bed every single day, starting from now."

With that, another member of the team produced a large box of cornflakes from behind his back. Thomson pushed Jack on to the floor and dragged down the duvet. He emptied the whole box of cornflakes all over Jack's sheet, and then Patel took a carton of milk out of his pocket and poured it everywhere. Another boy shook sugar over the top, and yet another produced a jar of marmalade and smeared it across Jack's pillow.

"There you are, wimp," said Thomson. "A nice nourishing breakfast for a weedy little wimp."

Jack got up off the floor. He was trying not to cry but it wasn't easy.

Thomson said, "And here's a warning, too. Mr Brabham has gone stark staring mad and picked you for next Wednesday's game against Villiers. If we lose that game, you won't need breakfast in bed anymore because you'll be dead and buried."

Mr Brabham was sitting at his desk marking exam papers. He was a young man who always wore a tweedy jacket and whose hair always stuck up at the back.

Jack knocked at the door and waited. Eventually Mr Brabham looked up and said, "Ah, Matthews. What can I do for you?"

"Actually sir it's next Wednesday's game against Villiers, sir."

"What about it?"

"I don't want to play in goal sir."

"Oh. So what position do you want to play? You're not much of a runner so I don't want to put you out on the wing."

"I don't want to play at all sir."

Mr Brabham put down his pen and sat back. "Is that because of what happened yesterday?"

"Sort of."

"I thought it might be. But the fact is that I don't really have anybody else except you. And there's something else besides. I think that everybody should be given a chance to show that they can put things right. Next Wednesday's game is your chance. If you don't play, everybody will think that you're a coward. If you do, and we win, then Thomson and all his cronies will forget about yesterday, and they'll be calling you a hero."

"Yes sir."

"Here it is," said the club secretary, as they reached the second-to-last photograph on the wall. "Whetstone FC, 1912–1913 Season." He peered at it more closely, and then took out his pen and pointed at a tall, good-looking man with a small moustache and hair parted in the middle. "That's your man. Bertram Matthews. One of the best goalkeepers we ever had, according to the records. What's your interest in him?"

Jack found himself staring at the man who had walked across No Man's Land in 1915 singing "O Little Town of Bethlehem." Well, *half* of it, anyway.

"He was my great-grandfather's brother. I'm trying to find out how he got killed in the war."

"Killed, was he? Poor chaps, look at them. Most of them were. The best thing you can do is go to the Imperial War Museum, or maybe the Public Records Office. I was reading the other day that they've started to release a lot of secret Army papers from the First World War. Might be worth a look, mightn't it?"

"Yes. Thank you, I'll try it."

Together they walked back along the dark panelled corridor. "So you're a Matthews, too?" the club secretary asked him. "I'll bet you're a great goalie, too. Runs in families, skill with a ball. Inherited. You'll have to come and see us when you're older."

"Yes," said Jack, although he didn't mean it.

He forged a letter from his grandfather, saying that he wanted to take him to a race meeting at Kempton Park. Mr Toffy, his housemaster, was mad keen on horse-racing, so he waved his hand and gave Jack permission to go without even reading it. Jack took a train to London and then the tube to the Public Records Office at Kew, where he spent most of the gloomy Saturday morning searching through books, papers and photographs. He had made himself some peanut-butter sandwiches, and he snatched quick bites out of them when nobody was looking.

He came across great-uncle Bertie's name quite unexpectedly, in a file on desertion, acts of cowardice and summary execution. During the war, over three hundred British soldiers had been shot at dawn for refusing to fight, or dropping their weapons and running away from the front line.

And here it was: "Report by Captain T.C. Watson, of the London Regiment, on the summary execution of Pte B.R. Matthews, December 25, 1915, by Second-Lieutenant W.W. Pearson."

Second-Lieutenant Pearson had been warned by his superior officers that he needed to keep an eye on great-uncle Bertie because he was "a threat to general morale . . . a coward and a waverer." He had seen great-uncle Bertie "defecting to the Hun in the full sight of the entire platoon." He had shouted a warning, and when the warning was ignored "I felled him with a single shot."

But Captain Watson had also talked to other eye-witnesses. Because it was beginning to snow, most of them hadn't noticed great-uncle Bertie until he was twenty or thirty metres into No Man's Land. But Pte H. Rudd had been standing next to him before he climbed out of the trench.

"It was very silent. The snow was falling and there was no gunfire. Pte Matthews suddenly said to me, 'Listen. I can hear somebody calling.' I listened and sure enough I could hear somebody shouting out for help, in English. Pte Matthews said, 'I'm going to go over the top and find him. He's probably wounded, or trapped in a shell-hole. He can't spend Christmas Day freezing to death.'

"He made himself a white flag. I said he was mad, and that he would only end up getting himself shot by a German sniper. He said that instead of calling out he would sing a carol as a way of finding his man, and then the Germans would think that he was just trying to show them some Christmas goodwill.

"I couldn't make him see that what he was doing was folly. He said, 'That's somebody's son out there, Rudd,' and up the ladder he climbed and off he went.

"I heard him sing the first line of 'O Little Town of Bethlehem' and then listen – and, sure enough, the second line came back from far away. He sang the second line, and waited, and the third line came back. It was then however that I heard Second-Lt Pearson challenge him to stop; and then the shot was fired.

"I tried to protest and to tell Second-Lt Pearson that there was a wounded man out there, but Second-Lt Pearson would have none of it and in the mood he was in I thought it wiser not to argue with him. Besides, his shot had started off a heavy exchange of rifle-fire with the enemy and there was no chance of saving the poor beggar after that.

"There was a heavy artillery bombardment the next morning at dawn and the body of Pte Matthews was never recovered, neither was that of the fellow he tried to save."

At the end of his report, Captain Watson had written: "I recommend that this evidence be kept secret. It would do no good to have a man of Pte Matthews' opinions made into a national hero; nor to suggest that the British Army is in the habit of shooting its own heroes in the back."

So that was what had happened. Great-uncle Bertie hadn't been a deserter at all. He had risked his life to rescue a man he didn't even know.

Jack made a photocopy of the evidence. The librarian said, "Serious subject for a young chap like you, isn't it?"

Jack said, "*Very* serious."

That weekend, he wrote a report all about great-uncle Bertie. He made copies of it and sent them to all the television news companies and all the national papers – as well as the local paper to which great-uncle Bertie had written, all those years ago.

At break on Tuesday morning, Mr Toffy came across the yard and said, "Matthews, you'd better come inside. Some reporters want to talk to you."

For a day, Jack was famous. On Wednesday his picture was in almost every newspaper, alongside great-uncle Bertie's, underneath the headlines "Great War Coward Was Hero After All" and "Great-Nephew Clears Local Footballer's Name."

But just before lunch Thomson came up and pushed Jack in the back. "Think you're some kind of celebrity, do you, you creep? You will be this afternoon, when I kill you for losing the game against Villiers."

*　　*　　*

Out on the football field, it was starting to snow. Jack's grandfather was standing on the touchline in a hat and a scarf and a thick brown tweed coat.

"That was a very fine thing you did for great-uncle Bertie," he told Jack. "I only wish his parents could have known what a hero he was."

"Hurry up, Matthews, you worm!" called out Patel. "The sooner we lose this game the sooner we can all go home!"

Villiers were a fit, quick, well-trained team. Their sports master was an ex-Army gym instructor who jogged and bounced up and down the touchline screaming at his forwards until he was red in the face – not like Mr Brabham, who stood under his snow-laden umbrella calling out, "Come on, Barrons!" from time to time, sucking throat-sweets, and coughing.

No matter how much he disliked them, Jack could see that Thomson and Patel were playing their best. As the snow whirled thicker and thicker, they kept the ball in the Villiers half for most of the first half-hour, and in the twenty-third minute Patel scored a cracking goal from a cross by Woods.

A minute before half-time, however, the Villiers forwards came weaving through the Barrons defence and left them all wrong-footed. Jack crouched ready in the goal-mouth with the snow blowing against his face. A small black boy came running up to him with the ball dancing around his feet. He feinted left. Jack jumped – he jumped with all his heart, his arms outstretched – but the ball swung to the right. He touched it with his fingertips, just a glancing blow, but he wasn't tall enough and he couldn't jump high enough, and the ball whacked into the back of the net.

"You muppet," sneered Thomson, at half-time. "We're going to lose this, because of you."

In the second half, with the snow falling so thickly that they could barely see, Villiers really stormed into them. Their sports master shouted from the touchline like a maniac. This was obviously their plan – to play a calm, defensive game in the first half, and then attack Barrons in the second half with everything they had.

Jack was good. He kept his eyes stuck to the ball and he threw himself wildly into save after save. Villiers attacked his goal eleven times, and every time he managed to keep them out.

"Come on, Villiers!" roared their games master. "We can't have a draw! We've got to annihilate them! Sack and pillage!"

There were only three minutes left. Villiers launched a fast, well-organized attack, passing the ball so quickly that the Barrons team couldn't touch them. Thomson was tackled and fell to the ground with a twisted ankle.

Jack, in goal, saw the Villiers forwards coming nearer and nearer, jinking and dodging their way through Barrons' last line of defence. He was so cold and frightened that his teeth were chattering. The small black boy was running toward him with the ball skipping around his toes. Villiers' star player, thought Jack. I don't stand a chance.

With less than a minute to go before the final whistle, the black boy ducked and spun around, avoided a tackle from Patel, cut around the back of him and came flying toward the goal.

"Keep your eye on the ball. Matthews, not the player," Mr Brabham had always told him, so he did.

The small black boy left Barrons' full-backs standing still like a pair of postboxes. He came running up toward the goal and Jack *knew*, just knew, that this was it. This was where he lost the game. This was the moment for which Thomson and Patel would punish him, for the rest of his school career. After this, he would be lucky to find nothing more revolting in his bed than cornflakes and milk and marmalade.

The small black boy was smiling as he kicked the ball. The winning shot, that was what he obviously thought. And the funny thing was that Jack was affected by that smile, and liked him, and almost wanted him to score. But he jumped all the same, his arms outstretched, trying to reach the ball and deflect it from the goal. He heard himself say "*Unh!*" with effort.

And he knew, even as he jumped, that the ball was just too high, and just too far away. He wasn't tall enough or strong enough to reach it. He tried to stretch his arms out in mid-jump, but it was impossible. The ball was nearly into the net, and he was already falling.

But as he fell, he felt two strong hands seize him around the waist. He felt somebody lifting him, lifting him, and it seemed as if he were flying. He reached for the ball with a last desperate effort and he caught it. It slammed right into his outstretched fingers, gritty with mud. He pulled it close to his chest and then he dropped to the ground, rolling over and over, just as the final whistle blew.

He sat up. People were cheering and clapping. Even Thomson was limping toward him, with both thumbs stuck up. Patel was slapping him on the back, and Woods was shouting, "Fantastic! Fantastic! The best save in the history of saves!"

He stood up, dazed, looking around. Somebody had lifted him. Somebody had picked him up. He could never have reached that ball on his own. But there was nobody there. The goal-mouth was empty, except for the snow that kept tumbling into it.

It was then, for the briefest of moments, that he saw the dark shadow of a man walking away across the playing fields. The man looked as if he were wearing a thick khaki overcoat, and a helmet on his head.

Jack lifted his hand to his forehead to keep the falling snow out of his eyes.

"Great-uncle Bertie?" he whispered.

"What?" said Thomson. "What are you talking about?"

Jack began to run. The figure turned, and stopped. Jack stopped, too, less than ten metres away. There was a moment's silence between them.

Then the figure sang, "O little town of Bethlehem," in the softest and deepest of voices.

Jack hesitated, and sang back, "How still we see thee lie."

"Above thy deep and dreamless sleep," sang great-uncle Bertie.

Jack swallowed. Tears were running down his cheeks, unstoppable, and he could hardly manage to sing the last line, "The silent stars go by."

Great-uncle Bertie stood and smiled at him, his face so kind and sad, and white as a memory. Then he turned and walked off into the snow, and it wasn't long before it swallowed him up altogether.

Jack walked back to the pitch where his grandfather was waiting for him. His grandfather squeezed his hand and said, "Come on. Let's have some tea, shall we? You must be frozen."

There was a light smattering of applause as they walked back to the changing rooms. Jack turned and looked back, just once, but there was nothing to be seen but the snow and the gathering darkness.

At the school carol service, however, when they sang "O Little Town Of Bethlehem." Jack sang only the alternate lines, and listened, and listened, for somebody else to sing the lines in between.

Jack be Quick

S he called him on his private number at three seventeen in the morning, and she was hysterical. "It's Jack! I can't wake him up!"

"Hey, ssh, calm down, will you? What do you mean, you can't wake him up?"

"He's just lying there . . . I shook him and I shook him but nothing happened."

"Listen, calm down. Is he still breathing?"

"I don't know. I couldn't wake him, that's all."

"How about a pulse? Is his heart still beating?"

"I don't know. I didn't try."

"Well, go try. I'll wait while you do it. And for Christ's sake get a grip on yourself."

There was a lengthy silence. Next to him, Ethel turned over and said drowsily, "Who is it? Couldn't they wait till the morning?"

He reached out and squeezed her hand. "It's OK. Something came up, that's all."

After more than a minute she came back to the phone. "He's not breathing and I can't find a pulse. I lifted up his eyelid and his eye was all stary."

"OK, then. Where are you?"

"The Madison, the Presidential Suite."

"What security do you have?"

"Two men in the hall outside. Bobby – what am I going to *do*?" Her voice rose almost to a squeal.

"Don't do anything. Don't touch him anymore. Get your clothes on and leave as quickly as you can. Don't say anything to the agents, nothing at all. Just smile and try to act normal."

"But what about a doctor?"

"Leave the doctor to me. Just get dressed and get out of there." Ethel turned over again. "Bobby? What's all this about a doctor?"

"Henry Kissinger," he said. He put down the phone, and switched on his bedside lamp. "Listen, honey, I have to go out for a while. I'll give you a call later."

"Is it really so urgent?"

Bobby was already unbuttoning his pale yellow pajamas. He gave her a quick, ambiguous nod, which was all that he could manage. Urgent wasn't the word for it. This was the end of the world as everybody knew it. He went into the dressing room and found a pair of gray pants, a shirt and a blue golfing sweater. When he was dressed, he leaned across the bed and gave Ethel a quick kiss. She said, "Look at you. You look so pale. Are you sure that you're feeling all right?"

"I'm fine. I'm really fine." And that was when he realized that he had told her three lies already.

From his car, he called just three people: Jack's private doctor, Toussaint Christophe; Harold Easterlake, from the State Department; and his own closest confidant from the Attorney General's office, George Macready. He didn't tell them what had happened, but he asked them all to meet him at the Madison as soon as they could. "And for Christ's sake be discreet," he said.

He thought of calling Ted Sorensen, Jack's closest counsel, but he decided against it, just for now. If Jack were really dead, he would want his own people around him not Jack's. And he didn't want to be out-maneuvered by LBJ.

He went up in the elevator directly to the penthouse floor. His reflection in the elevator mirror looked unshaven and strained, and his hair stuck out at the back. He tried to smooth it down but it kept springing up again. Outside the Presidential Suite the two Secret Service agents were sitting on folding chairs. One was staring at the ceiling and the other was reading *To Kill A Mockingbird*. They jumped to their feet as soon as they saw him coming.

"Good morning, Mr Kennedy. Something we can help you with?"

"I have to see the President right now," he said.

"He specially asked not to be disturbed, sir."

"That's all right. Just let me in and I'll wake him myself. Has his – uh, friend left already?"

The agent's eyes scarcely flickered. "About fifteen minutes ago, sir."

He unlocked the doors and let Bobby into the suite. The large sitting-room was lit with a single lamp. A room-service trolley was still parked in one corner, with the remains of two lobsters on it, and an empty bottle of Perrier Jouët rosé. A damp white bathrobe lay on the couch as if somebody had shed it like a pelt.

Bobby walked quickly across to the bedroom and opened the door. The ceiling light was on, which made the scene look even more sordid than it really was, a badly lit B-picture. The sheets of the king-size bed were twisted, and on the far side lay Jack, face-down, one arm crooked behind him and the other arm dangling. There were bright red smudges on the sheets which Bobby thought were blood; but as he came closer he could see that they were lipstick.

Jack. My brother. Oh God.

Bobby went around the bed, knelt down, and laid his hand on his brother's tanned, freckled back. He was still warm, but his muscles felt oddly flaccid. "Jack? It's Bobby! Jack, what's wrong?"

Jack's eyelids slowly opened and for one wonderful terrible instant Bobby thought that he was still alive. But Jack wasn't looking at him at all. He was staring at his bedside alarm-clock with an expression of total disinterest, and Bobby didn't need to feel his pulse to know that he was dead. Jesus. He stood up, his knees quaking, and took deep, slow breaths to steady himself. He felt as if his larynx were crammed with broken glass, and his eyes filled up with tears. He had always believed that they would live for ever, he and Jack, as gilded and youthful as they always were.

He let out a howl that sounded barely human, frightening himself; and he had to wedge his hand between his teeth to stop himself from doing it again.

After the first surge of grief, however, came overwhelming panic. What the hell were they going to do now? How were they going to explain what the President was doing in the Madison Hotel? And how long was it going to take before some bellboy leaked the information that he hadn't gone there alone? Even more catastrophic than that, they were supposed to be confronting the Soviet Foreign Minister Andrei Gromyko tomorrow morning, for further talks on Cuba. They were facing the most stressful test of their entire administration, and now Jack was lying dead in a lipstick-stained bed.

Harold Easterlake arrived first, quickly followed by Dr Christophe. "Have you touched anything?" asked Dr Christophe, trying to be matter-of-fact, although he was clearly very shaken. Harold Easterlake, pale and puffy-eyed, stood in the far corner and smoked furiously, and silently cried.

Dr Christophe gave Jack a quick examination. He was neat-bearded, lean, dark and handsome, in a French-Caribbean way, with liquid black eyes and a long curved nose. Jack had brought him to Washington seven months ago to help to deal with his twenty-three-year-old back pain. "If the regular doctors can't help me, I don't mind trying somebody irregular." And Dr Christophe was highly irregular. He had founded the Saturday Clinic in Sausalito, California, which promoted "spiritual solutions for every ill," including his controversial trance therapy, an out-of-body rest cure, and whole-skeleton manipulation that was supposed to disperse all of the bad spirits that clung to your joints and gradually paralyzed you.

It was the whole-skeleton manipulation that had particularly appealed to Jack; and Dr Christophe had kept him active and free from pain, even when he was highly stressed. He hadn't found it necessary to wear his back-brace for almost three months.

"Any idea what he died of?" asked Harold. "I mean, shit, he's only forty-five."

Dr Christophe picked up the small brown-glass bottle on the nightstand. "Did the President have heart problems?"

"You're his doctor. You should know that."

"Mr Kennedy, sir, I was the doctor only for his soul, not his body."

"Well, he didn't have any heart problems. None that he told me about. Apart from his back, he was the fittest man I ever knew. The first thing he did when he moved into the White House was to tell his staff to lose five pounds apiece."

Dr Christophe handed him the bottle. "Mr Kennedy, sir, this is amyl nitrite. It is a vasodilator, usually used in the treatment of angina pectoris."

"But Jack didn't have angina. I'm sure of it. You don't think that—"

"No, Mr Kennedy, sir. I don't think that his companion had angina, either. Apart from the treatment of heart disease, amyl nitrite is commonly used as a sexual stimulant. It dilates the *corpus spongiosum*, the spongy tissues of the penis, so that it can accommodate more blood, and thence become stiffer and larger. Unfortunately, there are associated risks, one of which is heart seizure."

Bobby pressed his hand over his mouth. He simply couldn't speak. Harold lifted his hand in resignation. "Oh, fuck," he said. "Oh, fuck." He repeated himself over eleven times before Bobby turned and stared at him, and he stopped.

At that moment George Macready arrived, looking as haggard as the rest of them. He was big and paunchy with a shock of white hair and a face that looked like a prizewinning Idaho potato. They didn't need to tell him what had happened. He took one look at Jack's body lying on the bed and he turned to Bobby with such pain in his eyes that it was hard for Bobby not to start crying again.

"We'll have to get him out of here," said Harold, lighting another Winston. "We'll have to put him in a laundry basket or something and get him back to the White House."

"I guess that Jackie doesn't know about this," said George.

Bobby shook his head. "As far as she's aware, he's working late on the Cuba crisis, and he's sleeping alone so that he doesn't disturb her."

"Maybe we can prop him up between us and make it look like he's walking," Harold suggested. "I saw that in a movie once."

"Are you crazy?" George hissed at him. "This is the President of the United States and he's dead, and naked, in a hotel suite where he's not supposed to be, after having sexual congress with somebody he wasn't supposed to be having sexual congress with." He turned to Bobby. "Was it—?"

Bobby said nothing. He didn't really need to. "God almighty," said George. "Look on my works, ye mighty, and despair."

"What the hell are we going to do?" said Harold. "If Jack isn't there tomorrow, Khruschev will wipe the floor with us. This is eyeball-to-eyeball."

"Maybe it'll save the situation," George suggested. "If we announce that Jack's dead, the Russkies can hardly keep up all this aggression, can they? It'll make them look like A-1 shits."

But Bobby shook his head. "If we announce that Jack's dead, then Lyndon will have to be sworn in as President, and he's going to go after Khruschev like a beagle with a firecracker up its ass. Jack was playing this cool and calm. Lyndon could screw it up completely." He looked down at the bottle of amyl nitrite. "Jesus. Talk about a heartbeat away."

"Well, then," said George, "what are the options?"

Bobby had another try at patting down his hair. "Either we try to get his body back to the White House and announce his death in the morning; or else we leave him here and cover up the evidence that anybody else was here – which will still leave us with the awkward question of why he came over to the Madison to sleep, when he has a whole selection of perfectly good beds in the White House."

"We could play for time," said Harold. "We could say that he's gone down with the grippe or something."

"Yes, but then his regular doctors will want to see him."

They all stared at each other. There didn't seem to be any alternative but to bite the bullet and call for the coroner, and announce that the President had died of heart failure. Maybe, with luck, they could keep his companion out of the news.

"There is one more alternative," said Dr Christophe, quietly. "It is a desperate measure, but then perhaps this is what you might call a desperate situation."

"Well, what? Anything."

"Apart from developing my trance therapy and my out-of-body experiences, I worked for many years with the drugs that they use in Haiti for bringing the dead back to life."

George said, "Am I hearing this right? Are you talking about zombies?"

"You can call them what you like," said Dr Christophe. "But there is nothing supernatural about what they are or how they are resurrected.

In many cases, people are deliberately given the drug tetrodotoxin, which comes from the puffer fish. Tetrodotoxin has an anesthetic effect 160,000 times stronger than cocaine, so somebody who has ingested some may appear to be dead. In Japan they call the puffer fish the *fugu* and eat it as a delicacy, and there have been many reported cases of tetrodotoxin victims being certified as dead, and then reviving after three or four days – in one case, in 1880, a gambler came back to life after a week in the mortuary."

"But Jack's dead already," said Harold, through a cloud of cigarette smoke.

"That is where my research may be of benefit. Apart from investigating the ways in which people were made into zombies, I researched the ways in which they were revived. The voodoo doctors use a drug derived from the *Bufo marinus*, which is a species of toad. It excites the heartrate, it promotes synaptic activity in the brain. It is the chemical equivalent of electro-convulsive therapy. If it can bring people back from tetrodotoxin poisoning, perhaps it can also bring people back from death."

"You really think you could revive him?" asked Bobby. He tried not to look at Jack's dull-staring eyes.

"I could only try. The *Bufo marinus* drug is capable of investing the human body with enormous strength. That is why you hear stories of zombies having to be restrained by six or seven people."

"Where can we get hold of this drug?" asked George.

"I have some myself. If you send somebody to my house, they can collect it."

Bobby looked at Harold and George, wracked with indecision. Dr Christophe's suggestion seemed like the only chance they had. But what if it didn't work, and a post-mortem showed that the Attorney General of the United States had tried to revive the dead President with a drug made from toads? The most sophisticated nation on earth, turning to voodoo? The administration would collapse overnight.

But George said, "Why don't you go ahead, Dr Christophe? We can't make it any worse than it is already."

"Very well," said Dr Christophe. "All I ask is that you give me immunity from prosecution, in case this fails to work."

"You got it," Bobby nodded. Harold picked up the phone and said,

"I need a despatch rider, right now. That's right. Put him on the phone. No, this isn't urgent. This is red-hot screaming critical. You got me?"

At three minutes past five in the morning, Dr Christophe tipped three spoonfuls of milky liquid between the President's lips – 500mg of the *Bufo marinus* powder in suspension. They had turned him over on to his back and covered him with a bedspread. Harold had already removed the lipstick-stained sheets and directed one of the two agents to wheel away the room-service cart and make sure that it was returned to the kitchens and its contents comprehensively disposed of. "I don't want one shred of lobster with the President's teethmarks on it, you got that?"

Bobby kept checking his watch. They were supposed to be having a working breakfast with State Department advisers and the Joint Chiefs of Staff at six thirty a.m. "How long do you think this will take?" he wanted to know.

Dr Christophe sat at the President's bedside. "If it happens at all, it will be a miracle."

Harold sat slumped in front of the dressing-table, his head in his hands, staring hopelessly at his frowsy face. George stood with his arms folded, tense but unmoving. It wouldn't be long before people would be asking where the President was – if they weren't asking already.

The sky lightened, and Harold opened the dark brown drapes. Outside, it was a gray, overcast October day. Traffic along M Street was beginning to grow busier, and the buildings echoed with the impatient tooting of taxis.

At a quarter to six, George switched on the television in the sitting-room and grimly watched the early-morning news: "The President has called Soviet Foreign Minister Gromyko back to the White House today to give him a strong warning about the placement of ICBM missile sites on Cuban soil . . ."

At six eleven a.m., Bobby called Ted Sorensen to say that he and Jack had talked all night and that the breakfast should be put back an hour. When Ted wanted to talk to Jack personally, Bobby told him that he was in the shower.

He went back into the bedroom, feeling exhausted. Jack was still lying there, and his face was grayer than it was before. Dr Christophe was leaning over him as if he were willing him to come alive, but it seemed as if willpower alone wasn't going to be enough. After a while, he turned to Bobby and said, "I'm going to try one last thing. If this doesn't work, this is the finish."

He reached into his leather satchel and took out a long pointed bone and a rattle decorated with hair and chicken's feathers.

"Oh come on," said Harold. "If your drug hasn't worked, you don't think bones are going to do the trick?"

"All medicine is a combination of drugs and ritual," Dr Christophe replied. "Even in America, you have your 'bedside manner', yes?"

"Jesus, this is nothing but mumbo-jumbo."

But George said, "Let him try." And Bobby, completely dispirited, said, "Sure. Why not?"

Dr Christophe pointed the bone so that it was touching the President's forehead. He drew a cross with it, and murmured, "*Il renonce de nouveau à Dieu aussi au Chresme . . . il adore le Baron qui apparait ici, tantôt en forme d'un grand bomme noir, tantôt en forme de bouc . . . il se rend compte de ses actions à lui . . .*" At the same time, he violently shook the rattle, so that they could scarcely hear what he was saying.

After a while he stopped murmuring and began to make an extraordinary whining sound, interspersed with hollow clicks of his tongue against his palate. He shook the rattle in a slow, steady, rhythm, knocking it against the bone. Sweat broke out on his forehead, and he clenched his teeth. Gradually his lips drew back, and his eyes rolled up, and his face turned into a grotesque, beastlike mask.

Bobby glanced at George in horror, but George reached out and held his arm. "I've seen this before. It's the way they conjure up spirits."

Dr Christophe's voice grew higher and higher, until he sounded almost like a woman crying out in pain. He lifted his rattle and his bone over his head and beat them faster and faster. The back of his shirt was soaked with perspiration, and his whole body was clenched with muscular tension. "*Je vous prie!*" he cried out. "*Je vous prie!*" Then he fell back as abruptly as if somebody had punched him, and lay shivering and twitching on the floor.

"This is it," said Harold. "I've had enough."

But at that moment, Jack opened his eyes.

Bobby felt a thrill of excitement and fright. Jack hadn't just opened his eyes, he was looking at him, and his eyes were focused, and moving. Then his mouth opened, and he tried to say something.

"He's done it," said George, in awe. "Son of a bitch, he's actually done it."

"Harold – help the doctor up, will you?" said Bobby. He went around the bed and sat next to Jack and took hold of his hand. Jack stared at him without saying anything, and then tried to raise his head from the pillow.

"Take it easy," Bobby told him. "You're fine. Everything's going to be fine."

Jack spoke in a slow, slurry voice, his chest rising and falling with the effort. "What's happened? What are you doing here? Where's Renata?"

"You had a heart attack. We thought we'd lost you."

"George," said Jack, trying to smile. "And Harold, how are you? And you, Dr Christophe."

"It was Dr Christophe who saved you."

"Well done, Dr Christophe. You'll have to increase your fees."

Dr Christophe was patting the sweat from his face with a bath towel. "You take it really easy, Mr President. You've just made medical history."

Jack tried to sit up, but Bobby gently pushed him back down again. "It's OK . . . the best thing you can do is rest."

He went through to the sitting-room, where Dr Christophe was packing his bag and putting on his coat. "It's a miracle," he said. "I don't know what to say."

"You don't have to say anything, Mr Kennedy. I didn't think it was going to work either. That's why I tried the invocation." He paused, and then he added, "I never tried the invocation before. I never dared. I don't know what the consequences are going to be."

"He's alive. He's talking. You'd hardly think that he ever had a heart attack."

"Yes, but I called on Baron Samedi; and I'm not at all sure that was wise. The President doesn't just owe his life to a drug, Mr Kennedy. He owes his life to the king of death."

Bobby laid a hand on his shoulder, and grinned widely. "He faced up to Nikita Khruschev. I'm sure he can face up to Baron Samedi."

"Well, we'll see," said Dr Christophe. "In the meantime, keep a very close eye on him. Make sure that he keeps on exercising . . . the worst thing for heart recovery is too much sitting around. No more amyl nitrite, ever. And watch for any sign of depression, or moodiness, or violent temper. Also . . . watch out for any behavior that you can't understand."

"You got it," said Bobby. "And doctor . . . thanks for everything."

Bobby was astonished by the speed of Jack's recovery. He was able to dress and return to the White House by mid-morning; and that afternoon he confronted Andrei Gromyko and gave him one of the sternest dressings-down that Bobby had ever heard. He appeared confident, energetic, quick-witted. In fact he seemed to have more energy than ever. He almost *shone.*

"You should call it a day," he said, after Gromyko had left.

"What the hell for?" Jack asked him. "I never felt better."

"Jack, you had a heart attack."

"A minor seizure, that was all. Things got out of hand. Lobster, champagne . . . too much excitement. That Renata reminds me so much of Marilyn."

"It wasn't a minor seizure, Jack. You were technically dead for more than three hours. I'm amazed you don't have brain damage."

"Listen," said Jack, jabbing his finger at him. "I'm fine."

The Russians shipped their missiles back to the Soviet Union. Afterward, Moscow agreed to the President's scheme to connect the Kremlin and the White House with "hot line" teletypewriters, so that he and Khruschev could communicate instantly in times of danger. Jack was ebullient, full of new ideas. He broke a Cold War precedent and allowed the Russians to buy American wheat.

In mid-July, Bobby came up to Hyannisport to spend a few days sailing and relaxing. Ethel and the kids were there already, and although Ethel was distracted and fraught and kept complaining about Rose, the kids were tanned and happy and having a good time. The first day, Bobby and Jack went for a walk on the beach. There was a strong southwest wind blowing and the grass whistled in the dunes.

Jack said, "I've been having these strange dreams."

"Oh, yeah? What about? The Civil Rights movement?"

"No, nothing like that. Not political dreams. I've been having these dreams about blood, about killing things."

The sand was very deep and soft here, and Bobby's bare feet plunged into it with every step, right up to the ankles. "I guess it's the responsibility, you know. The whole responsibility for life and death, having your finger on the button."

Jack shook his head. "It's more personal than that. It's like I want to kill something, and kill it for a reason. An animal, a child. I can almost feel myself doing it. I can feel the knife in my hand. I can smell the blood."

"You're tired, that's all."

"Tired? I never felt better. I hardly need any sleep; my appetite's terrific. I feel like sex about every five minutes of the day."

"So what do you think these dreams are all about? Why do you want to kill things?"

Jack stopped, and looked around. The wind was fresh and salty and the sea sparkled like hammered glass. He was tanned and fit. His eyes were clear, and he had never looked so strong and charismatic.

"I don't know," he said. "I just feel the need to make a sacrifice. You remember that time at the Madison Hotel, when I had that heart attack? I feel like somebody gave me my life; and I owe them a life in return."

"Listen, I shouldn't worry about it. What do you say we take the dinghy out?"

"No," said Jack. "I've got too much to think about. Too much to do."

Bobby was about to say something, but couldn't. They started to stroll back to the compound together, their bare feet kicking the sand, their hands in their pockets. An amateur photographer took a picture of them which later appeared on the cover of *Life*, and they couldn't have looked more carefree, two brothers with their hair blowing in the wind.

94

"Do you still see Dr Christophe?" asked Bobby, as they reached the house. John-John was sitting on the porch swing wearing a white sun-hat and determinedly stroking a white kitten that didn't want to be stroked. The swing went *sqqueeaakkk-squikkk, sqqueeakk-squikk,* over and over.

"Christophe? That quack?"

"He saved your life."

"I recovered, that's all. I was naturally fit. There wasn't any mystery about it."

"But you want to make a sacrifice to somebody that saved you, even if it wasn't him?"

Jack hooked his arm around Bobby's neck, almost throttling him. "Hey . . . these are dreams, that's all. Don't get upset."

But later that night, unable to sleep, Bobby put on a toweling robe, left the house, and walked down to the beach. The moon had concealed itself behind a cloud, but the night was still bright, and the sky was the color of laundry-ink. The sea glittered and sparkled, but its waves wearily washed against the shore, as if they were tired of washing, as if they had really had enough washing for one millennium.

He walked westward for a while, but then he began to grow chilly and he decided to turn back. Suddenly the idea of a hot, restless night next to Ethel seemed much more attractive, stringy sheets and all. As he started to trudge back, however, he saw an orange flame flickering not far away, among the dunes. It was almost like a flag waving. He hesitated, and then he started to walk toward it. Some students, most likely, camping on the beach.

He climbed the long, soft side of the dune, and then he reached the top. At first he couldn't understand what he was looking at: his brain couldn't work it out. But then he gradually made sense of it; and it was the worst carnage that he had ever seen in his life.

On the far side of the hollow, a driftwood fire was crackling and spitting. In the middle of the hollow, there were three bodies, all cut wide open, their entrails and their stomachs dragged out of them, and all piled together. There was gristle and blood-red connective tissue and frills of fat, and yellowish heaps of glistening intestine. Hunkered over this grisly array was Jack, wearing nothing but his green swimming shorts, his body spattered and smeared with blood. He was tossing ashes on to the bodies, and chanting, in the same distinctive voice with which he had said, "Ask not what your country can do for you, but what you can do for your country." But the words he was saying tonight were not the words of a political speechwriter. They were the words of a religious supplicant. "I offer you these bodies, Baron. I offer you their lives and their agony. You gave me life. You gave me strength. Take these lives in return, as my homage."

Bobby stood staring for almost half a minute, numbed with shock and terrible fascination. He watched Jack loping and crawling from carcass to carcass, cutting off legs and ribs, and gouging out eyes. His sacrificial victims were three sheep, but it was no less horrifying because of that. The shadows from the fire danced across the hollow, and made the scene look even more lurid.

He retreated down the sand dune before Jack could see him. He walked stiffly to the ocean's edge, his stomach churning. He stood in the surf and vomited, and the warm, thick vomit was washed around his ankles.

He called Dr Christophe in Washington; and discovered that he had left his house in Georgetown more than three months ago and returned to Sausalito. It took two and a half hours before he found him at a supper party in Mill Valley. The line was crackly, and there was a hubbub of guests in the background.

"It's Jack. He killed three sheep today, cut them right open."

"They were a sacrifice, Mr Kennedy. Nobody gets anything for nothing. The President has to repay his debt to Baron Samedi – not just once, or twice, but a thousand times over. Baron Samedi is a very demanding creditor, particularly when it comes to human life."

"Why the hell didn't you warn me?"

"I beg your pardon, Mr Kennedy. I did warn you. But you wanted the President back to life at any cost."

"Shit," said Bobby. "If anybody finds out about this—"

"That is the least of your worries," said Dr Christophe. "Now you must watch for even greater sacrifices. Not just sheep, but children, and women . . . Baron Samedi always wants more and more, and it is very hard to say no. If you don't make the sacrifice, you lose whatever he gave you. In your brother's case, your very life."

"But most of the time he seems so normal. In fact, he's very much *better* than normal."

"That was Baron Samedi's gift, Mr Kennedy. But one never gets anything for nothing; and a gift can always be taken away."

"So what do I do?"

"You have to make a decision, Mr Kennedy. That is what you have to do. I thought that was what politicians were especially good at."

"What decision? What in God's name are you talking about?"

"You have to decide whether to continue to protect your brother, or whether you might have to take steps to protect those who might innocently cross your brother's path."

Bobby said nothing for a long time. Then he hung up.

During the fall, Jack made a number of trips around the country. Next year was election year and he wanted to rouse up as much support as he could. He visited Pennsylvania, Minnesota and Nevada; then Wisconsin, North Dakota, Montana, California, Oregon, and Washington.

He seemed to have endless reserves of energy, and his back trouble had left him completely. He was always smiling and handshaking and he was full of optimism for 1964 – even in Washington, which hadn't supported him in 1960.

Bobby flew out to Seattle to join him. It was late October, and it was raining hard when he stepped off the plane. He had brought Harold with him and a new junior assistant, a pretty young Harvard law graduate, Janie Schweizer. Jack and his entourage were staying with a wealthy Seattle Democrat, Willard Bryce, at his huge Gothic-style townhouse overlooking Washington Park.

Willard appeared in the porch as Bobby's limousine came curving up the driveway. He was portly and affable, like W.C. Fields without the vitriol. "Welcome to the Emerald City. Or should I say the Soaking City. Don't worry. The forecast says it should clear by May."

They went inside, and found Jack in the drawing-room, holding an informal conference with twenty or thirty local Democrats. He was leaning back in a rocking-chair, dressed in his shirt-sleeves, and he

97

looked unexpectedly tired and strained. All the same, he made the introductions and cracked a joke about Seattle voters. "They never get it right. I came here asking for a landslide and they gave me a downpour."

When he saw Janie Schweizer, however, his smile completely changed, and he lifted his head back in that way that Bobby had so often seen before. Janie was a tall girl, with blonde hair bobbed in the style that Jackie had made almost obligatory, and a strong, Nordic-looking face. She was wearing a dark, discreet business suit, with a knee-length skirt, but it didn't conceal the fact that she had a very well-proportioned figure.

"This is Janie," said Bobby. "Just joined us from law school. I thought the experience would do her good."

Janie flushed. This was the first time that she had met the President. "Honored to meet you, Mr President."

"How come you get all the lookers, Bobby? Most of my staff look like the wicked witch of the west."

And all through the morning's discussions, in the gloom of Willard's drawing-room, with the rain trickling down the windows and the cigarette-smoke fiddling to the ceiling, Jack hardly ever took his eyes away from Janie Schweizer, and once Bobby caught him licking his lips.

That night, Willard held a formal fundraising dinner for one hundred local supporters. It was a glittering white-tie affair with a string quintet and the cutlery glittered like shoals of fish. Jack gave a speech about the future of world democracy, and his hopes for an end to the arms race. They didn't manage to get to bed until three a.m., and there was still laughter and talking in the house until well past four.

Bobby found that he couldn't sleep. He lay on his bed staring at the elaborately plastered ceiling, listening to the rain as it trickled along the gutters. He hadn't liked the way that Jack had been looking at Janie today; although he guessed that he couldn't blame him. She was younger and prettier than Marilyn, and she had a law degree. He would have been interested in her himself if the timing had been different.

An hour passed and still he couldn't sleep. He switched on the bedside lamp and tried to read another chapter of *Specimen Days in America*, by Walt Whitman. "I had a sort of dream-trance the other day, in which I saw my favorite trees step out and promenade up, down and around, very curiously, with a whisper from one: 'We do all this on the present occasion, exceptionally, just for you.'"

Eventually, he climbed out of bed, put on his warm maroon bathrobe, and went outside into the corridor. Jack had the largest bedroom, on the other side of the galleried landing. A Secret Service agent sat outside, reading a magazine. Bobby went round to Jack's door and pointed at it. "Is the President asleep yet?"

"I shouldn't think so, Mr Kennedy, sir."

Bobby paused. There was something in the agent's tone of voice that aroused his suspicion. "Are you trying to tell me that the President isn't alone?"

"Well, sir, it isn't for me to—"

"Who's he got in there?"

"Sir, I couldn't—"

Bobby came right up to him and seized hold of his necktie. "*Who – has – he – got – in – there?*"

He burst open the double doors and stepped into the bedroom. Behind him, the agent said, "Jesus Christ."

The far side of the room was dominated by a huge, louring four-poster bed, more like a ceremonial barge than a place to sleep. All its blankets had been stripped off and heaped on to the floor. On the bed itself, naked, hunched up like a wolf, Jack was kneeling in the sliced-open body of Janie Schweizer – *kneeling* in it, so that he was thigh-deep in bloody intestines. He had cut her apart from the breastbone downward, and all her internal organs were strewn across the bed.

Quivering, he slowly turned around and stared at Bobby with suspicious, animal eyes.

Bobby didn't say anything. He was too shocked to think of anything to say. He backed away, one step at a time, and then he closed the doors behind him.

"He's killed her, for Christ's sake," gasped the Secret Service agent. His face was the color of wet newspaper. "He's cut her to pieces."

"Don't do anything," said Bobby. "Just stay by the door and make sure that nobody else goes in there."

"What if he comes out? What if he tries to do the same to me?"

"What do you think? Run like hell."

"I don't see any other way," said George, tiredly. "We've been over it time and time again, and it's the only way out."

"What if he misses?" asked Harold.

"He won't miss, not at that range."

"What if he gets caught?"

"He won't be. We'll have three other guys there to help him get clear."

"How about this Oswald character?" Bobby wanted to know.

"*He'll* get caught, don't you worry about that."

"And there is absolutely no way that Oswald can be connected with us?"

"Absolutely none. He thinks he's being paid by something called the Communist Freedom League, and that they're going to give him political asylum in Russia."

"Supposing *he* manages to hit the target, too?"

"Pretty unlikely. But if he does – well, the more the merrier, if you know what I mean."

After Bobby had left, George said, "When it's all over, there'll be one or two loose ends that will need to be tied up. You know, such as that Secret Service agent, and Dr Christophe. Especially Dr Christophe. We don't want him bringing the President back to life a second time, do we?"

Harold lit a Winston, and nodded through the smoke.

On November 22, 1963, the Kennedy motorcade approached the triple underpass leading to Stemmons Freeway in Dallas, Texas. The sun was shining and crowds were cheering on both sides of the street.

Under the shade of a tree, discreetly shielded by three other men, ex-Marine sharpshooter Martin D. Bowman took a high-powered rifle out of a camoflaged fabric case, lifted it, and aimed it. As the Presidential limousine passed the grassy knoll on which he was standing, he fired three shots in quick succession.

It seemed to five or six of the eyewitnesses that "the President's head seemed to explode." But there was more than a spray of blood and brains in the air. For a fleeting second, a dark shadow flickered over the limousine – a shadow which one eyewitness described as "nothing but a cloud of smoke", but which another said was "more like a cloak, blowing in the wind, or maybe some dark kind of creature."

A third witness was even more graphic. "It came twisting up out of the car dark as a torn-off sheet of tarpaper blowing in the wind, except that I could swear it's face was all stretched out in agony with hollow eyes. I thought to myself, I'm seeing a man's soul leaving his body. But if it was his soul, it was a black, black soul, and more frightening than anything I ever saw."

The shadow appears on two frames of amateur movie stock that was shot at the time, but it was dismissed by photographic experts as a fault caused by hurried development. But 2,000 miles away, in Sausalito, California, a feathered rattle that was hanging on a study wall began to shake, all on its own. Dr Christophe raised his eyes from the book he was reading, and took off his spectacles.

"You're back then, master?" he said. "They took away your host?"

He stood up. He knew, with regret, that it was time for him to pack up and leave. They would be coming for him soon. "They want everything, don't they, Baron, even life itself; but they're never prepared to pay the price."

He went to the window and looked out over the garden. He wondered what Brazil would be like, this time of year.

Anaïs

He was talking to his wife on his mobile phone when he first saw Anaïs. He stopped in mid-sentence and stared at her. Even though she had her head half-turned away from him, he felt as if the paving-stones of the Pointe-à-Callière had dropped beneath his feet like an express elevator.

"Yes – you told them what?" asked his wife.

"What?" said George.

"You were telling me about the city planning department." Her voice was tiny and far away.

"Oh, yes," he said. "The planning department. What a collection of clowns." But he couldn't take his eyes off Anaïs. She was wearing a long black trenchcoat with the collar turned up, and she was sitting right on the very end of a cast-iron bench on the opposite side of the redbrick square, her head slightly lowered. The square had eleven black lamps and eleven trees. She had a small sketch-pad on her knee and she was drawing them – occasionally stopping to feed cracker-crumbs to the scruffy little brown birds that pecked around her feet. Her hair was cut in a long dark bob that swung and shone as she moved her head, and she had the profile of an angel – dreamy, heavy-lidded eyes, the straightest of noses, and teeth that were poised on her full lower lip in the faintest suggestion of underbite.

"George . . . can you speak up? I can't hear you very well."

"Sure, yes, sorry. Maybe I'd better call you later, from the hotel."

"You won't make it *too* late? I have to be up early tomorrow for a faculty meeting."

"No, no. I promise you. I won't make it later than nine."

Without even saying goodbye, he pushed down the aerial and

dropped the phone into his raincoat pocket. He waited for a moment, licking his lips with indecision, but then he stood up and walked across the square and stood close beside her – closer than a stranger normally would. The little brown birds all flustered into the air, and perched in the branches of the nearest tree.

Anaïs turned and looked up at him, one hand raised to shield her eyes from the bright grayness of the afternoon sky. Her eyes were green, as green as laurel-leaves frozen in ice.

"Sorry to scare off your birds," he told her. She didn't say anything, but continued to stare up at him, her hand across her forehead. God, she was beautiful. Even though she was wearing a trenchcoat he could tell that she had a good figure by the way that it was so tightly cinched in at the waist. All he could see of her legs were her ankles, in sheer black nylon. She wore shiny black patent shoes with unusually high heels.

"I was, ah, looking for the Rue de la Commune," he said. "Somebody told me there was some kind of monument there – some kind of obelisk or something."

Anaïs said nothing. She stared up at him for one moment longer, then she turned and pointed to the other side of the square.

"That way?" he asked her. Why didn't she speak? He was desperate to know what her voice sounded like, whether she was Québecois or American. But she continued to point, and she twitched her index finger a little to indicate that *oui*, or yes, that was the way to go. Her fingernails were very long and polished in dark maroon.

"Well, thanks very much," he said. "*Merci beaucoup.* I have to say that I'm really enjoying your city. First day I've had enough time to take a walk."

Anaïs turned away and tossed another handful of Saltine crumbs on to the ground. The first two or three birds began to twitter back down from the branches. George stood where he was until it was obvious that she wasn't going to turn back again.

"I – ah – it's kind of chilly, isn't it?" he said. "Maybe you'd like to join me in a cup of coffee. You know, just for the company."

She didn't answer. She didn't even shake her head. George waited for a moment longer and then gave an exaggerated shrug. "Please yourself." He started to walk slowly toward the Rue de la Commune.

Just once he stopped and looked back. She was still sitting there, among the eleven black lamps and the eleven trees, her head lowered over her sketchpad. George covered his mouth with his hand and felt that he could scarcely breathe.

He went to the Rue de la Commune although he didn't know why. He hadn't wanted to go there at all. He crossed it and found himself in a well-manicured, grassy square. The sky was still gray and overcast, but the grass was the same strong laurel-leaf color as Anaïs' eyes. On the right stood the obelisk honoring the first inhabitants of Montreal. In front of him stood an old customs house, its windows blind and its walls still streaked with damp from this morning's rain.

George felt that he had walked out of the world he knew into a new and different world altogether. He felt deeply changed. He had never realized that just *seeing* a woman could have that effect on him. But Anaïs was the girl that he had always wanted, if only he had known it. The girl he couldn't bear to be without.

It started to rain again, and so he turned up the collar of his coat and walked back to his hotel.

Two hours went by. George stood by the window in his hotel suite, drinking a Molson from the mini-bar and watching the rain ceaselessly dredging across the piers and cranes and grain-elevators of Montreal harbor.

The dark-tinted glass made his reflection look even more haggard than he really was. He was a tall, skinny, loose-limbed man of thirty five with brown brushed-back hair and a slightly gone-to-seed face, like a recently retired tennis-player.

He had been in Montreal seven weeks now, but up until today, he had been too busy to think about anything else except concrete and steel and structural analyses. He was an architect, the youngest and brightest partner in Novaks Safdie & Rain, and he was here to finalize his daring design for a new forty-two-story hotel on Sherbrooke Street West, a challenging competitor to Le Westin Mount-Royal and the Ritz-Carlton Kempinski. It would have over one hundred more rooms than either, more restaurants, a huge conference center and a state-of-the-art leisure facility.

The *pièce de résistance* would be a ten-story atrium, with bridges to symbolize the city's position on Montreal island, and three waterfalls to symbolize the confluence of the Ottawa and the St Lawrence rivers.

He walked over to the drawing-board that was set up in the middle of his living-room, and switched on his angle lamp. He hesitated for a moment, then he lifted aside his sketches for the hotel's elevator doors, and flipped back the cover of a white cartridge drawing block. Choosing a soft black pencil, he began to draw.

He had never been particularly good at likenesses. For instance, he had never attempted any portraits of Helen or Charlie, but his first portrait of Anaïs flowed from his pencil as if she were drawing herself. He sketched her head and shoulders, the way her hair swung along her jawline, her slightly pouting lips. She came to life from the page and stared at him in the same way that she had stared at him in the Pointe-à-Callière, aloof, disinterested, but with a very subtle hint of slyness in her eyes.

This was when he named her Anaïs. It was after the French erotic authoress, Anaïs Nin, but it was also a reminder of the perfume that his last girlfriend had worn, the girlfriend who had left him just before he met and married Helen. Anaïs Anaïs, a sweet flowery fragrance that always reminded him of being in love, and of being hurt.

Under the sketch, he wrote, "Today, in the Pointe-à-Callière, I met Anaïs as arranged. She was sitting on one of the six benches, feeding the little birds. Immediately she saw me she stood up, came toward me and put her arms around me. She knew that she couldn't ask me where I had been, but her green eyes filled with tears, and she said, 'George . . . you don't know how much I suffer when you leave me. I miss you so much that my heart feels as if it is being crushed in a terrible fist.'

"I kissed her forehead and whispered to her not to make a scene in public. Then I told her to open her raincoat. She was about to protest. The square was busy that afternoon in spite of the rain. But then, with lowered eyes, she unbuckled her tight belt, and unbuttoned her coat. She stood with her arms by her sides, her eyes still lowered, because she knew that I would be angry if she tried to look challenging.

"I reached out with one hand and opened up the coat a little way. Underneath she was completely nude except for a black lace garter belt and black silk stockings with lace tops. Her full white breasts were veined with blue, and in the chilly afternoon air her wide nipples crinkled and tightened. In her belly-button I noticed with satisfaction the gold ring that I had given her the last time we met. She had shaved her dark pubic hair into a shape like a flame, or a serpent's tail.

"I ran my middle finger down between her breasts, and then further still, pausing for a moment to tug at the ring. Then I told her that she could fasten her coat. She was to meet me at nine o'clock at my hotel. She begged to know why she couldn't come with me immediately. I like it when she's so distressed. I lifted her chin and kissed her on the lips and told her that it wasn't possible. She would have to wait until I was ready for her."

He tore off the page, and on the next sheet he drew a full-length portrait of Anaïs standing in the square with her raincoat open, exposing her naked body. He gave her a crushed, vulnerable expression; a look of entreaty. He made her breasts much bigger than they probably were, but this was only a fantasy, right?

He sat back and finished his can of beer. Anaïs looked back at him. He wrote the date and the time of their meeting on the bottom of the drawing, and signed it. That evening, restless, he went for another walk. A south-west wind had picked up and the rain had been blown away north-eastward. The sidewalks along St Laurent, The Main, were rapidly drying. The city glittered with lights and echoed with taxi-horns.

He passed the Montreal Pool Room, where a fat cook in a white apron stared mournfully out of the window while an array of hamburgers broiled in front of him; and the Brasserie Alouette, where old men with berets and crumpled faces sat drinking Molson and smoking Gauloises. He turned right at Maisonneuve and made his way toward the Rue St Denis, where he found himself shuffling along a crowded sidewalk past cafés and bars and bistros, art galleries and L'Axe Disco Sex Club, *avec Couples Érotiques.*

At last he reached the Rue Notre Dame, where St Denis became Rue Bonsecours. The brightness and the brashness was left behind. He descended a steep cobbled incline and found himself con-fronted by the Notre-Dame-de-Bonsecours Chapel. He stood still for a moment, breathing in the wind, breathing in the atmosphere.

Then he continued, and he knew where he was going, back to the Pointe-à-Callière, in case by some impossible chance she was still sitting there.

He walked across the square, and of course the bench was empty. He reached down and touched the place where she had been sitting with the tips of his fingers. Then he circled around two or three times. He had to be realistic. He would never see her again in his life. He had never felt so bereaved.

"I opened the door and there she stood, her raincoat collar turned up. I stood back and let her walk into the room. Even before I closed the door I ordered her to drop her raincoat, which she did, so that she stood there in nothing but her garter-belt and her stockings and her six-inch heels. One of the housekeepers walked past and saw her, and looked at me, but said nothing. It was my privilege to show her naked to anybody I wanted, and she knew that.

"I closed the door and then told her to get down on her knees, which she did. I circled around her while she knelt silent and obedient, her head slightly lowered, her hands clasped together in front of her. I told her to keep her hands by her sides, I didn't want her to hide anything, and she mutely obeyed. I asked her if she had been touched by any other men since I had last seen her. Had any other man held her hand? Had any other man kissed her? Had any other man made love to her?

"Each time she shook her head, but I didn't know whether to believe her or not. I took hold of her hair and lifted her head so that she was looking me directly in the eye. 'Just remember,' I told her. 'You belong to me now. Completely.'

"I ordered her bring me a whiskey, which she did. 'Now, undress me,' I said, and I stood with the glass in my hand while she loosened my necktie, unbuttoned my shirt and unfastened my belt. When I was undressed, I climbed on to the bed and lay back, and she climbed on top of me like a beautiful animal, her big breasts swaying. She kissed me and bit my neck, and dug her fingernails into my shoulders. She whispered how much she adored me and how she would serve me for the rest of her life. She said that I could do anything with her, body and soul.

"She rode up and down on top of me, delirious, her dark hair swirling from side to side. Her eyes were closed, her lips were parted, sweat ran down her cleavage. She begged me to push it in deeper and harder. She begged me to hurt her, to punish her for being so jealous.

"I rolled over and forced her face-down on to the bedcover, with her bottom lifted into the air. She was wide open to me, and she reached between her legs and tugged herself even wider apart. I pushed myself into her, and I pushed myself into her so hard that she was gasping and screaming. When I was finished, I lay back for a moment to get my breath back. Then I got up, picked up her coat, and threw it at her."

Another sketch, with Anaïs lying back on the bed, her face streaked with eye-liner. He had never drawn so well. He touched Anaïs' cheeks with a little pastel blusher, and touched in the laurel-green of her eyes. "Anaïs," he whispered, out loud. He was still finishing off the detail of her hair when the phone rang and made him jump.

"George? It's ten after midnight. I've been waiting and waiting for you to call."

"Oh . . . I'm sorry. I've been busy working on some drawings. Guess I got carried away."

"George, are you all right? You sound different."

"I'm fine. What do you mean, 'different'?"

"I don't know, distracted."

"I'm tired is all. It's been one of those days."

A pause. Then, "George . . . if something was wrong, you'd tell me, wouldn't you?"

Goddamn woman's intuition. "What do you mean by 'wrong'?"

"Well, if something was wrong between you and me."

"Sweetheart, you know there's nothing wrong between you and me."

"You keep forgetting to call and you never say I love you."

"Well, I love you, OK?" He couldn't help looking at Anaïs' eyes, Anaïs' lips. The lips said, "kiss me." The eyes said "have me."

He talked to Helen for a few more minutes and then he hung up. He covered his drawing-block with a sheaf of architectural schematics and switched off his angle lamp. He went to bed without taking a shower, and he slept very deeply, without any memorable dreams.

"George, you're not listening to me."

George blinked. He was having lunch in a heavy-duty French restaurant on the Rue de la Montagne with his partner Ken Safdie and two directors of Hôtelleries Québécoises. One of the directors had gone to take a phone call; the other had taken the opportunity to go to the bathroom. Ken had tried to take advantage of their momentary absence by asking George what he thought about their finance package, but George was staring out through the window into the street.

"George, you've been acting weird all morning. Are you pining for something?"

"*Pining* for something? Pining for something like what?"

"The 'flu, maybe. You haven't even touched your food."

George looked down at his gold-rimmed plate, and the large piece of poached salmon that lay on it, in a brandy sauce. He had only broken off one flake of fish, and then he hadn't eaten it.

"I don't know, Ken. I guess I'm not too hungry. I've had enough of French cuisine to last me a lifetime."

Ken looked at him with slitted ginger-eyelashed eyes. He and George had been friends for years, ever since architectural college. Ken was four years older than George – sandy-complexioned, big, with sandy-freckled hands more like a boxer than an architect. "Come on, George. It isn't the food, is it? You can tell me. What is it? You're homesick? You're missing Helen and Charlie? Come on, pal, I'm missing Yolande, but there's nothing I can do about it. You and me, we've got ourselves a job to do, and when we've done it, we'll be ludicrously famous and insanely wealthy."

"It's nothing," said George. "Really, it's nothing."

"Well then, cheer up for Christ's sake. Listen – what's the difference between a wife and a hurricane?"

"Ken, please."

"There isn't any difference between a wife and a hurricane. When they come, they're both wet and noisy, and when they go they take half your house with them."

"Yeah, good," said George. But then he saw a young girl with swinging brunette hair walk past the window and he couldn't help lifting himself out of his chair a little to make sure that it wasn't her.

Ken glanced at the girl and then turned back again. "Play it straight with me, George. What's going on here? You and me, we've never had secrets before."

George took a breath. He drummed his fingertips on the tablecloth. At last he looked up at Ken and said, "I've met someone."

"You mean a *girl*? You mean here, in Montreal?"

George nodded. "For Christ's sake, Ken, it was an accident. If I'd known she was there, I would have walked the other way, and never met her at all. I mean, I wish to God that I *hadn't*."

"George, what the fuck are you talking about?"

"It was yesterday . . . I went for a walk in Vieux Montreal and there she was."

"And what?"

"She's incredible. I mean you never saw a girl so beautiful. Dark hair, green eyes. The kind of figure you only dream about."

"Yes? So? And?"

"And nothing. I'm in love with her, that's all."

"You met her just yesterday and already you're in love?"

"I can't explain it, Ken. It's one of those things that happens just once in a lifetime, and most of the time it never happens at all. We never get to meet the girl of our dreams so we end up making a compromise and marrying the least-offensive girl we know."

"Is that all that Helen is to you? The least-offensive girl you know? Have you told her that? Jesus, talk about a sweet nothing."

"Ken, believe me. I have no intention of hurting Helen. But Anaïs—"

"That's her name? Anaïs? What's that, French?"

At that moment, however, the two hotel directors returned, one huge and well-fed, in a voluminous blue suit, the other small and highly polished, with a clipped moustache. The huge one clapped George on the shoulder and said, "You haven't eaten your salmon, George. It's wild, it's the best. Don't tell me that it struggled all the way up-rivair for nozzing."

George said, "We all do, Monsieur Truchaud. Salmon and people both. We all struggle 'up-rivair' for 'nozzing'."

Monsieur Truchaud frowned at Ken in bewilderment. But it was just at that moment that another brunette passed the window of the restaurant, in the company of a tall dark-haired man. George pushed back his chair. He could see her only from the back, but it was her. He was sure it was her.

"George?" said Ken; but George was already walking quickly toward reception, and pushing his way through the revolving door out into the street.

She had almost reached the end of the block. George jogged after her, still clutching his table-napkin. He dodged a taxi, and almost collided with a bicycle. The cyclist shouted, "*Bazar!*" George caught up with her on the other side of the street, outside a brightly lit couturier's window. He touched her sleeve and said, "Hey! Hey, wait up a second!"

It really was her. Same hooded eyelids, same green eyes. Her companion was tall, at least six feet two inches, with oiled-back hair. He was handsome but his cheeks were pitted with acne scars. He was wearing an expensive black overcoat and a yellow spotted cravat.

"*Qu'est-ce que c'est?*" he wanted to know. His voice was thick, with a strong Joual accent, like shingle in a concrete-mixer.

"It's nothing. It's just that this lady and I met briefly yesterday, and I asked her to join me for a coffee and she couldn't. I mean she obviously didn't have the time. So all I'm saying is that the offer still stands, and in fact I'd like to invite her out for dinner if she'd care to."

The girl didn't look at George once. All the time her eyes were fixed on her companion. Her companion stared at George as if he had a slight headache. George said, "There's no strings attached. It was just that she was kind enough to direct me to the Rue . . . well, she was kind enough to direct me, that's all. And dinner was just a way of saying thanks. You know, stranger in a strange city. One of those little acts of kindness."

The girl's companion stepped up so close that George could smell his lavender aftershave. His chest was like a wall. Very quietly, he said, "*Va-t-en, étron* – off you go, asshole."

George backed away. "Listen, I'm just trying to show my gratitude, that's all."

"Don't you speak English?" said the girl's companion. "I'm telling you real polite to go away and to leave this lady alone. Otherwise I'll cut your head off and stuff it up your ass."

George said, "Now look, now, I was only trying to—"

But at that moment Ken came up and put his arm around him and said, "Come on, George, let's get back to our meeting, shall we?"

"You want to keep your friend indoors," said the girl's companion. "*Il est fou comme la merde.*"

"Please!" said George. He tried to take hold of the girl's hand, but her companion pushed him away. "Why don't you let *her* answer?"

"If she wanted to answer, she'd answer," her companion said. "Now leave her alone. She don't want nothing to do with you. Not tonight. Not never."

They walked back to the restaurant. Ken said, "Was that her? Was that Anaïs?"

George nodded. He had a catch in his throat and he could hardly speak.

"Monsieur Truchaud saw the guy she was with. Apparently he knows him. He's what they call a *maudit* – a real bad dude. He couldn't believe it when you went running after him."

Just before he pushed his way back into the revolving door, however, George turned to Ken with tears in his eyes and said, "Did you see her, though, Ken? Did you see her? Can you understand what's happened to me here?"

Ken said nothing, but shook his head. Ken never looked at really beautiful girls. He had learned to be content with Yolande.

"Tonight I caught her out on the town with her older brother Guillaume. Hadn't I given her firm instructions to stay in my hotel room and wait for me, naked, kneeling on the floor? But there she was on the Rue de Montagne strutting along as if she didn't have a care in the world.

"How many times have I warned her about going back to her family? The Royers are one of the heaviest mobs of organized gangsters in Quebec. Her father was shot last year and his body found floating in the St Lawrence, wrapped up in razor-wire. Since then Guillaume and her younger brother Francois have taken over. Both are criminal psychopaths but they don't worry me. Anaïs is better off with me. At least she'll be well-disciplined.

"I confronted Guillaume and told him that if he ever came near Anaïs again I would personally make sure that he would spend the rest of his life in a wheelchair. I dragged Anaïs back to my room and told her to strip completely naked and to kneel down in front of me. I told her that she had embarrassed me in front of Guillaume and that she would have to be punished for her own good. I had my leather belt looped in my hand and I kept snapping her with it, little sharp snaps on her shoulders and her back and her thighs. She wept and begged my forgiveness. She said she would do anything for me, so long as I forgave her. And I said, yes, you will."

Next to his sloping, handwritten words, there were thumbnail sketches of Guillaume and Anaïs together, and then a larger picture of himself and Anaïs in the hotel room. Anaïs' back and shoulders were already criss-crossed with red marks.

She was so beautiful, so subservient. But so she should be, after the way that she had treated him this afternoon.

He popped open another can of Molson and circled around the room. Then he returned to his drawing-board. "What do you think you deserve, Anaïs?" he whispered. "What do you think you deserve, for humiliating me like that?"

"I tied her face-down to the bed, fastening her wrists with ropes, and knotting her hair to the bedhead so that she couldn't move her head without hurting herself.

"I took my belt and lashed it across her bare bottom. She gasped, and her whole body tensed. I lashed her bottom again, leaving another crimson stripe. I lashed her six or seven times, but after the six lashes she stopped begging for mercy and started to beg for more.

"I lashed her until she suddenly clenched her fists and gritted her teeth and started to shake in the throes of a huge convulsive orgasm.

"At once I threw aside my belt, climbed on to the bed and forced myself into her. I knew that I was hurting her, but I loved her, and she needed punishment, she needed to be hurt, just like every beautiful girl who condemns a man to live with a woman he doesn't really love.

"I dressed and left her for more than an hour in total darkness, while I went down to the hotel bar for a drink with one of my partners. When I eventually came back I switched on the bedside light and angled it into her eyes. I asked her if she had learned her lesson and she swore that she had. I untied her and let her get off the bed. But after she had put on her coat, she turned around and said, 'My brother will kill you for this.' I snatched hold of her hair and banged her face-first into a framed picture on the wall. I was beginning to believe that she was humiliating me on purpose, so that I would beat her some more."

He drew an elaborate full-page picture of Anaïs' punishment. He wrote the date, and then the time. Tomorrow he would punish her some more. A whip, perhaps, or a cat-o'-nine-tails, and some nipple clamps. Perhaps it was time he branded her with his own branding-iron, the initials GR, intertwined.

He called Helen and they had a fragmentary conversation about Charlie's progress at school. "He doesn't like football. He says it's too rough."

"Hey – I hope I haven't fathered a wimp." He was only half-joking.

"He's a very quiet, boy, George. He bottles things up, just like you do."

"Me, quiet?"

"You used to be, anyway."

He looked across the room at his drawings of Anaïs. He wondered why it was almost impossible to find a woman you really wanted. He wondered why it was that when you did – by a hundred-million-to-one chance – she didn't want to know you, she didn't even want to open her mouth and waste her breath by saying no to you. It was wrong. It was all very wrong. The planets spinning all the wrong ways, the horoscopes all talking gibberish.

He couldn't sleep and so he went for a walk through Vieux Montreal. It was well after two o'clock in the morning. The streets were empty and echoing. He returned to the Pointe-à-Callière and sat on the bench where Anaïs had sat, his head tilted back, his legs outstretched. The wind was still fresh, and he could see the ghostly clouds racing over the rooftops of the renovated houses. He felt a deep sense of time and place.

He felt more rested, and relaxed. Maybe his crisis was over. He looked around the windy square, which had once been a fort surrounded by a wooden palisade. He thought of Helen, and Charlie, and for the first time he missed them. It was time for him to finish his work here in Montreal and accept his responsibilities at home. After all, hadn't he punished Anaïs enough?

He stood up to leave, but as he did so three men entered the square and began to walk toward him, directly toward him, with obvious purpose. They wore hats and long black coats and their shoes rapped on the brickwork. George walked away from them, at a sharp diagonal, but one of them cut him off. He stopped, and stood where he was, and all three of them approached him.

"George?" asked one of them. His voice sounded very harsh and very familiar. "George, I warned you, *n'est-ce pas?* I warned you to leave her alone."

George said, unsteadily "I don't know what you're talking about."

"Don't tell me that you're going to lie to me, George! I would have thought better of you. You're such *un grand-jack* after all, aren't you? Such a he-man! But I warned you to leave her alone and you didn't, did you? I saw her tonight. I saw what you did."

"Listen – *écoutez* – I didn't do anything to anyone."

The man took off his hat and the lamplight revealed the acne-pitted face of the girl's companion.

"You hurt Anaïs, you *écu.* You hurt her so bad."

"Anaïs? But there isn't any Anaïs! Anaïs is just a story . . . not even half a story, just a few pictures and some fantasy stuff. It's all a fantasy!"

The man came up close. His eyes were as pale and expressionless as agates. "What you did to her, that didn't look like any fantasy to me."

George looked around him, desperately, but there was nobody else in the square. "Listen," he said, "I don't understand this at all. I don't know how you know that I called her Anaïs, how you know about those things I wrote, those pictures I drew – they were only a fantasy, you know? They were just a way of –

I don't know – they were just a way of expressing my frustrations, that's all."

The man said, "*Eh bien*, we all have different ways of expressing our frustrations, don't we? First of all, when I saw what you did to Anaïs, I thought *vais t'crisser un coup de poing* – you know, I thought that I'd beat the shit out of you."

He put his arm around George's shoulders, and George's heart began to palpitate, quite painfully. "Then I thought, no, *fuck dat*, I'm not going to beat him. Me – Guillaume Royer – one of the most notorious gangsters in Montreal – bruise his knuckles with a beating?"

George said, "Listen to me, listen to me. I don't know how you managed to see those drawings and read all that stuff, but it was all a fantasy, all of it. It never happened. I just made it up, you know what I mean? I invented it. Maybe you think it's sick. Maybe it is. But I swear to God that none of it's real."

Guillaume Royer gave George a reassuring pat on the shoulders. Then, with his right hand, he reached around and stuck a long kitchen knife into George's stomach, just above his waistband. George gasped. Every nerve in his stomach cringed in pain. It was so cold, so intense, so intrusive. He had never imagined that anything could hurt so much. His abdominal muscles cramped up, his knees buckled. But Guillaume and one of his companions gripped the back of his raincoat and held him up, so that he was still standing.

George stared at him and said, "Christ, you've stabbed me!"

Guillaume smiled. "Now *you* know what pain is. Not so much fun, hunh?"

"I swear to God that all those drawings were fantasy. I swear it. I swear it. I never even—"

Guillaume said nothing, but his face was filled with contempt. He slowly drew the knife upward, through George's intestines, and up through his liver. George could hear the soft slicing sound it made, actually *hear* it, and then the soft bubbling exhalation of a punctured lung. He continued to stare at Guillaume, because he knew what had happened and he didn't dare to look down.

"I swear," he said. "I swear to you."

Guillaume took out the knife and it was then that George's

intestines spilled out of his gaping stomach and dropped down to his knees like a thick, glistening apron.

Guillaume's companion lowered George to the ground, almost tenderly. Guillaume bent over and wiped his knife-blade on his coat.

"Now you don't have to worry about Anaïs any more, whether she misbehaves or not. No more problems, hunh?"

George looked up at him. "Anaïs . . ." he whispered, and tried to raise his hand. But then the dark square darkened even more, and his head dropped against the bricks. The three men walked briskly away leaving him lying amongst the eleven trees and the eleven black lamps.

Inspector Fauve leafed through George's sketches and then turned away from the drawing-board. He was short, stocky man with short bristly hair. "You think these are true?" he asked Sergeant Piquot.

Sergeant Piquot pulled a lugubrious face. "They're very graphic, aren't they? Very true-to-life."

"I know they're true-to-life. What I want to know is, are they true? Did the events in these drawings really happen, or is this all just fantasy?"

"He's written dates and times."

"Well, yes. But there's no crime family called the Royers anyplace in Canada, and we can't trace any Guillaume Royer, or any Anaïs Royer. What's more, none of the staff here ever saw Mr Rain take anybody up to his room, boy or girl or anything in between."

Inspector Fauve picked up the sketch that George had first made of her, the day he had seen her in the square. "You know something?" he said. "I never saw a girl as beautiful as this. If I had have done, I would have married her."

"You're married already."

"So what? With a girl like this, you don't worry about details like that."

In the Pointe-à-Callière, the following day, the girl sat on a different bench, and this time she wasn't feeding the birds, although a tortoiseshell cat sat on the other end of the bench, watching her. She was wearing her black raincoat and her eyes were concealed behind large black sunglasses, although the later-afternoon sun was very weak.

The man came across the square and immediately she stood up. He took her in his arms and kissed her. "I'm sorry I'm so late. I couldn't get away from my meeting, and then Phoebe called up and gave me a huge long shopping-list."

She kissed him again and brushed back his hair with her hand. "It's just my luck, isn't it, that I meet a man I really adore, and he's already married?"

The man said, "It won't be like this much longer, I promise you."

Together they walked to the Carré Louis until they reached the narrow entrance to a block of apartments. The girl opened the door and led the way into a gloomy hall that smelled of floorwax and cooking. They went up four flights of stairs without saying a word. At the top, the girl opened another, white-painted door and entered her light, bright studio apartment. There were wide dormer windows all along one side, with a view of the jumbled rooftops of old Montreal. Under the windows there was a large bed covered with a white bedspread and heaped with cushions. On the walls, big splashy abstract paintings in intense blues and eye-burning reds. On the far side of the room, a drawing-board and a table cluttered with inks and paints and pots of tinted water.

The man and the girl undressed in silence. The girl was smooth-skinned and lithe, and her hair shone in the pale blueish light of the dying day. They made love slowly and romantically, completely lost in the dreamworld of their infatuation, as new lovers do.

Much later, when it was dark, the man sat on the high stool in front of the drawing-board, while the girl lay back on the bed, smoking.

The man casually leafed through some of the drawings. "These are new. I haven't seen these before."

"It's a story I'm working on for *Fantaisie* magazine. It's almost finished."

The man picked up one of the sheets and studied it. "Hey . . . this guy looks just like me."

The girl smiled and sat up. "I modeled him on you, that's why. And the girl I modeled on me. It's a story about an architect who falls in love with a strange girl and then draws erotic pictures of her. In his drawings he treats her like dirt but she always comes back for more."

"What's this, therapy for a guilty conscience? It's not your fault that my marriage is breaking up."

"Therapy? Maybe. A little. But in the end the man's fantasy goes too far, and then *he* has to be punished, too. That's only justice."

The man looked at the next sheet. A man who looked just like him, sitting alone in the Pointe-à-Callière. Eleven trees, eleven black lamps. Three men approaching and surrounding him. One of them laying his arm around his shoulders. Then, a close-up of a knife penetrating his stomach. His face, shocked and desperate. His intestines wallowing out, on to the bricks.

"Yuck," said the man.

The girl came over and kissed him. "Here's the last picture . . . the grieving wife weeping over his casket. But I don't know . . . do you think a man like that deserves any tears?"

"Do you think that *I* deserve any tears?"

The girl thought for a moment, and then she said, "No. Neither of you do."

She picked up her eraser and rubbed out the droplets that were coursing down the woman's cheeks; and at that very instant, in the Cypress Funeral Home in Van Nuys, California, Helen Rain lifted her hand to her eyes and found that they were suddenly and inexplicably dry.

Cold Turkey

". . . and, as usual, Tarquin wishes all of you a very merry Christmas," said Uncle Philip, stroking the pedigree British Blue cat that sat in his lap. It was obvious, however, that Tarquin was wishing for only one thing. His coppery eyes were fixed on the huge, well-bronzed turkey that had just arrived in the middle of the dining-table. His tension was almost palpable. Mandy felt that if the turkey had been capable of twitching just an inch, Tarquin would have launched himself at it, and nothing could have stopped him.

"A very merry Christmas to Tarquin," Kenneth replied, raising his glass. "Long may he live in the lap of luxury." Kenneth was floridly drunk; and two of his shirt-buttons were missing but he was not too drunk to be less-than-subtly sarcastic.

Nicholas raised his glass, too, although he had remained supremely, remotely sober. A new partner in a firm of Essex Street solicitors couldn't afford to be caught for drink-driving, and besides, he never liked to lose control. His wife Libby, however, was beginning to look distinctly disarranged. She had already pulled one of her crackers and she had awkwardly tugged a purple paper hat over her frizzy ginger hair.

"To Tarquin," said Nicholas, and gave Uncle Philip a waxy, colorless smile. "May all his dreams come true."

"Cats don't have dreams, do they?" frowned Libby.

"Oh, yes," Nicholas assured her, as if he had never met her before. "They have the same kind of dreams as any other creature. Lust, greed, and lost opportunities. Most of all, though, they dream of revenge."

"I don't think Tarquin dreams of revenge, do you, sweetie?" said

Mandy, reaching over and tickling his chin. "I think Tarquin has nice dreams, about mice, and turkey."

Caitlin, arty and vague, threw back her tawny mane and jangled her silver bangles. "I don't think he dreams about mice, either. Cats are too cerebral to dream of mice."

"Cerebral?" laughed Kenneth. "They're not cerebral. They're parasites. They're not much better than tapeworms with fur."

"Kenneth!" Mary scolded him. "We're just about to eat lunch!"

Mary was Mandy's mother. Mandy's father had died in April in a road accident in Newbury, bloody and white in his BMW, with a local doctor holding his hand. His life insurance had scarcely covered the mortgage, and ever since then Mary and Mandy had been living on a smaller and smaller budget. Mandy couldn't remember when she had last bought herself a new skirt.

She thought that Christmas at Box Hill was dull beyond endurance. For three days every year the Chesterton family sat in the gloomy drawing-room or the musty-smelling conservatory, picking at soft-centered chocolates and cracking stale Brazil nuts, or bickering about politics or who had cheated at Monopoly two Christmases ago and who had ripped the board in half in a rage.

For Mandy, Tarquin was the only consolation. At least he didn't argue and he didn't get drunk. He was so haughty. Apart from Uncle Philip, Mandy was the only member of the family by whom Tarquin would deign to be stroked.

This year there were only eleven of them, including Mandy herself. Ned and Alice had won a safari to Kenya in a competition on the side of a jar of Kenco instant coffee. Poor Uncle David's prostate cancer had spread and he wasn't expected to see the Spring. Mind you, he was only a curate, so he didn't really count. Jilly and Michael were having a trial separation after that business with Jilly and the muscular plumber, and so Michael had come on his own, and was tetchy and gloomy and tearful by turns. Kenneth called him "the Surrey Waterworks."

Grace had arrived late, with far too many bags. She had a loud voice and a big face. Mandy had always assumed that she was a lesbian, but her mother said that she was engaged to be married once, to a Hungarian violinist. One night, drunk, he had thrown himself off Putney Bridge, and that was that.

None of the family liked each other much; and none of them felt any affection for Polesden View: this great elaborate red-brick Edwardian pile, with its ugly mansard roof and its gardens full of gelatinous moss and dripping laurels. Mandy thought it was the most depressing house she had ever visited. She was seventeen now – still petite, with dark short-cropped hair and a pixie-like face. But she no longer knelt on the window-seats, the way she did when she was younger, and peered through the stained-glass windows in the hall, amber and crimson and bottle-green. In those days she used to imagine that she could see ladies with capes and umbrellas wandering sadly along the rainswept garden paths. But there were never any ladies; there were only ghosts, and memories, and echoes, and Uncle Philip was the last of them.

They wouldn't have come within fifty miles of Box Hill if it hadn't have been for Uncle Philip. He was the oldest member of the Chesterton family. He was mean, arrogant and so unremittingly condescending to all of them that Mandy wondered that he didn't grow tired of it. But he had inherited most of the family fortune, which was immense, and none of them were going to displease him until he had gargled his last breath.

Three generations ago, the Chestertons had struck it rich in Rhodesia, and upstairs on the second landing there was still a faded photograph of uncle Philip's grandfather shaking hands with the diamond magnate Barney Barnato on the terrace of the Natalia Hotel in Durban. In the background, a cheeky black boy was sticking his tongue out.

Apart from Polesden View, Uncle Philip owned a 230-acre farm in Oxfordshire, a seaside house in Southwold, on the east coast, and a three-bedroomed flat in Cheyne Walk, in Chelsea. There were safes stuffed with stocks and bonds, and private deposit boxes crammed with family jewelry.

The family may have hated their Christmases here on Box Hill, but none of them were going to risk their inheritance.

Christmas lunch was even more oppressive than ever. It was one of those dark, airless days when the cloud hangs low over the Surrey Downs and the dining-room windows were all steamed up, which made it seem even darker. Uncle Philip sat at the head of the table with Tarquin in his lap, a gaunt silhouette with thin silver hair and gleaming cheekbones, where his skin was stretched tightly over his skull. He reminded Mandy of a Hallowe'en mask. He stroked Tarquin with his right hand and twisted his turkey into small pieces with the edge of his fork. Tarquin stared at the half-carved turkey carcass and didn't even blink.

"He looks so hungry, poor thing," said Mandy.

Uncle Philip gave her a wide, emaciated smile. "He has to learn to wait for what he wants, like everybody else. We mustn't spoil him, must we?"

"I suppose not," said Mandy, and stroked Tarquin under his chin until his throat rattled with harsh, catarrhal purring.

Grace said, "Philip . . . I hear you've been ill."

"A bout of the 'flu, that's all," said Philip. "The Grim Reaper isn't going to get me yet."

"You should think of selling this house. It's so big. It's so damp. It's so impractical."

"It's my home," said Philip. "More than that, it's Tarquin's home. Tarquin would be lost, anywhere else."

"Even if you don't move, you should at least think of re-assessing your holdings," said Kenneth, after a while. "Some of your older portfolios, well . . ."

Philip didn't even raise his voice. "When I need advice from a bankrupted stockbroker, Kenneth, I'll ask for it. I promise."

"Now come on, Uncle Philip, that's not fair," protested Joy. In the days when Kenneth had been handsome, the blond-haired captain of the village cricket team, Joy had been deliciously pretty, in a scrubbed, country kind of way. Now her face had been disassembled by Kenneth's alcoholism and their children's delinquency. Her young and golden life had vanished and she didn't know where to look for it.

Uncle Philip raised his eyes from his plate, where he had been tirelessly pursuing a Brussels sprout. "Fair, Joy? Fair? You all inherited a hundred thousand each when Father died; and what you did with it afterward was up to you. If you decided to spend it on cars and holidays and ridiculous business ventures, that isn't any concern of mine; and there's nothing about it that isn't *fair*."

He turned to Mandy and laid his hand on top of hers. "What game shall we play after lunch, Mandy? Scrabble? Or shall we play charades?"

Tarquin had cautiously lifted one paw on to the tablecloth. His eyes were locked on to the turkey as if by laser. Uncle Philip rapped his paw with the flat of his knife, and said, "Tarquin! You can't always have what you want, just when you want it!"

Mandy smiled at her mother, and then she said, "Let's play charades. This family seems to be good at it."

After the turkey came the blue-flaming Christmas pudding, and mince pies with thick Cornish cream. They pulled their crackers and put on paper hats and read out all the jokes. "*Father*: Your hair needs cutting badly. *Son*: No it doesn't . . . it needs cutting well!"

Mandy was too full to eat any more so she helped to clear away the dishes. In the large, pine-paneled kitchen she found Avril, the cook, scraping heaps of sprouts and roast potatoes into the bin. "I don't know why he always orders me to cook so much. Nobody ever eats it. They're all to busy arguing and scoring points off each other. They're all too busy worrying about their inheritance; that's it. That's what Mr Chesterton says, anyway."

"Doesn't he *ever* believe that we come here because we want to?" said Mandy.

The cook shook her head. "He knows you don't want to. But that's all part of the fun."

"You don't think it's *fun*, do you?" asked Mandy.

"Yes, Miss, I do, in a way. My father used to say that there was nothing that made him laugh more than monkeys dancing for nuts. I didn't really know what he meant until I came here, and saw you lot visiting Mr Chesterton once every Christmas. No more, because you really can't stand him, can you, the horrible old shriveled-up creature? And no less, because he might decide to cut you out of his will."

Nicholas came in, carrying the remains of the turkey. The cook loosely covered it with a tea-towel and put it into the larder to cool. "Turkey," she complained. "I can't stand the stuff. But your Uncle Philip always wants his cold turkey salad on Boxing Day."

Not surprisingly, Tarquin appeared, on a foraging expedition away from the base camp of Uncle Philip's lap. He went up to the cook and rubbed her legs with the flat of his head, and mewed.

"No, Tarquin, you're not having any turkey tonight. He's a terror, you know, when it comes to any kind of birds. Pheasants, quail, chickens. He hangs around the larder until I chase him away with the sponge-mop."

Mandy hunkered down and stroked Tarquin's soft and fluffy fur. "Surely we could give him just one slice of turkey?"

"Sorry," the cook told her. "Tarquin doesn't get any left-overs until your Uncle Philip's had all of his. Your Uncle Philip will eat a gammon until you can see his teethmarks on the bone, I promise you. Doesn't believe in waste. How do you think he stayed so rich? You've seen his car, haven't you? He bought that in 1962 and he won't change it for anything. Waste of money, that's what he calls it. And you should see the meat he expects me to cook with. Neck-end and scrag-end and skirt.

"He's mean and he's grumpy and if I were you I wouldn't come for Christmas ever again. You're just making fools of yourselves."

Mandy gave Tarquin one last tickle and then she stood up. "Perhaps you're right. Perhaps we shouldn't come here, ever again."

The next morning, Mandy woke up early and went down to the kitchen in her slippers to make herself a cup of coffee. The gloom of the previous day had lifted, and the sun was shining weakly through the trees. In the distance, through a gilded mist, she could see the Surrey Weald and the spire of Dorking church. While she waited for the kettle to boil she switched on the old transistor radio on the window-sill.

"Boxing Day promises to be bright and clear over most of the area, although there is a threat of wintry showers across Essex and Kent . . ."

When she was young, Mandy had always imagined that people held boxing matches on Boxing Day; and she still didn't quite believe her mother's laborious explanation that it was a day when the rich used to give boxes of Christmas leftovers to the poor – any more than she could quite forget her father's joke that the box trees which had given Box Hill its name had real ready-made wooden boxes growing on them, instead of fruit.

The kettle started to dribble, and then to whistle, and she went to the larder to find the coffee-jar. The larder door was already slightly open, only three or four inches. But as she approached it she could see the leftover turkey on the marble shelf on the left – and, on the red-and-white tiled floor directly below it, she could see a blue-gray fluffy leg.

She opened the door wide and there was Tarquin, lying on his side, his coppery eyes wide open, and obviously dead.

Uncle Philip sat on a chair in the kitchen with Tarquin in his arms, rocking backward and forward. Tears dripped down his withered cheeks and clung to Tarquin's fur like diamonds.

Kenneth stood in one corner, his eyes half-closed like overripe damsons, his hand pressed against his forehead in the classic gesture of a man who is swearing to himself that he will never touch another alcoholic drink as long as he lives. Nicholas, in his red silk dressing-gown, was calmer and waxier than ever.

"He was eating the leftover turkey," said Paul, Caitlin's husband, who was all dressed up in a bizarre assemblage of socks and tracksuit bottoms and a frayed brown jumper.

"But that couldn't have hurt him," said Roger. "We all ate the same turkey, didn't we, and none of us are sick."

"He could have choked," Caitlin suggested.

"He could have had a heart-attack. He's almost fourteen, after all."

Paul knelt down beside Uncle Philip's chair and said, "Do you mind if I – you know, touch him?"

Uncle Philip didn't seem to care. He turned away and his face was a mask of terrible distress.

Paul carefully opened Tarquin's lips. "Look, he didn't vomit, you see. He's still got half-chewed turkey in his mouth." He leaned closer and sniffed, and sniffed again.

"What is it?" asked Nicholas.

"Prussic acid. Or cyanide, to you."

"You mean he's been *poisoned*?"

"I used to work for Kodak," said Paul. "You use a lot of potassium cyanide when you're developing photographs, and they taught us to recognize the symptoms. Blue face, blue lips. Well, poor old Tarquin was blue already. But you can't mistake that smell. Sweet, isn't it? One of the most pleasant-tasting poisons there is."

Grace boomed, "Who on earth would want to poison Tarquin?"

"Well, nobody, of course," said Nicholas. "The whole thing was an accident. Somebody must have injected the cold turkey with cyanide after we went to bed last night, with the intention of harming whoever was going to eat it. Fortunately for the intended victim – but very unfortunately for Tarquin – the larder door was accidentally left open."

Caitlin looked aghast. "But we were all planning to *leave* after breakfast, all of us. We always do, on Boxing Day. The only person who would have eaten the turkey was—"

Uncle Philip looked up, although he continued to stroke Tarquin's lifeless head. "Yes," he said. "In fact, I would have thought it was quite obvious. Somebody poisoned the turkey because they wanted to get rid of *me*."

Kenneth looked at Caitlin and Caitlin looked at Paul and Paul looked at Libby. "The house was locked up all night," said Nicholas. "You always switch on the alarm. That means that whoever did it – well, it must have been one of us."

"We should call the police," said Libby.

"But if it's one of us—"

"If it's one of us, the police will find out who it is, and presumably charge him or her with attempted murder."

"My God," said Libby. "I simply can't believe that one of us would be capable of such a thing."

"Why not?" Kenneth demanded. "We all have more than enough of a motive, after all. We're all practically broke, and here's Philip sitting on several millions of pounds worth of property and shares . . . and making sure, year by year, that he reminds us how foolish we've been, how wasteful we've been . . ."

"You *have* been foolish, and you *have* been wasteful," said Uncle Philip. He stood up, with Tarquin's heavy dead body cradled in his arms. He circled the kitchen, and his voice was cracking with emotion.

"I always thought that you were rotten, all of you. Rotten through and through. You were each given more money than some people can earn in a lifetime, and each of you wasted it, and ended up with nothing. That's why you come here for Christmas, every year, even though you hate me, even though you hate each other, even though you're so bored.

"Well, every Christmas has been my way of showing my contempt for each and every one of you, because I never had any intention of giving you any of my money. I just wanted to see you grovel, year after year. I just wanted to see how low you were prepared to crawl.

"In the whole of my life, I have never come across greed and arrogance like yours. Never. You assumed that I would bequeath you all of my money. You couldn't see that the world is full of far more deserving beneficiaries. But worse than that, you couldn't even wait till I died, could you? One of you tried to poison me. One of you actually tried to murder me. But all you succeeded in doing was killing the one creature who took me for what I was. Tarquin didn't love me because I was wealthy. Tarquin loved me without any conditions at all. I loved him more than life itself, and I can't imagine how I'm going to live without him."

He looked from one to the other with an expression of total wretchedness, and then he walked out of the kitchen with Tarquin still dangling in his arms. The family watched him go, and none of them said a single word.

Only a second later, however, they heard a thumping sound in the hallway, and the clatter of a table tipping over. They rushed out of the kitchen to find Uncle Philip lying on his back, his eyes open, his face convulsed, with Tarquin lying on top of him.

"Ambulance!" Nicholas shouted. "Call for an ambulance!"

Detective Inspector Rogers came into the drawing-room where they were all assembled, blowing his nose loudly on a grayish-looking handkerchief.

"Christmas," he complained. "I always get a cold around Christmas."

Nicholas looked at his watch. "I do wish you'd get this over with, Inspector. I was hoping to get back to town before it got dark."

It was New Year's Eve, five days after Boxing Day. During the week, the family had been allowed to return home, but they had all been warned not to leave the south east of England until the police had completed their preliminary investigations; and Inspector Rogers had been around to each of them, with a long list of penetrating questions. Now they had been called back to Polesden View – as fractious as ever.

"First of all," said Inspector Rogers, "a post-mortem examination has shown that Tarquin the cat died from ingesting hydrocyanic acid, and that the poison entered his system by his consumption of a small quantity of contaminated turkey.

"If the intention of contaminating the turkey was to cause harm to Mr Philip Chesterton, almost all of you who were present on Boxing Day had a motive. A mistaken motive, as it turns out, because Mr Chesterton had no intention of leaving you any money – but you didn't know that."

He walked over to Kenneth and Libby, and said, "Your brokerage business is bankrupt, sir, and you desperately need a substantial amount of money to avoid losing your house."

To Grace, he said, "You, madam, after a long period of living alone, have found a partner of whom you are extremely fond. Unfortunately, he is very much younger than you, and you are finding that you keep having to buy him gifts in order to keep him happy. He wants a car, which you can't afford."

He crossed over to Nicholas, and said, "Now that you're a partner in your law firm, sir, you want to move into town and live according to your new status . . . amongst other things." Nicholas looked relieved. What nobody else in the family knew was that "other things" was his secretary, with whom he had just started an affair.

Inspector Rogers came over to Mary. "Your husband died in spring last year, leaving you and your daughter almost penniless."

Then he went up to Caitlin. "The lease on your pottery studio has just run out, and unless you can find a new one, you'll be going out of business."

Lastly, he approached Michael. "You're separated from your wife, sir, and she's threatening to divorce you. You're certainly going to need all the funds you can lay your hands on."

Inspector Rogers returned to the center of the room. "To be frank with you, however, there is no evidence that links any of you directly with the contamination of the turkey. It could have been any one of you, or it could have been some of you, or all of you, in concert.

"There is also the legal problem that nobody ate any of the poisoned turkey except for the cat; and that it is unlikely that we can prove beyond a reasonable doubt that whoever poisoned it was specifically intending to kill Mr Chesterton. It isn't as if the turkey was set out on a plate that was solely intended for him.

"For that reason I am obliged to let you all go about your business, but I must caution you that our investigations will continue and that you should stay in the country until further notice."

"By the way," said Mary, as they gathered up their coats. "Do you have any idea who *is* going to inherit?"

"Well – this is the funny part," said Inspector Rogers, taking out his handkerchief again and trying to find a dry bit. "The whole estate was supposed to go to Tarquin. All eleven million of it. He would have been the richest cat in the country."

"What!" Kenneth exploded. "Eleven million to a *cat*! It's insane!"

"It's legal, I'm afraid," said Inspector Rogers. "Didn't you read about that woman who gave two million to her spaniel?"

"But Tarquin's dead. Who gets the money now?"

"Let's see . . . something called the British Blue Protection League."

"Bloody cats again," grumbled Kenneth. "I hate bloody cats."

Mandy and her mother drove back to their semi-detached house overlooking Ealing Common in West London and her mother asked her if she wanted to go out for a curry because she had nothing in the house.

Mandy flopped back on the sagging corduroy sofa and said, "No. I'd rather be hungry."

"Whatever for?"

"Because I'm never going to be hungry again, ever; and I want to remember what it's like."

"What on earth are you talking about?"

"I'm talking about Uncle Philip's inheritance."

"I still don't understand you."

"Uncle Philip never believed that any of you loved him, did he? He always thought you were after his money."

"He was right, wasn't he? We didn't, and we were."

"But he knew that Tarquin loved him, and that Tarquin never wanted anything but warmth and food and his bony old lap to sit in."

"So?"

"So none of you used your brains, did you? If you want a cantankerous old man like that to feel good towards you, you don't pretend to like him for what he is, because he won't believe you. In fact he'll be even more suspicious of you than ever. No – you make sure that you win the confidence of somebody he trusts. Or, in Uncle Philip's case, *something* they trust, which was Tarquin.

"I started to make a fuss of Tarquin because there was nothing else to do at Polesden View. But Tarquin began to trust me, and Uncle Philip began to trust me, too. He gave me bits of money and sweets and he told me that he was going to leave all his inheritance to Tarquin, just to show you how greedy and insincere you all were."

"You *knew* about him giving his inheritance to Tarquin? And you didn't tell us?"

"If I'd told you, you would never have gone down to see him at Christmas, would you, and he wouldn't have trusted me any more."

"But we suffered all of those horrible, horrible Christmases, and you *knew*?"

Mandy smiled. "We called it our secret, Uncle Philip and me."

"But what was the point, when the money was all going to go to that stupid cat?"

"Oh, mum! The point was that even the brainiest cats can't look after themselves, can they? Cats can't open bank accounts. They can't even open tins of catfood. When their owners die, cats have to have people to look after them . . . people that their owners trust. And when cats die, they have to leave their money to somebody, don't they?"

Mandy went to the bookcase and tugged out a file. She opened it up so that Mary could see the first page. In official-looking letters, she had typed British Blue Protection League: Annual Accounts. The column under "credits" was still blank.

"I put Uncle Philip in touch with them. He never realized it was only me."

"*You* poisoned the turkey," Mary whispered.

Mandy nodded. "And I opened the larder door, so that Tarquin could get in."

"You couldn't have known that Uncle Philip would have a stroke."

"No . . . that was something of a bonus, wasn't it?"

"My God," said Mary. "I can hardly believe it. Eleven million pounds."

"Not until he dies, of course. But we can wait, can't we? It'll give us time to think what we're going to spend it on. You know what I've really always wanted? A dog."

Picnic at *Lac du Sang*

"The girls here are very young," said Baubay, taking a last deep drag at his cigarette and flicking it out of the Pontiac's window. "But let me tell you, they'll do *anything*."

Vincent frowned across the street at the large Gothic-revival house. It wasn't at all what he had expected a brothel to look like. It was heavily overshadowed by three giant dark-green elms, but he could see turrets and spires and decorated gables, and balconies where net curtains suggestively billowed in the summer breeze. The outside walls were painted a burned orange color, and there was something strange and other-worldly about the whole place, as if he had seen it in a painting, or dreamed it.

"I'm not so sure about this," he told Baubay. "I never visited a bordello before."

"Bordello!" Baubay piffed. "This is simply a very amenable place where guys like us can meet beautiful and willing young women, discuss the state of the economy, have a bottle of champagne or two, play Trivial Pursuit, and if we feel like it, get laid."

"Sounds like a bordello to me," said Vincent, trying to make a joke of it.

"You're not going to chicken out on me, are you? Don't say you're going to chicken out. Come on, Vincent, I've driven over eighty miles for this, and I'm not going back to Montreal without at least one game of hide the salami."

"It's just that I feel like – I don't know. I feel like I'm being unfaithful."

"Bullshit! How can you be unfaithful to a woman who walked

135

out on you? How can you be unfaithful when she was screwing a *crotté* like Michael Saperstein?"

"I don't know, but it just feels that way. Come on, Baubay, I never looked at another woman for eleven years. Well, I *looked*, but I didn't do anything about it."

"So – after all those years of sainthood, you deserve to indulge yourself a little. You won't regret it, believe me. You'll be coming back for more. Hey – with your tongue dragging on the sidewalk."

"I don't know. Is there a restaurant or anything around here? Maybe I'll have some lunch and wait for you."

Baubay unfastened his seatbelt and took his keys out of the ignition. "Absolutely emphatically no you are not. How do you expect me to enjoy fornicating with some ripe young teenager while all the time I know that you're sitting alone in some dreary diner eating Salisbury steak? What kind of friend would that make me? You're not backing out of this, Vincent. You're coming to meet Madame Leduc whether you like it or not."

"Well, I'll *meet* her, OK?" Vincent agreed. "But whether I do anything else—"

Baubay took him by the elbow as if he were a blind man and propelled him to the opposite sidewalk. The morning was glazed and warm and there was hardly any traffic. The house stood in the older part of St Michel-des-Monts, in a street which was still respectable but which was suffering from obvious neglect. The house next door was empty, its windows shuttered and its front door boarded up, its garden a tangle of weeds and wild poppies. Behind the houses, through a blueish haze, Vincent could see the mountains of Mont Blanc, Mont Tremblant, and beyond.

They climbed the stone steps to the front door and Baubay gave a smart, enthusiastic knock. The door was painted a sun-faded blue, and the paint had cracked like the surface of an old master. The knocker was bronze, and cast in the shape of a snarling wolf's head.

"See that?" said Baubay. "That was supposed to keep evil spirits at bay. They're quite rare, now."

They waited and waited and eventually Baubay knocked again. After a while they heard a door open and piano music, Mozart, and a woman's voice. Vincent felt butterflies in his stomach, and he had a ridiculous childish urge to run away. Baubay winked at him and said, "This'll be Madame Leduc now."

The front door was opened by a tall, ash-blonde woman with her hair braided on top of her head. She was wearing a long silk negligée in pale aquamarine, trimmed with lace. She must have been forty-five at least, but she was extraordinarily beautiful, with a fine, slightly Nordic-looking face, and eyes that were such a pale, washed-out blue that they were scarcely any color at all. Her negligée was open almost to her waist, revealing a deep cleavage in which a large marcasite crucifix nestled. Judging by the way her breasts swung, she must have been naked underneath.

"François, what a pleasure," she said. Her accent was faintly Québecois, very precize and refined. "And – how exciting! You've brought your friend with you today."

"I couldn't keep you all to myself, could I?" asked Baubay. "Violette, this is Vincent Jeffries. He's a very talented man. A great musician. Like, eat your heart out, Johann Sebastian Bach."

Mme Leduc held out her hand so that it slightly drooped, and Vincent realized that she expected him to kiss it. He did so, and when he lifted his eyes he saw that she was smiling at him in amusement. Baubay said, "Let's go inside. I could do some serious damage to a bottle of cold champagne."

They stepped into the hallway and Mme Leduc closed the door behind them, blotting out the sunshine. "The tall one and the short one," she remarked, and then she gave a brittle, tinkling laugh. Baubay laughed too, like a dog barking, and gave her a pat on the bottom. His shortness had never given him any trouble with women, or so he said, and Vincent believed him, because he was always packed with energy and he was quite handsome in a roughly cut, unfinished way, with a square jaw and thick eyebrows and thick black curls. Apart from being taller, Vincent was much thinner and quieter, with blondish combed-back hair and a narrow, rather aquiline face, and a way of peering at people as if they were standing six or seven miles away. When she had first met him, Patricia had said that he looked like Lawrence of Arabia, trying to see through the glitter of a distant mirage. In the end, their marriage had turned out to be the mirage.

"So, you're a great musician, Mr Jeffries?" asked Mme Leduc. "Some of my girls are learning the piano. You will have to give them some pointers."

"François is exaggerating, as usual," said Vincent. "I write scores for television commercials – incidental music, links, stuff like that. Do you know the Downhome Donut music? That was mine. Right now François and I are working on a Labatt's beer ad together."

"You should hear what he's written!" said Baubay. "Is it dramatic? Is it sweeping? Do bears go to the woods to dress up as women?"

They entered a large, high-ceilinged living-room. It probably overlooked the garden, but Vincent couldn't tell because all the windows were tightly covered by bleached white calico blinds, through which the sunlight filtered as softly as the memory of a long-lost summer day. The floor was pale polished hardwood, with antique scatter-rugs, and the furniture was all antique, too, gilded and upholstered in creams and yellows. There were huge mirrors everywhere, which at first gave Vincent the impression that he had walked into a room crowded with fifteen or sixteen girls.

Mme Leduc clapped her hands and called, "*Attention, mes petites!* M. Baubay has arrived and he has brought a friend for us to entertain!"

Immediately, the girls came forward and clustered around them. Now Vincent could see that there were only seven of them, but he still felt overwhelmed, and more than anything else he wished that he were someplace else. He had never been simultaneously so aroused and so embarrassed in his whole life. All of the girls were pretty: two or three of them were almost as beautiful as Mme Leduc. There was a redhead with skin as white as milk, and a long-haired brunette with dark slanting eyes that he could have drowned in. There were three blondes – one bubbly and curly, the other tall and mysterious with hair so long that she could have wrapped herself in it, like a silky curtain. There was another brunette who stood more shyly behind her friends, but she had a face so perfect that Vincent couldn't take his eyes off her.

What struck him most of all, though, was the way in which the girls were dressed. He didn't quite know what he had expected: Fredericks of Hollywood lingerie, maybe, or satin wraps like the one that Mme Leduc was wearing. But they all wore plain white cotton nightdresses, almost ankle-length, and one of them was even wearing white socks. Vincent supposed that Mme Leduc had wanted them to look younger than they really were, like schoolgirls; but even so none of them could have been older than eighteen or nineteen.

"Mr Jeffries is a musician, girls," Mme Leduc announced. "Perhaps he'll be kind enough to play for us while we bring him something to drink." She winked at Baubay, and Vincent saw her wink. She must have sensed how nervous he was, and, yes, it was a good idea, asking him to play the piano. It would help to relax him. "You like champagne, Mr Jeffries? Or may I call you Vincent?"

"Sure you can call me Vincent. But right now I think I'd prefer a beer, if you don't mind."

"Anything you want," she said. She looked into his eyes for almost ten seconds without saying anything. Her eyes were extraordinary, like blue ink that has spilled across the surface of a mirror. He dropped his gaze and found himself looking at the cross that dangled in her cleavage. He could smell the perfume that she exuded from between her breasts. It was very summery and flowery, and for some reason it made him think of – what? He couldn't think. Something elusive. Something deeply emotional. Something that had happened a long time ago.

One of the girls came up and took his coat. Another loosened his necktie. "You like this?" said Baubay, walking up and down the room. "This is what I call pampering."

"Please, play," said the redhead, shyly, and pulled out the piano-stool for him. Vincent sat down, flexed his fingers, and played one of his party-pieces, a high-speed version of *Camptown Races*. The girls laughed and clapped when he had finished, and one of the blondes kissed him on the cheek. The blonde with the long hair, more daring and more sensual, kissed him directly on the mouth. "François is right. You are a great musician. Your music is terrible – but you – you are a great musician." Bold words, he thought, almost frightening. But he had never had an erection while sitting at the piano before, as he did now. He could feel the warmth of the girl's body through her plain white nightdress. It was unbuttoned, and he could see the curve of a small swelling breast.

Mme Leduc brought him a golden glass of beer in a frozen glass. He drank a little, and then he played something slower, more sentimental, a score he had written for a poem. The blonde with the long hair came and sat next to him, and put her arm around him, but he played this song for the brunette who stood away from the others, her eyes lowered, her fingers trailing through her hair.

"In your arms was still delight . . . quiet as a street at night;
And thoughts of you, I do remember,
Were green leaves in a darkened chamber,
Were dark clouds in a moonless sky."

The blonde girl massaged his shoulders, and then ran her fingers all the way down his spine. The redhead stood behind him and stroked his hair. On the opposite side of the room, Baubay sat with one of the curly blondes on his knee and another kneeling on the floor beside him. He lifted his glass of champagne and gave Vincent a blissful beam. "Don't tell me this isn't the life, my friend. This is the life."

"Love, in you, went passing by," sang Vincent. He looked toward the brunette and she was lifting her hair so that it shone in the softly filtered sunlight in a fine net of filaments. He didn't know whether she knew that he was looking at her or not. He didn't know whether she was flirting with him or not. She appeared to be indifferent, and yet . . .

"Love, in you, went passing by . . . penetrative, remote, and
*   rare,*
Like a bird in the wide air,
And, as the bird, it left no trace . . ."

He paused, and then he sang, very quietly, *"In the heaven . . . of your face."*

There was a momentary silence, and then Mme Leduc pattered her hands together like a pigeon trapped in a chimney. "You weave quite a spell, Vincent. You must play us some more."

"Why doesn't one of your girls play? I'd like to hear them."

"Well, of course. I'm forgetting myself. You didn't come here to entertain *us*. Minette, why don't you play *Curiose Geschichte* for

Mr Jeffries? Minette's been practicing very hard this month. And, Sophie, why don't you dance?"

Vincent left the piano and the girl with the long blonde hair guided him over to the couch next to Baubay's, and sat down almost in his lap. She stroked his thigh through his chino pants and then she cupped her hand right between his legs, and squeezed it. He looked up at her but all she did was kiss him all over his face. He had drunk less than half of his beer but already he was beginning to feel that he had lost touch with reality. His cock was so hard that it ached and it just wouldn't go down.

Minette was one of the curly blondes. She sat at the piano with her eyes closed and played the slow, plaintive notes with perfect timing and inflection. Mme Leduc was right: she had been practicing hard. She was almost concert standard. But if she could play like this, what was she doing here, in this godforsaken Canadian suburb, selling herself to any man who wanted her?

Sophie, the redhead, stood in the middle of the floor with her toes pointed like a ballerina. Then she swept her arms down, gathered the hem of her nightdress, and drew it over her head. It landed on the rug with a soft parachute rustle, leaving Sophie completely naked. She was full-breasted but she was very slim, with narrow hips and long, long legs. Her breasts were marbled with blueish veins and her nipples were a startling pink that clashed with her hair. Between her legs arose a bright red flame, although it did little to conceal the plumpness of her labia.

Sophie danced: fast, and very stylistically, Isadora Duncan on speed. She waved her arms as if she were spinning through a storm and her breasts responded with a wild, complicated dance of their own. She whirled around the room, around and around. Then she covered her face with her hands and knelt on the floor only two or three feet away from Vincent. She swayed from side to side, staring at him as she did so, until he felt hypnotized. Then she slowly arched backward until her shoulders were touching the rug, and the lips of her vulva peeled apart, revealing the glistening depths of her vagina.

As if this wasn't enough, she reached down between her legs and pulled her lips even farther apart, exposing the tiny hole of her urethra, playing with her clitoris and sliding her long, manicured fingertips right inside her. The piano music. The succulent clicking of fingers and juice.

Vincent was breathless. As he watched, and he couldn't help watching, the blonde girl was gripping his cock through his pants, squeezing it hard and rhythmically, and he knew that if he didn't make her stop, he was going to be finished before he had even begun.

Suddenly, Minette stood up and the music wasn't there any more. Sophie rolled away across the rug. Mme Leduc's hands pattered together again.

"Now, perhaps, a little something to eat, before we get down to the principal entertainment of the day?"

Vincent was trying unsuccessfully to fend off the blonde, who was licking his neck with the flat of her tongue and trying to slide her hand down the front of his pants. "You're wet," she breathed. "Your shorts are wet. I can feel it."

"Yes, food!" Baubay enthused. "I hope you made some of your crabcakes, Violette! Vincent, you should try Violette's crabcakes! And her *andouilles!*"

"I want to try your *andouille*," the blonde breathed in Vincent's ear, and then draped her hair all over his head, so that he was tangled in it, suffocated in it.

They sat at a long table covered in an extravagantly long white linen cloth that poured over their knees and trailed across the floor. The windows of this room, too, were covered by bleached white blinds. Mme Leduc sat at the head of the table, and the girls sat along either side. Vincent and Baubay sat side by side, each of them being cossetted and spoonfed by the girls next to them. The food was like nothing that Vincent had ever eaten before: not all at the same meal, anyway. Cold spiced beef and fruit-flavored jellies; salads with endive and oranges; crabcakes served with fragments of honeycomb. There was a strange fried flatfish stuffed with peaches, and bowls of clear chilled soup that tasted like women's sexual juices lightly flavored with cilantro.

The shy brunette sat on the opposite end of the table, eating only a little and saying nothing at all. Vincent deliberately stared at her while he ate, but she never once raised her eyes to look at him. The blonde sitting next to him reached beneath the flowing tablecloth and started to massage him between the legs again. When he was hard, she jerkily tugged down his zipper and took out his erection, her fingers running up and down it like a piccolo player. He suddenly realized that he was beginning to enjoy himself.

"Do you think you could love me?" she asked him, in a hoarse, dirty whisper.

He kissed her on the lips. "You don't exactly make it easy to say no."

"But do you think you could *really* love me? Or any of us?"

"What? And marry you? And take you away from all this?"

She shook her head. "You could never do that, ever."

"But you're not going to do this for the rest of your life, are you? I mean, how old are you?"

"Eighteen."

"There you are, then. One day you'll meet the right guy, and you'll be able to put all of this behind you."

Again she shook her head. Vincent tried to kiss her again, but this time she raised her fingertips and pressed them against his lips.

Mme Leduc stood up and tapped her spoon against her wine-glass, so that it rang. "There!" she said. "We have been fed very well . . . now for some other pleasures. François, have you chosen who you would like to share your afternoon with?"

Baubay put his arm around Sophie's shoulders. "I can never resist a redhead, Violette, especially when she is a redtail, too."

"And perhaps Minette to accompany her?" asked Mme Leduc.

"Wonderful! But not on the piano, this time!"

Baubay got up from the table, and took Sophie and Minette by the hand. Giggling, they led him out of the dining-room, into the hallway, and up the stairs. Vincent could hear them laughing all the way along the landing.

"Vincent, how about you?" asked Mme Leduc. "Has any one of my girls caught your eye yet?"

The blonde gave him a dreamy, creamy look, and rubbed his penis again. Vincent didn't want to hurt her feelings, but he was too fascinated by the shy brunette. He nodded down the table and said, "I don't even know her name, but if she doesn't mind—?"

The blonde immediately pushed his erection back into his pants

143

and tugged up his zipper, almost catching him in it. "Look, I'm sorry," he said. "I think you're stunning, but—"

"But you prefer Catherine, I know. I've seen you staring at her."

"Catherine?" said Vincent, and the girl looked toward him and nodded, although she didn't smile. Vincent stood up and walked along the length of the table and held out his hand.

"This is only if you want to," he said.

"It is not her place to say if she wants to or not," said Mme Leduc, with a slight snap in her voice.

Catherine stood up, gathering up her white nightdress in front of her so that it was raised above her knees. Vincent had never seen a girl so beautiful or so quietly alluring, and he had certainly never met a girl so subservient. She had a high, rounded forehead and huge violet eyes. Her nose was straight with just a hint of a tilt at the end. Her lips were full, as if she were pouting a little, but that suggestion of sulkiness only aroused Vincent all the more.

"One girl will be sufficient?" asked Mme Leduc.

"Am I allowed to come back for seconds?"

Mme Leduc came up close to him and ran her hand up the back of his head, like rubbing a cat's fur the wrong way. It was an electrifying feeling, especially since he could feel her breast swaying against him through the silk of her negligée.

"Perhaps, next time, I can amuse you myself."

God, thought Vincent. Baubay was right. I feel like I've died and gone to heaven.

Without a word, Catherine took his hand and led him out of the room. She walked quite quickly on her pale bare feet, as if she were in a hurry. Her hand was small and cool. She didn't lead him upstairs, but across the hallway and along a corridor with a polished parquet floor. The corridor was light, but all of the windows were covered with the same white blinds.

They reached a door at the end of the corridor and Catherine opened it. Inside, Vincent found himself in a large downstairs bedroom. In the very center stood an iron-framed four-poster bed, draped with yards and yards of white gauze curtains, and covered in giant-sized white feather pillows. The only other furniture was a chaise-longue upholstered in plain cream calico, a French-style closet painted in dragged white paint, a washbasin, and a cheval mirror at the end of the bed, tilted in such a way that whoever was lying on the bed could see themselves. On one wall hung a large, vividly colored painting of a woman in a pearl necklace, lasciviously clutching a horse's erect penis, and staring directly at the viewer as if she were challenging everything he believed in.

Catherine closed the door. She walked across to the bed and drew back the curtains. Then, without turning around, she lifted off her nightdress, so that she was naked. She had a long, flared back, and very high, rounded buttocks. Her breasts were so big that Vincent could see the half-moon curves of them on either side.

However it was when she turned around that he had the greatest shock. He saw now why she had gathered up her nightdress when she stood up from the table. She had been concealing the fact that she was at least five or six months' pregnant. Her breasts were enormously swollen and big-nippled, and her stomach was like a lunar globe. Her vulva was swollen, too. She had shaved herself so that Vincent could see the dark blush color of her lips.

Pregnant she might have been, but Vincent still thought she was achingly beautiful. In fact, her pregnancy made her look even more beautiful. That was why her hair shone. That was why her skin glowed. That was why she had the secretive, knowing, self-protective look that had attracted Vincent in the first place.

She came up to him and unfastened the top button of his shirt. He looked down at her – at her calm, perfect face; at the trees of pale blue veins in her breasts; at her stiffened, rouge-brown nipples.

"How old are you?" he asked her, with a phlegmy catch in his throat.

"Eighteen and a half," she replied, unfastening another button, and another, and running her fingernails lightly through the hair on his chest.

"You're having a baby, and yet you're still doing *this*?"

"What else can I do?"

"You can contact your local department of welfare, for starters. You can get all kinds of financial help. You're a single mother-to-be, for Christ's sake, you're entitled. You don't have to work for Mme Leduc."

"But I do."

"No, listen to me, you don't. This really isn't suitable work for anybody who's pregnant."

She looked up at him. "So what are you trying to tell me? That you wouldn't have picked me if you'd known that I was fat?"

"You're not fat, you're pregnant, and if you want to know the truth I find you extremely attractive. But this isn't socially responsible."

"You don't want me, then? You want Eloise instead? Or Martine?"

"I didn't say that. I simply said that in your condition you shouldn't be working in a bordello."

"I don't have any choice."

"Yes, you do. You *do* have a choice. There are plenty of people you can turn to. I mean, what about your parents?"

She looked away. "Dead, both of them."

"Brothers or sisters? Aunts or uncles?"

She shook her head.

"Then, listen, maybe *I* can help you."

She said, "I don't want you to help me. I don't want you even to try. This is what I do. This is what I am. Other men have offered to help me, too, and every time I have to tell them the same thing."

Vincent didn't know what to do. He walked over to the white-blinded window and then he walked back again.

"You came here for pleasure," said Catherine, standing exposed in front of him, making no attempt to hide her complete nakedness with her hands. "Why don't you enjoy it while you're here?"

She came up to him and stood close so that her distended stomach touched the bulge in his pants. "Pleasing men is what I do best. I got pregnant, pleasing a man. Let me please you too."

"I don't know. I—"

She kissed his chest. She unbuttoned the last of his shirt buttons and then she started to unbuckle his belt.

"What about the baby?" he said, weakening. "Isn't it dangerous or anything?"

"There's plenty of room inside me," she said, pulling down his zipper. "Once I had three men inside me all at once, and baby, too." Without any hesitation, she wrested his rising cock out of his shorts, and pushed him back toward the bed. He sat down on it, and she dragged off his pants and his socks.

"Listen," he said, "maybe a blowjob'll do it . . . I don't want to take any risks." But he could hear his own voice and he knew how ineffectual he sounded. He wanted her desperately, he wanted her so much that his cock was visibly pulsing with every heartbeat. She pressed him down so that he was lying amongst all of those white downy cushions, and then she knelt beside him and took his cock into her mouth, running her tongue around his shiny purple helmet, sucking at it, licking it, and then sliding her tongue all the way down to his walnut-crinkled balls.

From where he was lying he could see underneath her body, her big swaying breasts, her rounded stomach. He reached out and cupped her breasts, feeling her rigid nipples brushing against his palms. Then he smoothed his hands around her stomach. He was surprised how hard it was, how tight it was. He thought to himself: *another man has fucked her, and left life inside her, and here it is, growing.* Although he couldn't understand why, he found the idea of it unbelievably erotic.

As she sucked him, he looked down the length of the bed toward the cheval mirror, and through the curtains of her hair he could see her lips enclosing his red, glistening shaft. She glanced up, and caught sight of his reflection. She smiled, and gave the head of his cock a long, lascivious lick.

In return, he lifted her right leg so that she was kneeling right over him. Right in front of him was her smooth crimson vulva, her lips thickened with pregnancy, her vagina flooded with juice. He buried his face in it like a man burying his face into a watermelon, licking as deep inside her as he could, then taking whole mouthfuls of her and sucking her until she let his cock out of her mouth and gasped, and pushed her hips even more forcefully into his face.

He lost all awareness of time. He gave her one orgasm after another, until her stomach was rock-hard and he was afraid that she was going to give birth. At the same time, she played with him, bringing him right to the edge of ejaculation and then letting him subside, until his balls ached and he was right on the edge of anger.

The bedroom was dark when she led him over to the chaise-longue and made him lie on his back. She straddled him, looking down at him, and it was so gloomy now that he couldn't see her face beneath the shadows of her hair. He could smell her, though. Her sex and her perfume and the same smell that he had detected on Mme Leduc: the smell of memories.

"I think you should make love to me properly," she whispered. "It's what you want, isn't it, to share my body with my baby?"

He half-rose, saying, "I can't." But she pushed him back again. She took hold of his erect penis and positioned herself right over it. She rubbed the head of his penis backward and forward between her lips until it was slippery with juice. "You want to meet my baby?" she teased him. "Don't tell me that you don't want to meet my baby."

She sank down on him, until he was buried right inside the warm elastic tightness of her body. She leaned forward so that her nipples touched his chest, and then she kissed him, and made a snorting sound of satisfaction in his ear. He climaxed with such violence that his whole world went dark.

It was almost eight o'clock when he left her sleeping on the four-poster bed. He dressed, and crept out, taking one last look at her. She was lying on her back with her hand lying idly between her legs, her hair fanned out across one of the pillows. It unnerved him to think that he had probably started to fall in love with her. He knew for sure that he would have to see her again. You can't have an encounter like this and just forget about it, just let it go.

He had never experienced an afternoon like it in his life. The way she had eaten his balls as if they were fruit. The way she had rubbed him until he had climaxed all over her breasts, and it had dripped from her nipples like milk.

"I want to feed my baby, when it's born," she had told him, massaging his sperm around and around.

"So when will that be, exactly?"

"I looked at my horoscope and my horoscope said soon."

"What about your gynecologist?"

She had frowned at him as if she didn't understand what he meant.

He walked back along the gloomy corridor feeling both elated and deeply guilty. He loved her, he wanted her, but he knew that he had to save her, too. He had to save her from Mme Leduc. Most of all he had to save her from men like him.

He had almost reached the hallway when he saw the shield-shaped plaque on the wall. He stopped, and peered at it, like Lawrence of Arabia peering at a mirage. It said "*École St Agathe, fondée 1923*," and underneath the lettering was an emblem of a goose flying from a blood-red lake.

He was still peering at it when a voice said, "Did you have a good time, Vincent?" He turned to see Mme Leduc standing in the hallway. He didn't know whether it was the dim evening light or maybe his own sexual satiation that made her look older, much older, and far less beautiful. She looked rather like the Snow Queen, from the story that his mother used to tell him when he was young, frigid and stern.

"I had a very good time, thank you," he told her. "Well . . . let's put it this way, I had a very interesting time."

She reached out and stroked his cheek. Her colorless eyes were almost sad.

"Why do you—" he began, and hesitated. Then he managed to say, "Why do you *do* this? These girls, they're all so young. They have so much in front of them . . . so much life to lead."

"You disapprove," she said. "I thought, from the moment that I opened the door, that you would disapprove."

"It's not that I disapprove. It's more like I don't understand."

She gave him a smile like diluted milk. She unfolded and refolded her negligée and gave him the briefest flash of heavy white breasts, with areolas the color of rose-petals, as they turn to brown.

"It isn't necessary for you to understand, Vincent. All you have to do is to enjoy yourself, and pay."

"I mean, how did you *discover* this place?" Vincent asked Baubay, as they drove back toward Montreal along the Laurentian Autoroute. "It's great, I'll grant you that, but it's so strange."

"What's strange about it? I think it's very normal. I went to a club in San Francisco where everybody was jerking off all over the place and there were three guys trying to make out with a one-legged woman. You've been closeted, Vincent. You don't know the half of what goes on. Group sex, leather clubs, bestiality. Compared to all of that, Mme Leduc is respectability itself."

"So how did you find it?"

"Some guy at Dane Shearman Philips told me about it. Mme Leduc encourages her clients to pass on her card to anybody who might appreciate what she has to offer."

"Seven young girls, not much more than eighteen years old. One of them six months' pregnant."

"Don't tell me you didn't enjoy it. Don't tell me you won't be going back."

Vincent said nothing, but looked ahead at the glittering lights of downtown Montreal. It looked unreal, like a city painted on the sky.

And of course he did go back, only three days later, and on his own this time. The hot weather had broken into a thunderous electric storm, and even though he parked his rental car right outside the house he was soaked by the time he reached the porch. He was still drying his face with his handkerchief when the door opened and Mme Leduc appeared – dressed in a robe of peach-colored silk.

"Why Vincent. I didn't expect you so soon."

"I should have called, I know, but I didn't know your number."

"And you didn't want to ask François for it, because you didn't want François to know that you were coming here?"

Vincent gave an awkward shrug. "I just wanted to see Catherine, that's all. Well, I wanted to see you, too."

"You'd better come in, then," she said, as another deafening burst of thunder shook the roof of the house.

Vincent followed her inside. "I'm worried about Catherine, if you must know. I haven't been able to get her off my mind."

"You're not the first."

"It's just that it isn't right, a pregnant girl having unprotected sex with strange men. Think of the infections she could pick up. Think of the baby."

"*You* had sex with her."

"Yes, I did. And I feel more guilty about it than I can possibly tell you."

"So what do you propose to do?"

"I propose to make you an offer. Let me take Catherine away from here so that she can have her baby someplace quiet and comfortable, with a decent clinic nearby. I'll make sure you're not out of pocket. If you work out her potential earnings for, say, the next six months, I'll pay you in advance."

Mme Leduc took him through to the living-room. The blinds were still drawn tight and it was so gloomy that he could barely see her. "Why don't you sit down?" she asked him. "Would you like some tea, or a glass of wine?"

"No, no thank you. I just want to hear you say that Catherine can come with me."

Mme Leduc stood facing the mirror over the fireplace, so that Vincent could see only her dim reflection. "I'm afraid that's impossible, Vincent. None of us can leave this house, ever."

"Why the hell not? What happens when the girls get older, and lose their looks? You can't run a cathouse with a collection of senior citizens, can you?"

Mme Leduc was silent for a long time. Then she said, "If I tell you why Catherine can't leave, will you promise me that you'll leave here, and never come back, and forget all about her?"

"How can I make a promise like that?"

"It's for her own good, that's why."

"Well, I don't know. I'll think about it, okay? That's as far as I'm prepared to go."

"Very well," said Mme Leduc. "I suppose that'll have to do." She turned around and came toward him, standing so close that he could have lifted his hand and touched her face. "A long time ago, in the 1920s, this used to be a school, an academy for young girls."

"I saw the noticeboard in the corridor. St Agathe's, right?"

"That's right. It was quite a famous school, and diplomats and wealthy businessmen used to send their daughters here during the summer to learn cookery and dressmaking and riding and all the social skills."

"I see. Kind of a finishing school."

Mme Leduc nodded. "One July day, in 1924, some of the girls were taken by their teacher to Lac du Sang, for a picnic. Lac du Sang is a local beauty spot, and very beautiful it is, too. They call it Lac du Sang because it's surrounded by maples, and in the fall, when the leaves turn red, the lake reflects them, and looks as if it's filled with blood. They say it was a magic place, a sacred place, where even the Indians would never venture.

"Anyway, the girls set out their picnic and the day was perfect. There was never such a day in the history of days. The lake, the trees, the sky so blue that it could have been ceramic. The teacher stood up and looked around at her girls and said, "What a perfect, perfect day. I wish we could all stay young forever. I wish the day could last for twenty-four years, instead of twenty-four hours."

Mme Leduc stood looking at Vincent and Vincent waited for her to continue, but she didn't. After a while, he said, "Go on. She wished that it would last for twenty-four years. Then what?"

"Then it did."

Another long pause. "I don't understand," said Vincent.

"It's not difficult," said Mme Leduc. "The day lasted for twenty-four years. At least, it did for them. The sun stayed high in the sky and they didn't notice the time passing by. It was all like a dream. When at last they returned to the school they found that it was closed, and that all their friends had gone. It was no longer 1924. It was 1948."

She went over to a rosewood bureau on the opposite side of the room and returned with a yellowed newspaper. "Here," she said. "This is what happened."

It was a copy of *The St Michel-des-Monts-Sentinel*. The front-page headline read SEARCH FOR ST AGATHE GIRLS CALLED OFF – Little Hope of Finding Missing Nine and Teacher, say Mounties.

Vincent read the first paragraph. "Police now believe there is little or no hope of them ever finding the teacher and nine girls from St Agathe's Academy who went missing three months ago on a picnic at Lac du Sang. The entire area has been thoroughly searched and there is no evidence to suggest that they all ran away together or that their disappearance is a practical joke. RCMP inspector René Truchaud called the Lac du Sang incident, "The greatest single mystery in Canadian police history."

Mme Leduc said, "They came looking for us on the day after we disappeared, but of course we weren't there. To them, we were still in yesterday, still lying in the grass by the lake."

"It was *you*? It was you and your girls?"

Mme Leduc gave him a sad, elegant nod. "We had a day like no other day has ever been; or ever will be. But we came back here and found that half of our lives had passed us by. I still don't know what happened to us; or why. I still don't know whether it was supposed to be a gift or a curse. But the first part of my wish came true, too, and so long as we stay here, inside the house, we remain as we were, all those years ago. It's almost as if my wish diverted us out of the stream of time, into a backwater, and that me and my seven girls are doomed or blessed to stay here forever."

"It says here nine girls."

"Yes . . . there *were* nine. Two of them left – Sara five years ago, and Imogene just before Christmas. Sara tried to come back but she didn't look like a young girl any longer. Time had caught up with her, and aged her over forty years in a single week. I received a letter from Imogene. Only two lines. Do you want to read it?"

She passed over a sheet of paper that had been folded and refolded until it was soft. The handwriting on it was so crabbed and spidery that Vincent could barely decipher it. It said, *"Chère Mme Leduc, I am very old and close to death. Tell all of the girls that I will wait for them in Heaven."*

Mme Leduc said, "It appears that the further time leaves us behind, the quicker we will age if we try to leave. So . . . the rest of us decided to stay."

"I can't believe any of this," said Vincent. "Days can't last for twenty-four years. People don't stay young forever. Who are you kidding? You're just trying to stop me from taking Catherine away from you. All you care about is how much you can make out of her. A pregnant teenager, what an attraction! Jesus, if you cared about any of these girls you wouldn't be selling their bodies to every lecherous old guy with a fat enough wallet."

"You exclude yourself from that category, I suppose," said Mme Leduc.

"I was tempted, I admit it. She's a beautiful girl, she tempted me. But that doesn't stop me from trying to put things right."

"Vincent . . . has it occurred to you that this is the only way in which we can make a living? None of us can leave the house, so what else are we supposed to do? We may stay young forever, but we still need to eat; and we still have bills to pay."

Vincent laughed and then abruptly stopped laughing. He looked at Mme Leduc and said, "You're seriously crazy, you know that? If you really believe that you disappeared in 1924 for twenty-four years and that you're never going to grow old . . . well, I don't know. I'd just like to know what stuff you're on."

At that moment Catherine walked into the room in her long white nightgown. Her hair was tied back and she looked especially young and vulnerable. It had only been three days since Vincent had seen her, but he had forgotten how mesmerising she was. The way she looked up at him from underneath her long, long eyelashes. The way she pouted. The way her breasts moved underneath the fresh-pressed cotton.

Mme Leduc took hold of her hand. "Mr Jeffries here wanted to take you away with him, Catherine. I had to explain why he couldn't."

"And of course I believed every word," said Vincent. "That must have been some picnic, out at Lac du Sang. Don't tell me you didn't run short of sandwiches – you know, in twenty-four years?"

Mme Leduc said, "Why don't you take Vincent to your room, Catherine? I expect that he'd like to talk to you alone."

Without a word, Catherine took his hand and led him along the corridor. She opened the door of her room and let him in. "I just came to talk," he told her.

"You mean you don't like me any more?"

"I came to ask you to leave this place. I came to persuade you to do the best for your baby."

Catherine took a few steps away from him, and then pirouetted, and lifted her nightgown over her head, so that she was standing in front of him completely naked. *"Now* tell me that you don't like me any more."

"Catherine, you can't go on doing this. I've found an apartment for you. It's pretty small but the landlady can take good care of you, and there's a clinic only four blocks away."

Catherine stood up close to him, smiling her dreamy smile. Her nipples were knurled and stiff, and she pressed the hard globe of her stomach up against his reluctantly rising erection. "There," she said, "you *do* still like me, after all."

"I don't just *like* you, Catherine."

"Then prove it," she challenged him. She tugged down his zipper and pried his cock out of his shorts. He said, "No, not that," but she gave him two or three irresistible rubs with her hand and he didn't say anything else after that.

He watched her as she knelt in front of him, her eyes closed, her pouting lips encircling his reddened erection. Her cheek bulged as she took him in deeper, and her tongue swam around his glans like a warm seal. He ran his hands through her hair and fondled her ears and he felt so weak, but so transported with pleasure, that he knew he had to have her for ever, for himself. He would raise her and he would raise her baby, both. He would guard her and protect her and make love to her all night.

His sperm flew into her hair and crowned her with pearls. She looked up and smiled at him, and outside the house the thunder rumbled and rattled the windows.

"Would you like to live with me?" he asked her.

She squeezed his softening penis with her hand. "Of course . . . if only it were possible."

"Then let me take you away from here. Tomorrow night, I'll come for you, yes?"

She held out her hand and he helped her on to her feet. "If only it were possible," she repeated, and kissed him, very frankly, on the lips.

"You're nuts," said Baubay. "You know what the penalty is for kidnap?"

"She wants me," Vincent told him. "She said she'd come to live with me, if I got her out of there."

"Those girls say anything you want to hear. It's what you pay them for."

"Catherine's different."

"The only thing different about Catherine is that she's got a bun in the oven."

"François, if you don't help me with this then I'll do it on my own."

"I still say you're nuts."

They drew up outside the house. Vincent had persuaded Baubay to bring him up here for another evening with Mme Leduc and her girls, with the promise that he would pay, but as they approached St Michel-des-Monts he had explained his plan to take Catherine away with him.

"Supposing Violette was telling you the truth about Lac du Sang?"

"Oh, come on, François. Get real. A bordello full of immortal schoolgirls?"

"I guess, when you say it like that."

They knocked at the door and Mme Leduc answered, dressed in scarlet silk. "Well, well," she said, as she took them inside. "Like a bee to the honeypot, Vincent? Can't keep away?"

Vincent gave a self-deprecating shrug.

The girls were all in the living-room, and Minette was playing Brahms on the piano. They stood up when Baubay and Vincent came in, and twittered around them, giving them little kisses of welcome and touching their hair. Only Catherine remained seated, and Vincent deliberately didn't catch her eye.

"Who takes your fancy tonight, François?" asked Mme Leduc.

Baubay looked around the room. He glanced at Vincent, and then he said, "You, Violette. It's you that I want tonight."

Later, after champagne, Baubay and Violette climbed the stairs together while the girls clapped and giggled and whistled their encouragement. As soon as they had gone, Vincent went over to Catherine and took hold of her hand. "Our turn?" he suggested.

He held her hand quite tightly as they left the living-room and crossed the hallway. Then – as they passed the front door – he suddenly pulled her and said, "This is it! Come on, Catherine, this is our chance!"

Catherine tried to wrench herself away from him. "No!" she cried out. "What are you doing?" But Vincent twisted open the doorhandle, flung the door wide open, and dragged Catherine out on to the porch.

"*No!*" she screamed. "*No, Vincent, I can't!*"

She deliberately sank to her knees, but Vincent bent down, and bodily picked her up. "No!" she shrieked at him. "I can't! I can't! No, Vincent, you'll kill me!"

She pulled his hair and dug her fingernails into his face, but he found the pain almost exciting. He carried along the pathway and out into the street, where his car was parked. He opened the driver's door and managed to force her inside, pushing her across to the passenger seat. Then he climbed in, started the engine, and sped away from the house with a high-pitched squealing of tires.

"*Go back!*" she shouted, trying to snatch the steering-wheel. "*You have to go back!*"

"Listen!" he shouted back at her. "Whatever Violette told you, it's garbage! She said it to scare you, so that you wouldn't leave! Now stop worrying about her and start thinking about yourself, and your baby."

"*Go back!*" Catherine howled. "Oh God, you can't do this to me! Oh God please go back! Oh God, Vincent, please take me back!"

"Will you shut up?" Vincent told her. "Shut up and put on your seatbelt. Even if you don't feel protective toward your baby, I do."

"*Take me back! Take me back! I can't go with you, Vincent! I can't!*"

She punched him again and tried to tear at his ear, and the car swerved wildly across the highway. But in the end he managed to catch hold of both of her wrists in his right hand, and restrain her. She stopped trying to hit him, and she curled herself up in her seat, and softly sobbed.

She was asleep by the time they reached Montreal. He parked

outside the apartment building and switched off the engine. He looked across at her and brushed the hair from her face. She was so beautiful that he could hardly believe she was real. He lifted her out of the passenger seat and carried her in through the entrance hall. It was stark and brightly lit, but it was late now and there was nobody else around. He went up in the elevator and by the time they reached the sixth floor she was beginning to feel heavy.

He opened the door and carried her into the apartment. It wasn't much – a plain, furnished place with two bedrooms, a bathroom and a small kitchenette. By day it had a narrow view of the Prairies River, partly blocked out by another apartment building. He took her through to the bedroom and laid her on the bed. Over the white vinyl headboard hung an almost laughably incompetent painting of a forest in the fall.

He sat beside her and took hold of her hand. "Catherine?" he coaxed her. "Come on, Catherine. We're here now, sweetheart. We've escaped."

Her eyes flickered open. She stared at him, first in bewilderment, and then in horror. She sat up and looked around her. "Oh God," she said. "Oh God, this can't be true."

"Come on, it's not that bad," said Vincent. "A few flowers, a couple of loose covers."

But Catherine ignored him. She climbed off the bed and went directly to the mirror over the dressing-table. "Oh God," she kept repeating.

Vincent stood beside her as she peered frantically at her face. "Catherine, nothing's going to happen to you. That story that Violette tells . . . it's only a way of frightening you."

"But I was *there*. I was there at Lac du Sang in 1924."

"You couldn't have been. It simply isn't possible. I don't know what Violette did. Maybe she brainwashed you or something. But no day ever lasted longer than twenty-four hours and nobody ever stayed young forever."

"You have to take me back. I'm pleading with you, Vincent. I'm pleading on my child's life."

"You want to go back? Back to what? Back to being a whore?

Back to sucking men's cocks and opening your legs to anybody who can pay the price?"

"Is that your problem? Is that why you took me away? Because you wanted me to open my legs but you didn't want to pay for it?"

"For God's sake, Catherine, I took you away because I love you."

For the first time she took her eyes away from her reflection in the mirror. There was an expression on her face that he had never seen on any girl's face before. It laid him open right to the bone, as if she had cut him with a ten-inch butcher's knife.

It was after eleven o'clock. He asked her if she wanted anything to eat or drink but she said no. He switched on the television in the living-room but there was nothing on but lacrosse and an old Errol Flynn movie. Catherine stayed in the bedroom, staring at the wall. In the end he came in and sat next to her again. "Listen," he said. "Maybe I made a mistake."

She glanced up at him, and she looked very pale and very tired.

"If you want to go back, I'll take you back. I just thought I was doing the right thing, that's all.

"Why don't you get some sleep and we'll make an early start in the morning."

She said nothing, but closed her eyes.

"I'm sorry," he said. "I'm sorry for being in love with you. I'm sorry for being human. What else was I supposed to do?"

He watched television until just after midnight, and then he undressed and climbed into bed with her. She was breathing softly against the pillow. He reached out and touched her arm, and then her breast. Then he ran his hand over the swelling of her stomach. He could feel the baby stir and kick, like somebody kneading dough.

He slept uneasily until four minutes past three. He kept having fragmentary dreams about people laughing and talking in other rooms. He woke with a strong hard-on and he reached out for Catherine again. She was still quietly breathing. He caressed her breasts through her nightgown and then he drew her legs apart and climbed on top of her. Maybe it was wrong of him to fuck her while she was asleep, but he needed her so urgently. She felt dry, in the darkness, but he spat on his fingers to moisten the end of his cock. Then he pushed himself into her, and started a deep, plunging rhythm.

She woke up. He sensed her wake up. But he was too close to his climax to stop, and he kept on thrusting himself into her, harder and harder. He heard her panting, quick and harsh, and he thought, great, she's getting into it too. He said, "Come on, baby, you're wonderful. Come on, sweetheart, you're fantastic."

It was then that she screamed. It was a piercing, gargling scream, and he could feel spit fly all over his face. He jerked upright, his skin freezing in fright, and then she screamed again. He scrabbled to find the bedside lamp, and managed to switch it on, but then it dropped on to the floor, so that what he saw was illuminated by an angled, upward light that made it look even more terrifying than it was.

He was kneeling between the legs of a shriveled old woman. Her sparse white hair was coming out in clumps. Her eyes were sunk into their sockets and her lips were drawn tightly back over orange, toothless gums. All that identified her as Catherine was her huge, swollen belly.

"Oh Jesus," Vincent whispered. "Oh Jesus, tell me this is a nightmare."

The old woman tried to scream again, but all she managed this time was a thick gargle. She lifted one of her bony arms, and clawed feebly at Vincent's shoulder, but Vincent pushed her away. She was collapsing in front of his eyes. Her face was tightening over her cheekbones and her breasts were shriveling. Her collarbone broke through her skin, and her chin dropped on to her chest.

"Catherine!" Vincent quivered. "Catherine!"

He lifted her head, but it dropped sideways on to the pillow and it was obvious that she was dead. Vincent climbed off the bed, wiping his hands on the sheet. He was trembling so much that he had to hold on to the wall for support.

It was then that he thought: *the baby – what about the baby? Even if Catherine's dead, maybe I can save the baby!*

He thought for one moment of calling for an ambulance – but how the hell was he going to explain an old, dead woman in his bed –

an old, dead *pregnant* woman? He approached Catherine cautiously, and laid his hand on her stomach, and, yes, he could still feel the baby kicking inside her. But how long could it survive if he didn't get it out?

He went to the kitchen, opened the drawer, and took out a carving-knife. He returned to the bedroom and stood beside Catherine gray-faced. He nearly decided to do nothing, to let the baby die, but then he saw Catherine's stomach shift again, and he knew that he had to give it a chance.

He inserted the point of the knife into her wrinkled skin, just above her pubic bone. Then, slowly, he pushed it in through the muscle, until he felt something more yielding. He was terrified of cutting the baby as well, but he kept on slicing her stomach open, and she was so decayed and dry and papery that it was more like cutting open a rotten old hessian sack. At last he had her stomach wide open, and he drew aside the two flaps of flesh to reveal her womb.

Shaking and dripping with sweat, he cut the baby out of her. One foot emerged, and then a hand. Miraculously, it was still alive. It was purple and slithery and it smelled strongly of amniotic fluid. He turned it over so that he could cut the umbilical cord, and then he lifted it up in both hands. It was so tiny, so frail. A baby girl. Her eyes were squeezed shut and she clasped and unclasped its fingers. She snuffled, and then she let out two or three pathetic little cries.

Vincent was overwhelmed. He started to sob out loud. Tears ran down his cheeks and dripped from his chin. He couldn't understand what had happened to Catherine, but he knew that he had saved the baby's life. He carried her through to the living-room, laid her on the couch, and then went to the bathroom to find some towels.

He sped to St Michel-des-Monts through driving, sunlit rain. At times his speedometer needle wavered over 110kph. He managed to reach the house just after eleven o'clock. He ran to the front porch, vaulted up the steps and banged furiously on the knocker.

Mme Leduc appeared, with Baubay close behind her. "You came back," she said. "I'm amazed that you had the nerve."

"Well . . . I don't think I had any choice."

"Catherine?"

He lowered his head. "You were telling me the truth. Catherine's gone. But I managed to save her child. I wanted to bring her back here before it was too late."

He went back to the car, and opened the door. Very hesitantly, like somebody who has never felt rain on their skin before, or had sunlight shining in their eyes, a young girl climbed out, barefoot, but wrapped up in green bath towels. Vincent took her hand and led her toward the house. Violette and Baubay watched in silence as she came up the steps. She looked at least seventeen or eighteen years old, with long brunette hair, like Catherine's, and she was almost as pretty, although her features were a little sharper.

"There," said Vincent, as he led her into the house. "You'll be safe here."

There were tears in Mme Leduc's eyes. "I wish that I had never wished," she told Vincent.

"Well," Vincent told her. "Sometimes we all think that."

They drove away from the house just as the rain was beginning to clear. Baubay said, "Where are you going? Montreal's back that way."

Vincent handed him a folded route map. "Lac du Sang," he said. "There's one more thing I have to do."

In the woods, he dug a shallow grave and buried Catherine's dessicated body. He filled her face with earth and leaves. "I'm sorry," was all he could think of to say. Afterward he stood by the edge of the water under a clear blue sky.

"They came here and they wished," he told Baubay. "God, they couldn't have known what they were wishing for, could they?"

"All I wish for is a new Mercedes," said Baubay.

"I just wish that I could have woken up every night and found Catherine lying next to me."

"You can go back to Violette's and try out her daughter."

"Forget it. I feel like her father. I brought her into the world, didn't I? I watched her grow up."

"In three hours? That's not fatherhood."

"All the same, it was incredible. She just grew bigger and bigger, like one of those speeded-up movies."

"Sure she did."

"She did, I swear it."

"Sure."

They climbed back into the car and drove away, leaving the waters of Lac du Sang as still as ever.

Six weeks later, Baubay phoned to tell him that he had been promoted and given a metallic gold 500SL as a company car. After that, Vincent awoke two or three times every night, and fearfully reached out to make sure that there was nobody lying on the other side of the bed.

The Ballyhooly Boy

Rain came dredging down the street in misty gray curtains as we drew up outside the narrow terraced house in the middle of Ballyhooly. All of the houses in the row were painted different colors: sunflower yellows, crimsons, pinks and greens. In sullen contrast, Number 15 was painted as brown as peat.

Mr Fearon switched off the engine of his eight-year-old Rover and peered at the house through his circular James Joyce glasses. "I'll admit it doesn't look much. But prices have been very buoyant lately. You could get eighty-five thousand for it easy, if you put it on the market today."

I took in the peeling front door, the darkened and dusty front windows, the sagging net curtains in one of the upstairs rooms. I guessed that I *could* sell it straight away; but then it might be worth smartening it up a little. A coat of paint and a new bathroom suite from Hickey's could make all the difference between £85,000 and £125,000.

I climbed out of the car, tugging up my collar against the rain. A small brindled dog barked at me for invading its territory without asking. I shaded my eyes and looked in through the front window. It was too grimy to see much, but I could just make out a black fireplace and a tipped-over chair. The living-room was very small, but that didn't matter. I might redecorate Number 15, but I certainly wouldn't be living in it. Not here in Ballyhooly, which was little more than a crossroads ten miles north of Cork, with two pubs and a shop and a continuous supply of rain.

Mr Fearon made a fuss of finding the right key and unlocked the front door. He had to kick the weatherboard to open it; and it gave a convulsive shudder, like a donkey, when it's kicked. The doormat was heaped with letters and free newspapers and circulars. Inside the hallway, there was a strong smell of damp, and the brown wallpaper was peppered with black specks of mold.

"It'll need some airing-out, of course, but the roof's quite sound, and that's your main thing."

I stepped over the letters and looked around. Next to the front door stood a Victorian coat and umbrella-stand, with a blotchy, yellowed mirror, in which Mr Fearon and I looked as if we had both contracted leprosy. On the opposite wall hung a damp-faded print of a dark back street in some unidentifiable European city, with a cathedral in the background, and hooded figures concealed in its Gothic doorways. The green-and-brown diamond-patterned linoleum on the floor must have dated from the 1930s.

The sitting-room was empty of furniture except for that single overturned wheelback chair. A broken glass lampshade hung in the center of the room.

"No water penetration," Mr Fearon remarked, pointing to the ceiling. But in one corner, there were six or seven deep scratchmarks close to the coving.

"What do you think caused those?" I asked him.

He stared at them for a long time and then shrugged.

We went through to the kitchen, which was cold as a mortuary. Which *felt* like a mortuary. Under the window there was a thick, old-fashioned sink, with rusty streaks in it. A gas cooker stood against the opposite wall. All of the glass in the cream-painted kitchen cabinets had been broken, and some of the frames had dark brown drips running down them, as if somebody had smashed the glass on purpose, in a rage, and cut their hands open.

Outside, I could see a small yard crowded with old sacks of cement and bricks and half a bicycle, and thistles that grew almost chest-high. And the rain, gushing from the clogged-up guttering, so that the wall below it was stained with green.

"I still can't imagine why your woman wanted to give me this place," I said, as we climbed the precipitous staircase. Halfway up, there was a stained-glass window, in amber, with a small picture in the center of a winding river, and a dark castle, with rooks flying around its turrets.

"You'll be watching for the stair-carpet," Mr Fearon warned me. "It's ripped at the top."

Upstairs, there were two bedrooms, one of them overlooking the street and a smaller bedroom at the back. In the smaller bedroom, against the wall, stood a single bed with a plain oak bedhead. It was covered with a yellowing sheet. Above it hung a damp-rippled picture of the Cork hurling team, 1976. I went to the window and looked down into the yard. For some reason I didn't like this room. There was a sour, unpleasant smell in it, boiled vegetables and Dettol. It reminded me of nursing-homes, and old, pale people seen through rainy windows. It was the smell of hopelessness.

"Mrs Devlin wasn't a woman to explain herself," said Mr Fearon. "Her estate didn't amount to much, and she left most of it to her husband. But she insisted that this house should come to you. She said she was frightened of what would happen to her if it didn't."

I turned away from the window. "But she wouldn't explain why?"

Mr Fearon shook his head. "If I had any inkling, I'd tell you."

I still found it difficult to believe. Up until yesterday morning, when Mr Fearon had first called me, I had never heard of Mrs Margaret Devlin. Now I found myself to be one of the beneficiaries of her will, and the owner of a shabby terraced property in the rear end nowhere in particular.

Not that I was looking a gift horse in the mouth. My Italian-style café in Academy Street in Cork hadn't been doing too well lately. Only three weeks ago I had lost my best chef Carlo, and I had always been badly under-financed. I had tried to recoup some of my losses by buying a £1,000 share in a promising-looking yearling called Satan's Pleasure, but it had fallen last weekend at Galway and broken its leg. No wonder Satan was pleased. He was probably laughing all the way back to hell.

We left the house. Mr Fearon slammed the front door shut behind us – twice – and handed me the keys. "Well, I wish you joy of it," he said.

As I opened the car door, a white-haired priest came hurrying across the road in the rain. "Good morning to you!" he called out. He came up and offered me his hand. "Father Murphy, from St Bernadette's." He was a stocky man, with a large head, and glasses that enormously magnified his eyes.

"You must be Jerry Flynn," he said. "You're very welcome to Ballyhooly, Jerry."

I shook his hand. "Difficult place to keep a secret, Ballyhooly?"

"Oh, you'd be surprised. We have plenty of secrets here, believe me. But everybody knew who Margaret Devlin was going to give her house to."

"Everybody except me, apparently."

Father Murphy gave me an evasive smile. "Do you know what she said? She said it was destiny. I have to bequeath my house to Jerry Flynn. The wheel turning the full circle, so to speak."

"And what do you think she meant by that?"

"I believe that she was making her peace before God. The world is a strange place, Jerry. Doors may open, but they don't always lead us where we think they're going to."

"And this door?" I asked, nodding toward Number 15.

"Well, who knows? But when you're back, don't forget to drop in to see me. My housekeeper makes the best barmbrack in Munster. And we can talk. We really ought to talk."

I hadn't planned on going back to Ballyhooly for at least ten days. I was interviewing new chefs and I was also trying to borrow some more money from the bank so that I could keep the café afloat. I had already re-mortgaged my flat in Wellington Road, and even when I told my bank manager about my unexpected bequest he shook his head from side to side like a swimmer trying to dislodge water out of his ears.

But only two nights later the phone rang at half-past two in the morning. I sat up. The bedroom was completely dark, except for a diagonal line of sodium street-light crossing the ceiling. I scrabbled around my nightstand and knocked my glass of water on to the floor, the whole lot. The phone kept on ringing until I managed to pick it up. I don't like calls in the middle of the night: they're always bad news. Your father's dead. Your son's been killed in a car crash.

"Who is it?" I asked.

There was nothing on the other end of the line except for a thin, persistent crackling.

"Who is it? Is anybody there?"

The crackling went on for a almost half a minute and then the caller hung up. *Click.* Silence.

I tried to get back to sleep, but I was wide awake now. I switched on the bedside light and climbed out of bed. My cat Charlie stared at me through slitted eyes as if I were mad. I went to the bathroom and refilled my glass of water. In the mirror over the washbasin I thought I looked strangely pale, as if a vampire had visited me when I was asleep. Even my lips were white.

The phone rang again. I went back into the bedroom and picked it up. I didn't say anything, just listened. At first I heard nothing but that crackling noise again, but then a woman's voice said, "Is that Mr Jerry Flynn?"

"Who wants him?"

"Is that Mr Jerry Flynn who has the house in Ballyhooly?"

"Who wants him? Do you know what time it is?"

"You have to go to your house, Jerry. You have to do what needs to be done."

"What are you talking about? What needs to be done?"

"It can't go on, Jerry. It has to be done."

"Look, who is this? It's two-thirty in the morning and I don't understand what the hell you're talking about."

"Go to your house, Jerry. Number 15. It's the only way."

The woman hung up again. I stared at the receiver for a while, as if I expected it to say something else, and then I hung up, too.

For a change, it wasn't raining the next morning when I drove back to Ballyhooly, but the hills were covered with low gray clouds. The road took me over the Nagle mountains and across the stone bridge that spans the Blackwater river. I drove for almost twenty minutes and saw nobody, except for a farmhand driving a tractor heaped with sugar-beet. For some reason, they reminded me of rotting human heads.

When I reached Ballyhooly, I parked outside Number 15 and

climbed out of my car. I hesitated for a few moments before I opened
the front door, pretending to be searching for my keys. Then I turned
around quickly to see if I could catch anybody curtain-twitching. But
the street was empty, except for two young boys with runny noses
and a dog that was trotting off on some self-appointed errand.

I pushed open the shuddering front door. The house was damp
and silent. No new mail, only a circular advertising Dunne's Stores
Irish bacon promotion. I walked through to the kitchen. It was so
cold in there that my breath smoked. I opened one or two drawers.
All I found was a rusty can-opener, a ball of twine and a half-empty
packet of birthday-cake candles.

I went through to the living-room. Out on the street, an old man in
a brown raincoat was standing on the opposite corner, watching the
house and smoking. I picked up the fallen chair and set it straight.

The silence was uncanny. A truck drove past, then a motorcycle, but I couldn't hear them at all. I felt as if I had gone
completely deaf.

I returned to the hallway and inspected myself in the blotchy
Victorian mirror. I certainly didn't look well, although I couldn't
think why. I felt tired, but that was only natural after an interrupted
night. More than that, though, I felt unsettled, as if something were
going to happen that I wasn't going to be able to control. Something
unpleasant.

It was then that I glanced up the stairs. I said, *"Jesus!"* out loud,
and my whole body tingled with fright.

Standing on the landing was a white-faced boy, staring at me
intently. He looked about eight or nine, with short brown hair
that looked as if it had been cut with the kitchen scissors, and
protruberant ears. He wore a gray sweater with darned elbows
and long gray-flannel shorts. And he stared at me, in utter silence,
without even blinking.

"What are you doing here?" I asked him. "You almost gave me
a heart-attack."

He didn't say anything, but continued to stare at me, almost as if
he were trying to stare me into non-existence.

"Come on," I said. "You can't stay here. This house belongs
to me now. What have you been doing, playing? I used to do

that, when I was your age. Play in this old derelict house. Ghost-hunters."

Still the boy didn't speak. His fists were tightly clenched, and he breathed through his mouth, quite laboriously, as if he were suffering from asthma.

"Listen," I told him. "I'm supposed to be back in Cork by eleven. I don't know how you got in here, but you really have to leave."

The boy continued to stare at me in silence. I started to climb up the steep, narrow staircase toward him. As soon as I did so, he turned around and walked quite quickly across the landing, and disappeared into the smaller bedroom at the back of the house.

"Come on, son," I called him. I was beginning to lose my patience. I climbed up the rest of the stairs and followed him through the bedroom door. "Breaking into other people's houses, that's trespass."

The bedroom was empty. There was nobody there. Only the bed with the yellowed sheet and the dull view down to the yard, with its weeds and its cement sacks.

I knelt down and looked under the bed. The boy wasn't there. I felt around the walls to see if there was a secret door, but all I felt was damp wallpaper. The sash window was jammed up with years of green paint; and the floor was covered in thin brown underlay, so the boy couldn't have lifted up any of the floorboards. I even looked up the chimney, but that was ridiculous, and I felt ridiculous even when I was doing it. The flue was so narrow that even a hamster couldn't have climbed up it.

My irritation began to rearrange itself into a deeply disturbing sense of creepiness. If the boy hadn't hidden under the bed, and he hadn't climbed up the chimney, and he certainly hadn't escaped through the window, then where had he gone?

He couldn't have been a ghost. I refused to believe in ghosts. Besides, he had looked far too solid to be a ghost. Too normal, too real. What ghost has falling-down socks and darns in its sweater?

But he wasn't here. I had seen him standing at the top of the stairs. I had heard him breathing. But he wasn't here.

I went from room to room, searching them all. I didn't go up in the attic because I didn't have a ladder, but then the boy hadn't had a ladder, either, and there was a cobweb in the corner of the attic door which he would have had to have broken, even if he had found some miraculous way of getting up there. The house was empty. No boy, anywhere. I even opened up the gas oven.

I left the house much later than I had meant to, almost half an hour later. As I came out, and slammed the door shut, a woman approached me. She probably wasn't much older than thirty-five, but she looked forty at least. Her brown hair was tightly permed and she had the pinched face of a heavy smoker. She wore a cheap purple coat and a long black skirt with a fraying hem.

"Well, Jerry," she said, without any introduction, "you've seen what you have to do."

"Was it you who phoned me last night?"

"It doesn't matter who phoned you. You've seen what you have to do."

"I haven't the slightest idea what I have to do."

"You should be here at night then. When the screaming starts."

"Screaming? What screaming? What are you talking about?"

The woman took out a pack of Carroll's and lit one, and sucked it so hard that her cheeks were all drawn in. "We've been living next door to that for twenty-five years and what are *we* supposed to do? That house is all we've got. But my daughter's a nervous wreck and my husband tried to take his own life. And who can we tell? We'd never sell the property if everybody knew about it. Number 17, they're the same. Nobody can stand it any more."

It started to rain again, but neither of us made any attempt to find shelter. "What's your name?" I asked her.

"Maureen," she said, blowing smoke.

"Well, tell me about this screaming, Maureen."

"It doesn't happen all the time. Sometimes we can go for weeks and we don't hear anything. But it's November now, and that's the anniversary, and then we hear it more and more, and sometimes it's unbearable, the screaming. You never heard such screaming in your whole life."

"The anniversary?" I asked her. "The anniversary of what?"

"The day the boy killed his whole family and then himself. In that house. Nobody found them till two days later. The gardaí thought the house was painted red, until they realized it was blood. I saw them carry the mother and the daughters out myself. I saw it myself. And you never saw such a frightful thing. He used his father's razor, and he almost took their heads off."

I looked away, down Ballyhooly's main road. I could see Father Murphy, not far away, white-haired, leaning against the rain, talking to a woman in a blue coat.

"Can't the priest help you?"

"Him? He's tried. But this is nothing to do with God, believe me."

"I don't see what I can do. I was bequeathed this house, by somebody I never even knew, and that's it. I run a café. I'm not an exorcist."

"You've seen the boy, though?"

I didn't say anything, but the woman tilted her head sideways and looked at me closely. "You've seen the boy. I can tell."

"I've seen – I don't know what I've seen."

"You've seen him. You've seen the boy. You can't deny it." She sucked at her cigarette again, more triumphantly this time.

"All right, yes. Is he a local boy?"

"He's the very same boy. The boy who killed his family, and then himself."

I didn't know what to say. I was beginning to suspect that Maureen had been drinking. But she kept on smoking and nodding as if she had proved her point beyond a shadow of a doubt, and that I was just being perverse to question the feasibility of a dead schoolboy walking around my newly acquired house.

"I have to get back to Cork now," I told her. "I'm sorry."

"You've seen him and you're just going to leave? You don't think that you were given this house by accident? That your name was picked out with a pin?"

"Quite frankly I don't know *why* it was given to me."

"You were chosen, that's why. That's what Margaret always used to say to me – Mrs Devlin. She was chosen and there was nothing she could do about it, except to pass it on."

I unlocked my car. Maureen started to become agitated, tossing her cigarette away and wiping her hands on the front of her coat, over and over, as if she couldn't get them clean.

"You mustn't go. Please."

"I'm sorry. I have a business to run."

But it was then that I saw one of the grubby upstairs curtains being drawn aside. Standing in the bedroom window, staring at me, was the white-faced boy. Somehow he must have hidden from me when I was searching the house, and here he was, mocking me.

I kicked open the front door and ran upstairs. I hurtled into the front bedroom but the boy was gone. He wasn't in the back bedroom, either. There was a tiny linen cupboard between the two rooms, but it was empty except for two folded sheets and a 60-watt lightbulb. I slapped the walls in both bedrooms, to see if they were hollow. I lifted up the mattress in the smaller bedroom, in case it was hollowed-out, and the boy had been concealing himself in there. It was stained, and damp, but it hadn't been tampered with.

Underneath it, however, lying on the bedsprings, I discovered a book. It was thin, like an exercise book, with a faded maroon cover, and it was disturbingly familiar. I picked it up and angled it toward the window, so that I could see what was printed on the front.

Bishop O'Rourke Memorial School, Winter 1976. The same junior school that I had attended, in Cork. I opened it up and leafed through it. I could even remember this particular yearbook. The sports reports. The opening of the new classroom extension. The visit from the Taoiseach. And right at the back, the list of names of everybody in the school. Familiar names, all of them, but I couldn't remember many of their faces. And there was my name, too. Class III, Gerald Flynn, between Margaret Flaherty and Kevin Foley.

But what was it doing here, this book, hidden under the mattress in this run-down little house in Ballyhooly?

I looked around one more time. I still couldn't work out how the boy had managed to elude me, but I would make sure that he never got in here again. Tomorrow morning I would change the locks, front and back, and check that none of the windows could be opened from the outside.

As I left the house, Father Murphy came over.

"Everything in order?" he asked me, with that same evasive smile. A real priest's smile, always waiting for you to commit yourself.

"You said we ought to talk."

"We should," he said. "Come across and have a glass with me."

We crossed the street and went into a small pub called The Roundy House. Inside, there was a small bar, and a sitting-room with armchairs and a television, just like somebody's private home. Two young men sat at the bar, smoking, and they acknowledged Father Murphy with a nod of their heads.

We sat in the corner by the window. The afternoon light strained through the net curtains the color of cold tea. Father Murphy clinked my half of Guinness, and then he said, "Maureen hasn't been upsetting you?"

"She told me that she could hear screaming."

"Well, yes. She's right. I've heard it myself."

"I've seen a boy, too. I saw him in the house, twice. I don't know he got in there."

"He got in there because he's always in there."

"What are you trying to tell me, that he's a ghost?"

Father Murphy shook his head. "I don't believe in ghosts and I don't suppose that you do, either. But he's not alive in the way that you and I are alive. You can see him because he will occupy that house until he gets justice for what happened to him. That's my theory, anyway."

"You really think it's the same boy who killed his family? That's not possible, is it? I mean, how can that be possible? He killed himself, too, and even if he hadn't, he'd be my age by now."

Father Murphy wiped foam from his upper lip. "What's been happening in that house isn't recognized by the teachings of the Church, Jerry. I've tried twice to exorcize it. The second time I brought down Father Griffin from Dublin. He said afterwards that no amount of prayer or holy water could cleanse that property, because it isn't possessed of any devil.

"It's possessed instead by the rage of a nine-year-old boy who was driven to utter despair. A child of God, not of Satan. His father was a drunk who regularly beat him. His mother neglected him and fed him on nothing but chips, if she fed him at all. His older sister had

Down's Syndrome and he was expected to do everything for her, change her sheets when she wet the bed, everything. He lived in hell, that boy, and he had nobody to help him.

"My predecessor here did whatever he could, but it isn't easy when the parents are so aggressive. And he wasn't alone, this boy. He was only one of thousands of children all over the country whose parents abuse them, and who don't have anywhere to turn.

"Whatever it is in your house, Jerry – whatever kind of force it is – it's the force of revenge. A sense of rage and injustice so strong that it has taken on a physical shape."

"Even if that's true, father – what can *I* do about it?"

"You were chosen. I don't know why. Margaret Devlin said that *she* was chosen, too, when she inherited Number 15. And before her, Martin Donnolly. I never knew what became of him."

"So what happened to Margaret Devlin? How did she die?"

"Well, it was a tragedy. She took her own life. I believe she was separated from her husband or something of the kind. She took an overdose of paracetamol. Lay dead in the house for over a week."

On the drive back to Cork, under a late-afternoon sky as black as a crow's wing, I kept thinking what Father Murphy had told me. *A sense of rage and injustice so strong that it has taken on a physical shape.* It didn't really make any scientific sense, or any theological sense, either, but in a way I could understand what he meant. We all get angry and frustrated from time to time, and when we do, we can all feel the uncontrollable beast that rises up inside us.

Katharine was waiting for me when I got back to my flat. She was a neat, pretty girl with a pale pre-Raphaelite face and long black hair. She helped me in the café from time to time, but her real job was making silver jewelry. We nearly had an affair once, after a friend's party and too many bottles of Chilean sauvignon, but she was such a good friend that I was always glad that we had managed to resist each other. Mainly by falling asleep.

She wanted to know if I wanted to come to an Irish folk evening in McCurtain Street. She was dressed for it: with a blue silk scarf around her head and a long flowing dress with patterns of peacock feathers on it, and dozens of jangly silver bracelets. But I didn't feel in the mood for "Whiskey in the Jar" and "Goodbye Mrs Durkin". I poured us a glass of wine and sat down on my big leather sofa, tossing Bishop O'Rourke's Memorial Junior School yearbook on to the coffee table.

"What's wrong?" asked Katharine. "The bank didn't turn you down, did they?"

"As a matter of fact they did, but that's not it."

She sat close beside me, and she had some perfume like a pomander, cinnamon and cloves and orange-peel. "You've got something on your mind. I can tell."

I told her about Number 15 and the boy that I had seen on the landing. I told her about Maureen, too, and the screaming; and what Father Murphy had said about revenge.

"You don't believe any of it, do you? It sounds like a prime case of mass hysteria."

"I wasn't hysterical, but I saw the boy as clear as I can see you now. And I couldn't find how the hell he managed to get in and out of the house. There just wasn't any way."

She picked up the yearbook. "This is spooky, though, isn't it – finding your old junior school yearbook under the mattress?"

She read through the list of names in Class III. "Linda Ahern, remember her?"

"Fat. Freckles. The reddest hair you've ever seen. But when she turned fourteen, she was a cracker."

"Donal Coakley?"

"Thin. Weedy. We all used to chase him round the playground and pinch his biscuits."

"What a mean lot you were."

"Oh, you know what schoolkids are like."

"Ellen Collins?"

"Don't remember her."

"Martin Donnolly?"

I frowned at her. "Who did you say?"

"Martin Donnolly."

"I don't remember him, but that was the name of the man who owned Number 15 before Margaret Devlin."

"It's a common enough name, for goodness' sake."

"Yes, but who comes next? Margaret Flaherty. I wonder if she could have changed her name to Devlin when she married."

"Isn't there somebody you could ask?"

I called my old friend Tony O'Connell – the only former classmate from Bishop O'Rourke's who I still saw from time to time. He ran an auto repair business on the Patrick Mills Estate out at Douglas.

"Tony, you remember Margaret Flaherty?"

"How could I ever forget her? I was in love with her. I picked her a bunch of dandelions once and she threw them away and called me an idiot."

"Do you know if she married?"

"Oh, yes. She married some fellow much older than herself. A real waste of space. Estate agent, I think he was. Frank Devlin."

"And Martin Donnolly? Do you know what happened to him?"

"Martin? He moved to Fermoy or somewhere near there. They found him drowned in the Blackwater."

I put down the phone. "I may be making a wild assumption here," I told Katharine, "but it looks as if Number 15 is being passed from one old pupil of Bishop O'Rourke's to the next, alphabetically, down the class list. And everybody who owns it ends up dead."

"You'd better check some more," Katharine suggested. "See if you can find out what happened to Linda Ahern and Donal Coakley."

It took another hour. Outside, it started to grow dark, that strange foggy disappearance of light that happens over Cork some evenings, because the River Lee brings in cold seawater from the Atlantic, the same reaches where the *Lusitania* was sunk, and the city turns chilly and quiet, as if it remembers the dead.

I found Ita Twomey, who was Linda Ahern's best friend when they were at school, by calling her mother. Ita was Mrs Desmond now, and lived in Bishopstown. "Linda was a single mother. But she inherited a house, I believe. But she was killed in a car accident on the N20 . . . both herself and her kiddie. They burned to death. The gardaí said that she drove her car deliberately into a bridge."

And Donal Coakley? I managed at last to find Vincent O'Brien, our class teacher at Bishop O'Rourke's. "You'll have to forgive me for sounding so hoarse. I was diagnosed with cancer of the larynx only two months ago. I'll be having a laryngectomy by Christmas, God willing."

"I'm trying to find out what happened to a classmate of mine called Donal Coakley."

"Donal? I remember Donal. Poor miserable kid. I don't know what happened to him. He was always very unhappy at school. All of the other kids used to bully him, every day. I don't suppose you did, Jerry, but you know how cruel children can be to each other, without even realising what they're doing. He was always playing truant, young Donal, because he didn't want to stay at home and he didn't want to go to school. Poor miserable kid. They were always stealing his lunch money and taking his sweeties and hitting him around. You never know why, do you? Just because his parents were poor and he always smelled a bit and had holes in his socks."

"But do you know what happened to him, after he left school?"

"I couldn't tell you. He never finished Bishop O'Rourke's. He left at mid-term. He couldn't take the bullying any longer. I think his parents moved. There was some trouble with the social services. I never heard where they went."

My mouth was as dry as if I had woken up from drinking red wine all night. "Donal was bullied that badly?"

"It happens in every school, doesn't it? It's kids, they have a sort of pack instinct. Anybody who doesn't fit in, they go for, and they never let up. Donal had second-hand shoes and jumpers with holes in them and of course that made him a prime target. I'm not talking about you, Jerry. I know you were very protective of the weaker kids. But it was a fact."

Protective? I thought of the time that I had snatched the Brennan's bread-wrapper in which Donal's mother had packed his jam sandwiches for him, and stamped on it. I thought of the time that five of us had cornered him by the boys' toilets and punched him and beaten him with sticks and rulers until he knelt down on the tarmac with his grubby hands held over his head to protect himself, not even crying, not even begging for mercy, though we kept on shouting and screaming at him.

Donal Coakley. My God. The shame of it made my cheeks burn,

even after all these years. The day it was raining and we found out that he had lined his shoes with newspaper because they had holes in the soles. Wet pages from the *Evening Echo* folded beneath his socks.

"Is that all you wanted to know?" asked Vincent O'Brien.

I could hardly speak to him. "I'd forgotten Donal. I'd forgotten him. I don't think I wanted to remember."

I put down the phone and Katharine was staring at me in the strangest way. Or perhaps she wasn't. Perhaps I had suddenly realized what I had done, and everything was different.

"I – ah, I have to go back to Ballyhooly," I told her.

"You're not *crying*, are you?"

"Crying? What are you talking about? I have to go back to Ballyhooly, that's all."

"Tonight?"

"Yes, tonight. Now."

"Let me come with you. Something's happened, hasn't it? You'd be better off with somebody with you."

"Katharine – this is something I have to deal with on my own."

She took hold of my hands between hers. She stroked my fingers, trying to calm me down. "But you must tell me," she said. "It's something to do with Donal Coakley, isn't it?"

I nodded. I couldn't speak. She was right, damn it. She was right. I was crying. The boy on the landing was Donal Coakley. I had bullied him and tortured him and stolen his money and trodden on his lunch, and what had he ever had to go home to, except a drunken father who punched him and a mother who expected him to lay the fire and take care of his handicapped sister; and that damp bedroom in Ballyhooly.

I could have befriended him. I could have taken care of him. But I was worse than any of the others. No wonder his father's razor had seemed like the only way out.

You don't know how dark it is in the Cork countryside at night, unless you've been there. Only a speckle of distant flickering lights as we drove over the Nagle mountains. It was cold but at least it was dry. We arrived in the middle of Ballyhooly at eleven thirty-seven and the Roundy House was emptying out, three or four locals laughing and swearing and a small brown-and-white dog barking at them disapprovingly.

"I don't know what you expect to find here," said Katharine.

"I don't know, either."

I helped her out of the car, but all the time I couldn't take my eyes off Number 15. Its windows looked blacker than ever; and in the orange light of Ballyhooly's main street, its paintwork looked even more scabrous and diseased.

"Is this it?" Katherine asked. "It looks derelict."

"It is." I unlocked the front door and kicked the weatherboard to open it. I switched on the light and, miraculously, it worked, even though it was only a single bare bulb. I had called the ESB only yesterday afternoon to have Number 15 reconnected. The damp smell seemed even stronger than ever, and I was sure that I could hear a dripping noise.

"This is a seriously creepy house," said Katharine, looking around. "How many people died here?"

"That night? All four of them. Donal's father and mother, Donal's sister, and Donal himself. And Margaret Flaherty died here, too."

"It smells like death."

"It smells more like dry rot to me," I said. But then I took two or three cautious steps into the hallway and sniffed again. "Dry rot, and something dead. Probably a bird, stuck down the chimney."

"What are you going to do?" asked Katharine.

"I don't know. But I have to do *something*."

We took a look in the living-room. The broken ceiling-light cast a diagonal shadow, which made the whole room appear to be sloping sideways, and distorted its perspective. The wind blew a soft lament down the chimney.

"What are those scratches?" asked Katharine, pointing up at the coving. "It looks like a lion's been loose."

"I asked the estate agent."

"And?"

"Either he didn't know or he didn't want to tell me."

I took Katharine into the kitchen. It was deadly cold, as always. I didn't really know what I was looking for. Just some sign of what was really happening here. Just some indication of what I could do to break the cycle of Donal Coakley's revenge.

If it *was* Donal Coakley, and not some madman playing games with us.

"Nothing here," said Katharine, opening the larder door and peering inside. Only an old bottle of Chef sauce, with a rusty, encrusted cap.

We went upstairs together. I hadn't realized how much the stairs creaked until now. Every one of them complained as if their nails were slowly being drawn out of them, like teeth. The landing was empty. The front bedroom was empty. The back bedroom was empty, too. The chill was intense: that damp, penetrating chill that characterizes bedrooms in old Irish houses.

"I think you should sell," said Katharine. "Get rid of the place as soon as you can. And make sure that you don't sell it to the next person on your class register."

"You may be right. And there was me, thinking this was going to solve all of my problems."

Katharine took a last look around the bedroom. "Come on," she said. "There's no point in staying here. There's nothing you can do."

But at that moment, we heard an appalling scream from downstairs. It was a woman's scream, but it was so shrill that it was almost like an animal's. Then it was joined by another scream – a man's. He sounded as if he were being fatally hurt, and he knew it.

"Oh my God," Katharine gasped. "Oh my God what is it?"

"Stay here," I told her.

"I'm coming with you. I just want to get out of here."

"*Stay here!* We don't know what the hell could be down there."

"Oh, God," she repeated; but her voice was drowned out by another agonized scream, and then another, and then another.

I started downstairs, ducking my head so that I could see through the banistairs into the hallway. I was so frightened that I was making a thin pathetic whining noise, like a child.

The screams were coming from the living-room. The door was half-open, and the light was still on, but I couldn't see anything at all. No shadows, nothing. I reached the bottom of the stairs and edged my way along the hall until I was right beside the living-room door. The screams were hideous, and in between the screams I could hear a woman begging for her life.

I tried to peer in through the crack in the door, but I still couldn't see anything. I thought: there's only one thing for it. I've just got to crash into the room and surprise him, whoever he is, and hope that he isn't stronger and quicker and that he doesn't have a straight-razor.

I took a deep breath. Then I took a step back, lowered my shoulder and collided against the door. It slammed wide open, and juddered a little way back again. The screams abruptly stopped.

I was standing in a silent room – alone, with only a chair for company. Either we had imagined the screaming, or else it was some kind of trick.

I was still standing there, baffled, when I heard the bedroom door slamming upstairs, and more screaming. Only this time, I recognized who it was. Katharine, and she was shouting out, *"Jerry! Jerry! Jerry for God's sake help me Jerry for God's sake!"*

I vaulted back up the stairs, my vision jostling like a hand-held camera. The door to the smaller bedroom was shut – brown-painted wood, with a cheap plastic handle. I tried to open it but it was locked or bolted. And all the time Katharine was screaming and screaming.

"Katharine!" I yelled back. "Katharine, what's happening! I can't open the door!"

But all she could do was scream and weep and babble something incomprehensible, like *"no-no-no-you-can't-you-can't-be-you-can't—"*

I hurled myself against the door, shoulder-first, but all I did was bruise my arm. Katharine's screams reached a crescendo and I was mad with panic, panting and shaking. I propped my hands against the landing walls to balance myself, and I kicked at the door-lock – once, twice – and then the door-jamb splintered and the door shuddered open.

Katharine was lying on the bed. She was struggling and staring at me, her eyes wide open. She looked as if she were fastened on to the mattress with thick brown sticks – trapped, unable to move. But beside the bed stood a huge and complicated creature that I could hardly even begin to understand. It almost filled the room with arms and legs like an immense spider; and glossy brown sacs hung from its limbs like some kind of disgusting fruit. In the middle of it, and part of it, all mixed up in it, his head swollen out of proportion and his eyes as black as cellars stood Donal Coakley, in his gray flannel shorts and his patched-up jumper, his lips drawn back as if they had been nailed to his gums. He floated, almost, borne up above the threadbare carpet by the thicket of tentacles that sprouted out of his back.

The thick brown sticks that fastened Katharine to the bed were spider's legs – or the legs of the thing that Donal Coakley had created out of his need for revenge. This was revenge incarnate. This was what revenge looked like, when it reached such an intensity that it took on a life of its own.

In his right hand, Donal held a straight-razor, with a bloodied blade. It was only an inch above Katharine's neck. He had already cut her once, a very light cut, right across her throat, and blood was running into the collar of her green sweater.

I approached him as near as I dared. The whole room was a forest of spiderlike legs, and there was nothing on Donal's face to indicate that he could see me; or that he had any human emotions at all.

"What do you want me to do?" I asked him. "What do you want me to say? You want me to apologize, for bullying you? I bullied you, yes, and I'm sorry for it. I wish I'd never done it. But we were all young and ignorant in those days. We never guessed that you were so unhappy, and even if we'd known, I don't think that we would have cared.

"It's life, Donal. It's life. And you don't ease your own pain by inflicting it on others."

Donal raised his head a little. I didn't know whether he could see me or not. The criss-cross spider's-legs that surrounded him twitched and trembled, as if they were eager to scuttle toward me.

"You don't know the meaning of pain," he said; and his voice sounded exactly as it had, all those years ago, in the playground of Bishop O'Rourke's. "You never suffered pain, any of you."

"Oh God," said Katharine, "please help me."

184

But without any hesitation at all, Donal swept the straight-razor from one side of her neck to the other. If you hadn't been paying any particular attention, you wouldn't have realized immediately what he had done. But he had sliced her neck through, almost to the vertebrae, and from that instant there was no chance at all of her survival. Blood suddenly sprayed everywhere, all over the bed, all up the walls, all over the carpet. No wonder the gardaí had broken into this house and thought that it was all decorated red.

Katharine twitched and shuddered. One hand tried to reach out for me. But I knew that Donal had killed her – and so, probably, did she. The blood was unbelievable: pints of it, pumped out everywhere. Donal's hands were smothered in it, and it was even splattered across his face.

I shall never know to this day exactly what happened next. But if you can accept that men and women become physically transformed, whenever they're truly vengeful, then you can understand it, even if you don't completely believe it. When Donal cut Katharine's throat, something happened to me. I'm not saying that it was similar to what happened to Donal. But my mind suddenly boiled over with the blackest of rages. I felt hatred, and aggression, but I also felt enormous power. I felt myself lifted up, surged forward, as if I had legs and arms that I had never had before, as if I had unimaginable power. I hurled myself at Donal, and the thicket of limbs that surrounded him, and grasped him around the waist.

He slashed at my face with his straight-razor. I knew he was cutting me. I could feel the blood flying. He struggled and screamed like a girl. But I forced him backward. I gripped his hair and clawed at his face. His spidery arms and legs were flailing at me, but I had spidery arms and legs that were more than the equal of his, and we fought for one desperate moment like two giant insects. My urge for revenge, though, was so much fiercer than his. I hurled him back against the bedroom window.

The glass cracked. The glazing-bars cracked. Then both of us smashed through the window and into the yard, falling fifteen feet on to bricks and bags of cement and window-frames. I lifted my head. I could feel the blood dripping from my lips. I felt bruised all over, as if I had been trampled by a horse. I could hear shouting in the street, and a woman screaming.

Donal Coakley was staring at me, only inches away, and his face was as white as the face of the moon.

"I've got you now, Jerry," he said; and he managed the faintest of smiles.

And that's my testimony; and that's all that I can tell you. You can talk to Father Murphy, for what it's worth. You can talk to Maureen. If she doesn't admit to the screaming, then it's only because she's worried about the value of her house. But it's all true; and I didn't touch Katharine, I swear.

If you can't find any trace of Donal, then I don't mind that, because it means that he's finally gone to his rest. But I'd be careful of who I bullied, if I were you; and I'd steer clear of white-faced boys in second-hand shoes. And I wouldn't have a vengeful thought in my head, not one. Not unless you want to find out what vengeance really is.

The Sympathy Society

The phone rang just as Martin was cracking the second egg into the frying-pan. He wedged the receiver under his chin and said, "Sarah! Hi, sweetheart! You're calling early!"

There was an uncomfortable pause. Then, "Sorry, Martin. This is John – John Newcome, from Lazarus."

"John? What can I do for you? Don't tell me Sarah's left some more documents at home."

"No, no, nothing like that. Listen, Martin, there's no easy way of saying this. We've just had a call from the British Embassy in Athens. I'm afraid there's been an accident."

Martin suddenly found himself short of breath. "Accident? What kind of accident? Sarah's all right, isn't she?"

"I'm sorry, Martin. We're all devastated. She's dead."

Martin turned off the gas. It was all he could think of to do. Whatever John Newcome said next, he wasn't going to be eating the full English breakfast that he had planned for himself. The flat was silent now. The television had switched itself off. The birds had suddenly stopped chirruping.

"You're going to hear this sooner or later," said John Newcome. He was obviously trying to be stable but his words came out like a bagful of Scrabble tiles. "The press will be onto you. You know. Sarah had an accident on a jet-ski, late yesterday afternoon. It seems as if she went between two boats. There was a line between them. The chap from the Embassy said that she probably didn't see it. Only a thin line. Braided steel."

"No," said Martin.

"I'm sorry, Martin. But it's probably better that you hear it from me. She went straight into it and it cut her—"

Martin could never tell afterward if he had actually heard the words, or if he had imagined hearing them, or seen what had happened to Sarah in his mind's eye, as if she had sent him a Polaroid snap of it. Full color, blue sky, blue sea, yachts as white as starched collars.

"Head—"

No this can't be true. This is Thursday morning and as soon as I've finished my job in Fulham I'm flying out to Rhodes to spend the next ten days with her, swimming and snorkeling and going to discos. Not Sarah. Not Sarah with her long blonde hair and her bright gray oystershell eyes and her Finnish-looking face. And the way she laughed – wild exaggerated laughter, falling backward on the futon. And those toes of hers, kicking in the sunlight. And she hated fat, she used to take her ham sandwiches apart and put on her reading-glasses and search for fat like a gold prospector.

And her kisses, clicking on his shoulder, in the darkest moments of the night. And suggestive little whispers.

"Off."

His mother said that he was very brave. His father stood with his hands deep in the pockets of his brown corduroy trousers and looked as if he had just heard that interest rates had gone down again. He spent most of the weekend in his old room, lying on his candlewick bedspread, facing the wall. He saw so many faces in the floral wallpaper. Devils, imps, demons and fairies. But he couldn't clearly remember what Sarah had looked like. He didn't want to remind himself by looking at photographs. If he looked at photographs, he would remember only the photographs, and not the real Sarah. The real Sarah who had touched him and kissed him and waved him goodbye at Stansted Airport. Turning the corner. The sun, catching her hair. Then, gone.

After the funeral, he went for a long walk on the Downs, on the bony prehistoric back of Sussex, where the wind constantly blew and the sea always glittered in the distance. But no matter how often you walked up there, you always had to return. And, as evening turned the sky into veils of blue, he came down the narrow chalk path, clinging on to the hawthorn bushes to keep his balance, and he knew that he was going to go mad without her. He was going to kill himself, take an overdose, cut his wrists, fill his car with carbon monoxide. She was gone, and she had left him all alone in this world, and he didn't want to be here any longer. Not alone. What was the point? What was the purpose? Everything that he had ever done, he had done expressly for her. His whole life from the moment he was born had been leading him toward her, by all kinds of devious paths and diversions. They had given him her jewelry. Her necklace, her watch. What was the point of them, if she wasn't alive to wear them?

And more than anything, he kept imagining what it must have been like for her, rounding the prow of that yacht, laughing, revving up her jet-ski, only to see that steel cable stretched in front of her, far too late. Maybe she hadn't seen it at all. But what had she *felt*, when she hit it, and her head came flying off? Don't tell me she felt nothing. Don't tell me she wouldn't have suffered. Don't tell me that for one split-second she wouldn't have realized what had happened to her?

Nobody had any proof, of course, but didn't they always say that when they guillotined the nobles in the French Revolution, and their heads had tumbled into the basket, some of them had cried out in shock?

In their flat, two weeks later, he stood in front of the bathroom mirror and tried to cut his throat with the steak knife that he had stolen from a Berni Inn the previous summer. Because Sarah had dared him to. Now he believed that he knew why she had dared him. She wanted him to have a way of joining him, when she died. It was drizzling outside. One of the gutters was blocked with leaves and water was clattering intermittently into the basement area outside.

He drew the serrated blade across his neck. It tugged at his skin and blood suddenly poured on to his shirt. It didn't hurt, but the tugging was deeply unpleasant, and the knife obviously wasn't sharp enough. He had expected to cut through his carotid artery and send spurts of blood all over the bathroom, up the walls, over the mirror.

Sarah's neck must have pumped blood, when her head was cut off. He remembered reading about the beheading of a British soldier in a Japanese PoW camp. His commanding officer said that blood jumped out of his neck like a red walking-stick.

He lifted the knife again. His hand was already slippery and his fingers were sticking together. He tried to cut again, but his neck was so messy that he couldn't see what he was doing, and he was beginning to tremble.

He slowly dropped to his knees on to the floor. The knife fell in the washbasin. He stayed where he was, his head bowed, his eyes streaming with tears, his mouth dragged down in a silent howl of loneliness and agony.

Jenny came to see him in hospital. Jenny was plump and pale with scraped-back hair. She worked in the accounts department at Hiya Intelligence, but ever since he had started working there, she had made excuses to come up and see him in software. She had brought him a box of Milk Tray chocolates and a John Grisham novel.

"You've lost an awful lot of weight, Martin," she said, laying her little nail-bitten hand on top of his.

He tried to smile. "Throat's still sore. Besides, I haven't got much of an appetite."

"How long have you got to stay in here?"

"I don't know. The psychotherapist said he wasn't very happy with me. I said, 'What's happiness got to do with anything?'"

"So what did he say?"

"He said, 'If you don't know, you ought to stay in hospital.'"

Jenny reached down and fumbled in her big woven bag. She produced a folded copy of the *Evening Standard* and handed it to him. "There," she said. "Read that ad I've circled. I don't know if it'll help, but you never know."

It was a small display advertisement in the classified section, under Personal Services. It read: "Grieving? Suicidal? When you've lost a loved one, The Sympathy Society understands how you feel. Unlike all other counselors, we can offer you what you're really looking for." Underneath, there was a telephone number in Buckinghamshire.

Martin dropped the paper on to the floor. "I don't think so, Jenny. The last thing I need is even more sympathy. I've had so much sympathy I've been feeling sympathy-sick. Like eating a whole box of chocolates at one sitting.

"By the way—" he said, handing her back the box of Milk Tray, "I don't like milk chocolate. You eat them."

"It's all right. Give them to the nurses."

She looked so disappointed that he took hold of her hand and squeezed it. "I'm just pleased that you came, that's all. I can't expect you to understand how I feel. Nobody can. Sarah was everything to me. Everything. I'm not making a song and dance about it. I simply don't see the point of living without her."

"What about your family? Your mum and dad? What about all of your friends?"

"They'll get over me."

"You really think so?" she challenged him, with tears in her eyes, and her lower lip quivering. "You're hurt, of course you are. You're absolutely devastated. But why should even more people have to suffer?"

"I'm sorry, Jenny. It's my life and I have the right to do what I want with it. And that includes ending it."

Jenny stood up, and sniffed, and picked up her bag. "If that's the way you feel, I hope you make better job of it next time."

Martin gave a painful cough and held out his hand to her. "Don't be angry with me, Jenny. Please."

"I'm not. I just can't stand to see you giving in. I'd give my life for you, you know that."

He looked into her eyes and he could see how much she loved him. He had the dreadful, unforgivable thought that if only *she* had died, instead of Sarah. Hadn't she offered her life? And if it could make any difference, would he have taken it?

"Thanks for the book, and the chocolates," he said.

She didn't answer, but she leaned forward and kissed him on the forehead. Then she left the ward, dancing awkwardly in the doorway with a man on crutches.

Martin lay back on the bed. The sun crossed the ceiling like the spokes of a broken wheel. He dozed for a while, and when he opened his eyes it was almost four o'clock.

"You've been sleeping," said a soft voice, very close to his ear.

"Mmm," he said. Then he suddenly opened his eyes wider. That was Sarah's voice. He was sure that it was Sarah's voice. He turned sideways and she was lying right next to him, her eyes bright, her blonde hair spread across the pillow. She was smiling at him in that gently mocking way she had, when she caught him doing something embarrassing.

"Sarah," he whispered, reaching up and touching her hair. "I had this nightmare that you were dead. It seemed completely real. You don't have any idea."

She didn't reply, but very, very slowly closed her eyes.

"Sarah, talk to me. Don't go to sleep. I have to tell you all about this dream."

Her eyes remained closed. The color gradually began to seep out of her cheeks. Her lips were almost turquoise.

"Sarah – listen to me – Sarah!"

He tried to take hold of her shoulder to shake her, but his hand seized nothing but blanket. He sat up, shocked, and it was then that he realized that only her head was lying next to him. Her severed neck was encrusted with dried blood and part of her windpipe was protruding on to the sheet.

He made an awful moaning noise and half-jumped, half-fell out of the bed, tangling his feet in the sheets. His head struck the edge of his bedside table and his plastic water-jug dropped on to the floor, along with his book and his chocolates and his wristwatch.

A nurse came hurrying over. "Martin! Martin, what's the matter?"

She helped him up. He tilted on to his feet, and twisted around to stare at the bed. Sarah's head had vanished, and he knew that it hadn't really been there at all. It had been nothing more than a nightmare. He sat down on the side of the bed, feeling shocked and bruised. The trouble was, it was worse being awake. Sarah was dead and he was alone, and he could never wake up from that, ever.

*   *   *

Back at the flat, with the blinds and the curtains drawn, he sat at the kitchen table and smoothed out the page from the *Evening Standard* that Jenny had given him. He had read the advertisement for The Sympathy Society again and again, and every time he read it he had been left with an odd feeling of unease. "Unlike all other counselors, we can offer you what you're really looking for." How did they know what he was looking for? How did they know what *anybody* was looking for?

He ate another spoonful of cold spaghetti out of the can. That was all he had eaten since he came out of hospital. He didn't have to cook it, he barely had to chew it, and it kept him alive. It seemed absurd, to keep yourself alive when you wanted so much to die, but he didn't want to die a lingering death, through starvation and dehydration; and there was always a chance that somebody would find you, and resuscitate you, and feed you with drips and tubes. He wanted to die instantly, the way that Sarah had died.

After almost an hour, he picked up the phone and dialed the number in Buckinghamshire. It rang for a long time, with an echoing, old-fashioned ringing tone. Eventually, it was picked up. There was a moment's breathy pause, and then a clear voice said, "Miller."

"I'm sorry. I think I must have the wrong number. I wanted The Sympathy Society."

"You've reached The Sympathy Society. How can I help you?"

"I've, er – I saw your ad in the *Standard*."

"I see. And may I ask if you have recently been bereaved?"

"About six weeks ago. I lost my partner. She—" He found that he couldn't get the words out.

Mr Miller waited for a while, and then he asked, with extreme delicacy, "Was it *sudden*, may I ask? Or an illness?"

"Sudden. It was very sudden. An accident, while she was on holiday."

"I see. Well, that means that you're very suitable for Sympathy Society counseling. We don't counsel for illness."

"I've had some psychiatric counseling on the NHS."

"And?"

"It hasn't made me feel any better, to tell you the truth."

"That doesn't surprise me. Psychiatrists, on the whole, have a very conventional view of what it is to be 'better.'"

"I don't quite understand what you mean."

"Well, if you're interested in us, why don't you come to see us? It never did anybody any harm to talk."

"How much do you charge?"

"Financially, nothing."

"You mean there are no fees at all?"

"Let me put it this way. I do expect some output from all of the people we help. I'll explain it you when you come to see us."

"You sound pretty confident that I will."

"We word our advertisement very carefully. It appeals only to those who we can genuinely help."

It started to rain again. Martin couldn't see it through the blind, but he could hear the castanet-clatter of water on the concrete outside.

"Tell me how to reach you," he said.

The taxi dropped him off by a sagging green-painted gate, at the end of a driveway that was made almost impassable to motor vehicles by its overgrown laurel-bushes. His feet crunched up the wet pea-shingle until eventually a redbrick Victorian house came into view. Its windows were black and empty, and one of its side-walls was streaked green with lichen. Three enormous ravens were strutting on the lawn, but they flapped away when they saw him coming, and settled on the roof instead, like three bad omens.

Martin went to the front door and rang the bell. He waited for two or three minutes but nobody answered, so he rang it again. He couldn't hear it ringing anywhere in the house. A corroded brass knocker hung in the center of the door, with the face of a hooded monk. He banged it twice, and waited some more.

At last the door opened. Martin was confronted by a white-faced young woman with her hair twisted on top of her head in a messy but elaborate bun. She wore a simple gray smock and grubby white socks.

"You must be Martin," she said. She held out her hand. "I'm Sylvia."

194

"Hello, Sylvia. I wasn't sure I'd come to the right house."

"Oh, you have, Martin. Believe me, you have. Come inside."

Martin followed her into a huge gloomy hallway that smelled of frying onions and lavender floor-polish. On the right-hand side of the hallway, a wide staircase ran up to a galleried landing, where there was a high stained-glass window in ambers and browns and muted blues. It depicted two hooded monks in prayer and a third figure in a thick coat that looked as if it were made of dead stoats and weasels and water-rats, all sewn together, their mouths open, their legs lolling. This figure had its back turned, so that it was impossible to see who it was meant to be.

Sylvia led Martin along the hallway until they reached a large sitting-room at the back of the house. It was wallpapered and furnished in brown, with two dull landscapes on the walls. Here sat three others – two men and a woman. They turned around as Martin came in, and one of them, a silver-haired man in a baggy brown cardigan, stood up and held out his hand. The other man remained where he was, black-haired, with deep black rings under his eyes, hunched in his big worn-out armchair. The woman was standing by the window with a cup of milky coffee in her hand. She was so thin that she was almost transparent.

"Geoffrey," said the silver-haired man, shaking Martin's hand. "But you can call me Sticky, my dear Mary always did. Ardent stamp-collector, that's why."

"Sticky – the stamp-collector who came unhinged," put in the black-haired man, in a West Country accent.

Sticky gave Martin a tight little smile. "This is Terence. Sometimes Terence is extremely cordial but most of the time Terence is extremely offensive. Still, we've learned to take him as he comes."

"What he means is, they've learned to keep their gobs shut," said Terence.

Sticky ignored him. "Over here – this is Theresa. She used to be a very fine singer, you know. Cheltenham Ladies' Chorus."

Theresa gave Martin an almost imperceptible nod of her head. "It's a pity," said Sticky. "She hasn't sung a single note since she lost her family."

Terence said, "Where's the pity in that? I haven't plowed a single furrow and you haven't stuck in a single stamp, and Sylvia hasn't strung together a single necklace. There has to be a reason for doing things, doesn't there? A reason. And none of us here has a single reason for breathing, let alone singing."

"Come on, Terence," Sticky chided him. "You know we do. You know what we're here for, all of us."

At that moment another door opened on the opposite side of the sitting-room, and a tall man entered, leaning on a walking-stick. He was very thin, almost emaciated, with steel-gray hair scraped back from his forehead, and a nose as sharp as an ax. His eyes were so pale that they looked as if all of the color had been leached out of them by experience and pain. A triangular scar ran across his left cheek and disappeared into his hairline.

He wore a black double-breasted suit with unfashionably flappy lapels. As he walked into the room, Martin had the impression that beneath his clothes, his body was all broken and dislocated. It was the way he balanced and swiveled as he made his way across the carpet.

"Martin," he said, in a voice like glasspaper. "You'll forgive me for not shaking hands."

"Mr Miller," said Martin.

"Tybalt, please. Ridiculously affected name, I know; but my father was an English teacher at a very pretentious boys' primary."

He eased himself into one of the armchairs and propped his stick between his knees. "You must tell us who you have lost, Martin; and how. But before you do, your fellow-sufferers here will tell you why *they* sought the help of The Sympathy Society. Sticky – why don't you start?"

"Silly thing, really," said Sticky, as if he were talking about nothing more traumatic than allowing himself to be bowled lbw in a local cricket match. "I was looking after my grandson for the day. Beautiful little chap. Blond hair. Sturdy little legs. We were going to go down to the beach and look for crabs. I went to get the car out of the garage, and I didn't realize that I'd left the front door open. Little chap followed me, you see. I reversed out of the garage and he was so small that I didn't see him standing behind me. I ran over him. Slowly. And stopped, with the wheel resting on his stomach."

He paused for a moment and took out a clean, neatly pressed handkerchief. "He was lying on the concrete looking up at me. There was blood coming out of his ears but he was still alive. I'll never forget the expression on his face as long as I live. He was so *bewildered*, as if he couldn't understand why this had happened to him. I moved the car off him, but that might have been the wrong thing to do. He died almost at once.

He smiled, but tears were filling his eyes. "Of course, that was the end of everything. My marriage; my family. Do you think my daughter could ever look me in the eye again? I thought of killing myself by putting a plastic bag over my head. I nearly succeeded, but a friend of mine stopped me just in time. And I was glad. Suffocating like that – that was the coward's way out."

"Sylvia?" said Tybalt.

Sylvia stared at the floor and spoke in a hurried monotone. "My husband Ron was all I ever wanted in the whole world. He was loving and kind and generous and he was always bringing me flowers. He was a firefighter. About nine weeks ago he went out on a shout in Bromley. Paint factory on fire. He was the first in, as usual. His nickname was Bonkers because he was always rushing into things without thinking.

"He kicked open a door just as a tank of paint-stripping gel blew up. He was covered in it, from head to foot. The coroner said it had the same effect as napalm. It stuck to him, and it cremated him alive. He was screaming and screaming and trying to get it off him, but there was nothing that any of his mates could do. Two of them had to take early retirement with post-traumatic stress disorder. And me? I missed Ron so much that it was like a physical pain. I wandered around like a zombie for the first few weeks. I walked in front of buses, hoping that they wouldn't stop. I thought of pills. I bought two hundred paracetamol from different chemists. But then I thought, no. That's not the way. That's when I saw the ad for The Sympathy Society. And rang. And here I am."

"Your turn, Terence," said Tybalt.

Terence didn't say anything at first, but cracked his knuckles one by one. Theresa, at the window, winced with exaggerated sensitivity at every crack.

"Come on Terence," Tybalt coaxed him. "Martin needs to know what happened to you."

"Farming accident," said Terence, at last. "There's a kind of plow called a disk plow. It's got steel disks instead of shares. Ours got jammed last year, and my sister tried to fix it. It decided to unjam itself when she was right underneath. Dragged her halfway through it. She called for help for two hours before she died. I was plowing in the next field and I couldn't hear her. The doctor said he'd never seen anybody suffer such terrible injuries and stay alive for so long. Half her face was torn off and one of her legs was twisted around backward, so that the foot was pointing the other way.

"After the funeral I went home and I took out my shotgun. I sat in the parlor for nearly an hour with the barrel in my mouth. But I think I knew all the time that I wasn't going to do it."

There was another long pause and it became obvious that Terence wasn't going to say any more than that. "Theresa?" said Tybalt.

Theresa gave a wan smile. Without turning away from the window, she said, "It's extraordinary how your life can be heaven one second and hell the next. Just like that, without any warning at all. We were on holiday in Cornwall, my husband Tom and I and our daughter Emma. It was a beautiful, beautiful day. The sun was shining. The breeze was blowing off the sea. We went for a walk on the cliffs. Tom and I were holding hands and Emma was running all around us. Then suddenly she was gone. Vanished. We were frantic. We thought she'd fallen over the cliff, and we searched and searched but there was no sign of her anywhere. Not on the rocks. Not on the beach. It was just as if she'd vaporized; as if she'd never existed.

"I can't describe the panic I felt. Tom called the police and the coastguard, and they searched, too.

They had tracker dogs out, helicopters, everything. I overheard them saying things like, 'She'll probably be back on the five o'clock tide, three miles down the coast.' Tom was wonderful. He kept telling me that she was probably playing some silly game, and that she'd soon turn up, teasing us for being so worried.

"But she wasn't playing some silly game, and she didn't turn up. We did an appeal on television. You might even remember it. Somebody said they had seen her in Fowey, with a strange man in a raincoat. But that was all a mistake.

"A little Jack Russell terrier found Emma, in the end. She had fallen down a natural chimney in the ground, nearly sixty feet down, and so narrow that she was completely wedged, and scarcely able to breathe. The post-mortem showed that it had taken her five days to die."

"Tom went out the next day and it was only when I was putting away the ironing that I found the letter he had left me. It was too late by then. He had hanged himself in a lock-up garage in Ealing.

"Everybody was so kind. Once or twice my sister nearly persuaded me that it was worth going on, that life could still be worth living. I took too many pills, but I washed them down with vodka, and I was sick. I thought of cutting my wrists, they say you have to do it from wrist to elbow, don't they, so that nobody can stop the bleeding before you die. But what happens when you take pills? You fall asleep, and that's it. And what happens when you cut your wrists? You gradually lose consciousness. You don't stay wedged in a hole in the ground for five days, slowly dying of thirst and starvation, looking at the little circle of daylight sixty feet above you and wondering why your parents haven't come to rescue you. You don't suffer, as Emma must have suffered. You don't lose your faith in the people who are supposed to be taking care of you."

She stopped in mid-flow, and lifted one hand, as if she were trying to attract the attention of somebody in the garden. But there was nobody there. Only the overgrown bushes, and the apple trees heavy with half-rotten Worcesters.

Martin turned to Tybalt, and Tybalt raised one eyebrow, as if he were asking him if he was beginning to understand what was happening here, at The Sympathy Society. Martin looked from Theresa to Sylvia, and then at Sticky, who was making a show of folding up his handkerchief again.

"Martin?" said Tybalt. "Why don't you tell us *your* story?"

Later in the evening, they sat in the kitchen and ate a supper of chicken casserole with green peppers, and home-made bread – prepared, said Tybalt, by "Mrs Pearce . . . such a dear person . . .

she comes up from the village." The atmosphere at dinner was strained. Terence was twitchy and obnoxious. Sylvia couldn't stop dabbing her eyes and her nose with her paper napkin. Theresa wouldn't eat anything, except for a tiny nibble of bread, and Sticky was deeply distracted, as if he were thinking about something else altogether.

During the cheese course (when the table was messy with crumbs and stripped-off sticks of celery) Tybalt scraped back his chair and said, "Martin – you've realized by now what we're doing here, haven't you?"

"I'm not sure," said Martin. "I think perhaps I'm missing something."

"Understatement of the year," put in Terence.

Tybalt ignored him. "We're not here to cry for you, Martin; or mollycoddle you; or make you believe that life has to go on. What a fallacy that is! Life doesn't have to go on, if you don't want it to. Where were you, before you were born? You weren't anywhere. You didn't exist. In the same way, you won't exist after you're dead. There's no heaven, Martin. There isn't any hell. But there is one thing: in the instant when you die, there's *revelation*."

"Revelation?" Martin was used to being the center of attention, and he didn't like the way that Tybalt dominated the whole room, and everybody in it.

"Revelation like the Book of Revelations," said Terence. "Revelation like the scales falling from your eyes."

Tybalt smiled. "When you're dead, you're dead. That's all there is to it. Blackness, nothingness, that's it. We all know it, even if we're scared to admit it. But I believe there's a split-second, when you die, that you see the world as it really is. We probably see it when we're born, too. Why do you think babies cry, when they first come out of the womb? But babies forget; and babies can't tell us what they've seen."

"Neither can dead people," said Martin.

"Well, you're right there. Nobody comes back. But these days, there is a way to record what people are seeing, in their mind's eye. When people think, electrical impulses jump from one synapse to the other, inside of the brain. And we can catch those electrical impulses and record them, just like a DVD disk."

"What are you trying to tell me? That you can record what's happening inside of other people's brains?"

Tybalt nodded; and nodded. "You've got it, Martin. That's exactly what we can do. The technology is still in its infancy, but we've managed to recover five or six minutes of footage of living brain activity; and at least six seconds of post-mortem activity. We can see what people are thinking about, when they die."

He stopped for a moment, to light up a cigarette. Then he waved away the smoke, and said, "We can record those last split-seconds of human life. We can record it in pictures and sound, DVD no problem. The entire technology has been in place since 1996. What it needed was the will to make it work."

"And you think that *you* have that will?" asked Martin.

"Not me, you. You're the only one who can show us what happens when you go to meet your Maker. You and Terence, and Sylvia, and Sticky, and Theresa. You're the only people who can make this work."

Martin said nothing. He was beginning to grasp the enormity of what Tybalt was saying, but he needed to hear it spelled out. Tybalt said, "I have my suits tailored, but I'm a physical mess. When I was twenty-four, I borrowed my friend's motorcycle and took my girlfriend for a ride along the Kingston bypass. We went through the New Malden underpass at 125mph, and then I lost it. She came off the pillion and flew right over the central reservation, straight into the front of a Securicor van. I tumbled nearly half-a-mile down the road in front of me, and smashed up everything that was smashable. Ribs, pelvis, arms, legs, ankles. I was like a jelly filled with bits of bone. And I died. I lay there on the road, dead. And when I was dead, I saw something. Only for a few seconds. But I saw the world as it really was. Not the way we imagine it, when we're alive. *I saw the world as it really was.*"

"But you survived," said Martin.

Tybalt shrugged, and tapped his stick. "Yes, I survived. By good or bad fortune, an ambulance was passing, and they took me straight to Kingston Hospital. They thought I was past saving. They gave me so many electric shocks that they burned my nipples off. But after the seventh shock, I started to breathe; and I have never stopped breathing since.

"All the same, I know what I saw, after that accident, and I don't believe that it was shock that caused me to see it, or concussion, or psychological trauma. As I lay in the road, Martin, I saw things that would make your hair stand on end."

"So what are you saying to me?" asked Martin.

"I'm saying nothing. But you listened to all of your fellow society members this afternoon, didn't you? They're all bereaved, just as you are. None of them want to carry on without their family or their partners. They all want to die. But none of them want to kill themselves with tablets, or exhaust fumes, or by cutting their wrists. When they die, they want to feel what their loved ones felt. They want to suffer in the same way. Sylvia wants to burn; Sticky wants to be crushed; Theresa wants to be trapped below ground. This will be their redemption.

"You know what I'm talking about, Martin. How many mornings have you lain awake and thought about Sarah, and what she felt like, when that steel wire cut off her head? You want to experience that too, don't you, Martin? – or else you wouldn't have answered my advertisement. The Sympathy Society isn't the Samaritans. The Sympathy Society *really* sympathizes. We'll give you what you're craving for. The same death that your loved one suffered."

Martin's mouth was totally dry. "You'll do that – you'll burn Sylvia? You'll trap Theresa under the ground?"

Tybalt nodded. "Nobody else understands, Martin, but I do. You want to die. But trying to cut your throat with a steak knife . . . that doesn't even compare, does it? What did Sarah feel? After her head was cut off, did she still *think* for a second or two? Did she see her body, still speeding along on that jet-ski, with blood pumping out of her neck? You want to know that, don't you, Martin?"

Martin cleared his throat, and nodded.

Tybalt leaned forward and touched his knee with chalky fingernails. "The Sympathy Society can arrange for you to be killed in any way you choose. There's only one thing we ask in return. We need to record your impressions with synaptic monitors . . . we need to see what you see, think what you think, the instant you die. I saw something terrible when I lay on the road after my motorcycle accident, and I need to know whether I was hallucinating or not."

"What did you see?" asked Martin.

Tybalt shook his head. "I don't want to put any ideas in your head. Besides, if I tell you, you won't want to be killed at all."

"I want to die," said Martin. "I want you to cut off my head, and kill me. I need to know what Sarah went through. I need to know exactly what she felt like."

"There you are," said Tybalt, with unexpected gentleness. "That's why we call ourselves The Sympathy Society."

The following morning was chilly and overcast, and inside the house it was so gloomy that they had to switch the lights on. They gathered for breakfast in the kitchen, although Martin couldn't manage anything more than a cup of coffee. Sylvia sat at the head of the table, her hair all pinned up. She looked even paler than usual, and there were dark circles under her eyes. Around her neck hung a small silver crucifix.

At half past eight, Tybalt came in through the garden door. He was wearing a long black overcoat with the collar turned up. "Well," he said, chafing his hands together. "Everything's ready, Sylvia, if you are."

Sylvia set down her teacup. She looked around the table, at each of them, although she didn't smile. "I don't like goodbyes," she said. "Anyway, we're all going to meet again, aren't we?"

Theresa reached across the table and took hold of her hand. There were tears in her eyes. "I envy you," she said. "You don't know how much I envy you."

Tybalt said, "None of you have to come out and watch. This is Sylvia's moment, after all. But if you want to be with her, I'm sure she'll appreciate it."

Sylvia stood up. She was wearing a plain green linen dress, and she was barefoot. Tybalt went back out into the garden and she followed him, leaving the door ajar.

Theresa said, "I'm not going. I can't." Terence didn't say anything, but made no move to get up from the table. Sticky went through to the hallway and came back with his brown tweed overcoat and his checkered scarf. "I'm going. Poor girl deserves somebody there. Terrible thing, to die on your own."

"*Don't*," said Theresa. Sticky laid an apologetic hand on her shoulder. "Sorry . . . didn't mean it like that."

Martin didn't know whether he wanted to witness Sylvia's death or not; but Sticky said, "Come on, old boy. You never know. When you see this, you might change your mind."

They went out into the garden. The grass was wet underfoot and dew was clinging to the branches of the apple-trees. Martin was shivering, and it wasn't because of the cold. In the far corner of the garden stood a dilapidated shed with broken windows, and just in front of it, Sylvia was already kneeling on the ground. Tybalt was standing over her, taping electrodes to her temples with silver fireproof tape. A little distance away stood an old metal table with a PC standing on it, and a collection of equipment for recording Sylvia's heart-rate and brain activity.

Martin and Sticky stopped and stood at a respectful distance, close to one of the trees. A robin perched on the fence close by, beadily watching them. Sylvia looked so plain and pale she reminded Martin of St Joan, about to be burned at the stake. But her expression was completely calm, and her eyes were lifted toward the sky, as if she were quite prepared for what was going to happen to her. As if she were quietly looking forward to it.

It took nearly ten minutes for Tybalt to fix the last electrode, and Martin was beginning to lose his nerve. "I think I'll go back inside," he told Sticky. But Sticky took hold of his hand, and gripped it tight, and wouldn't let it go. "You're best staying," he said.

Tybalt went across to the metal table and switched on his PC and his recording equipment. Then he went to the shed and came back with a large blue petrol-can. He told Sylvia to cover her face with her hands, and then he unscrewed the lid and poured the contents all over the top of her head. Sylvia shuddered, and let out a muffled, high-pitched *ah*! It wasn't petrol. It was a thick, greenish gel, which dripped slowly down her neck and over her shoulders. Martin could smell it, even from twenty feet away. It was paint-stripper, and it must have been searing the exposed skin on Sylvia's hands and neck already.

Tybalt's expression was grim, and he worked as quickly as he could.

He picked up a large paintbrush and smeared the gel all down Sylvia's dress, back and front, and over her legs. She was trembling in agony already, but she kept her hands pressed over her face, and the only sound she made was a thin, repetitive *"eeeshh – eeeshh – eeeshh—"* But the pain that she was suffering was nothing to the pain she would be suffering next.

Without any hesitation, Tybalt took a cigarette lighter out of his pocket, and snapped it into flame.

"Are you absolutely sure you want to do this?" he asked her, in a voice so quiet that Martin could scarcely hear him.

With her hands still clamped over her face, Sylvia nodded. Tybalt lit the top of her piled-up hair, and instantly her head burst into flame.

Martin jolted with shock, but Sticky kept gripping his hand. He had never seen anybody burn before, and it was so horrific that he couldn't believe what he was looking at. Sylvia's hair caught fire in a whirl of tiny sparks, and then her ears shriveled and curled over like blackened bacon-rinds. She kept her hands over her face even though the tips of her fingers were alight. But then the fumes from the paint-stripper exploded with the softest *whoomph* and she was completely buried in flames.

Martin couldn't understand how she could bear the pain without moving. The flames were so fierce that he could hardly see her, only her blackening elbows and her scarlet-charred feet. But then she threw open her hands and screamed the most terrible scream that he had ever heard in his life. It wasn't just a scream of agony, it was a scream of total despair.

Sylvia tried to stagger on to her feet. Martin instinctively tried to move forward to help her, but Sticky held him back. "It's what she wants, man! It's what she came here for!"

Sylvia toppled sideways on to the grass, with flames literally pouring out of her face. She opened and closed her mouth two or three times, but her lungs were too burned for her to scream again. The flames ate through her dress and turned the flesh on her thighs into charcoal. She quivered, as her nerve-endings were burned, but eventually she stopped quivering and it was clear that she was dead. Thick smoke rose into the gray morning sky, and the smell of roasted meat brought a surge of bile into Martin's throat.

Tybalt switched off his equipment and approached them gravely. "I think she understood what her husband went through. I hope so."

"Did you record anything?" asked Martin.

"I won't know till later, when I analyze all of the images."

"I wouldn't like to think that she died like that for nothing."

"She didn't die for nothing. She died because she's a human being, and human beings should have the choice to die in any way they want to. You haven't changed your mind, have you?"

Martin thought about Sarah speeding toward the cable. "No," he said. "I haven't changed my mind. But I wouldn't want to burn, like Sylvia did."

They went back into the house. Theresa was sitting in the corner, in tears. Terence was hunched in his chair, saying nothing.

"She's gone," said Sticky, unnecessarily. "A good girl, a very brave ending."

Later that evening, Martin knocked on the door of Tybalt's study. Tybalt was sitting in front of his PC, frowning at the blurry, silvery-gray images that danced on the screen. As soon as Martin came in, he switched it off.

"Anything?" asked Martin.

Tybalt shook his head. "Not so far. It's too soon to tell. There's a lot of filtering to do, a lot of enhancing. But I think I caught *something* today."

Martin hesitated. Tybalt appeared tense, and anxious for him to go, as if he had recorded some images from Sylvia's last agonized seconds of life that he didn't want to discuss.

"Of course – as soon as I come up with anything . . ." Tybalt began.

Martin nodded. Then he said, "Who's next?"

"Theresa. Hers will take the longest, of course. There's an old dry well, right at the end of the garden, beyond the orchard. I had it bored deeper, fifty feet or so. She's going to go down tomorrow morning."

"Isn't anybody going to miss us? What about our bodies? Aren't you worried about the police?"

Tybalt gave a small, secretive smile. "By the time the police come looking, The Sympathy Society will have moved to pastures new. And everyone here has written a letter, explaining that they have taken their own lives. As will you, when your turn comes."

"Yes," said Martin, at last.

Theresa dropped herself down the dry well at the end of the garden just after dawn the following day. It was drizzling slightly, and her hair was stuck wetly to her forehead. They kissed her, each of them, before she went. She was obviously frightened, but she was smiling.

Tybalt attached the last electrodes to her forehead, with reels of cable so that he could monitor her alpha-rhythms right down at the bottom of the well. She knelt down in the brambly grass, and then, quite abruptly, she slithered out of sight.

They heard her cry out. "My leg! I think I've broken my leg!" But they didn't answer, and she didn't cry out again. She had chosen to suffer the same death as her daughter, and her daughter had broken her left wrist and her collarbone, when she fell.

There was nothing more to do. They walked through the orchard and back to the house.

Three days later, it was Terence's turn. Tybalt had arranged to hire a tractor fitted with a disk plow. It was delivered to the top of the lane that ran down the side of the house, and Terence himself drove it down to the paddock past the orchard. He whistled as he steered it on to the grass. For the first time since Martin had met him, he seemed cheerful and contented.

This was one death that Martin really didn't want to witness. But, again, Sticky insisted. They walked to the paddock by way of the orchard, and Martin stood for a while by the well, listening. Theresa had insisted that nobody should peer down the well to see how she was, because that would mean that she wasn't completely forgotten, the way her daughter had been forgotten.

He listened, but he heard nothing. Tybalt had checked this morning and said that she was still alive, but "very, very weak."

The tractor was parked beside the paddock gate, with its engine chugging over. Terence was already lying underneath the plow, between its shining circular disks. He was stripped to the waist, with Tybalt's electrodes fastened to his forehead. He caught sight of Martin and Sticky making their way across the grass, and he gave them an elated thumb's up.

Martin went up and hunkered down next to him. "Are you all right?" he asked him.

"Couldn't be better. I've been looking forward to this. You don't know how much."

"Aren't you frightened at all?"

"Frightened? What of? Pain? Dying? If we were all frightened of pain and dying, we'd all sit at home with a blanket over our heads, wouldn't we?"

Tybalt came over. "Are you ready, Terence? This is what you really want?"

Terence's eyes were bright. "Come on, Mr Miller. Let's get this over with. The sooner the better."

Tybalt reached out and touched Terence's lips with the tips of his fingers, as if he were a cardinal giving benediction. Then he stood up and said, "Better stand clear, Martin."

He went to the tractor and climbed into the cab. He revved the engine two or three times, and each time Terence grinned in anticipation. Then, with no further warning, he engaged the plow.

"*Oh, Christ!*" shrieked Terence. The shining steel disks dragged him in like gristle into an old-fashioned meat mincer. His right arm was crushed into a bloody rope of bones and thin white tendons, and twisted around the spindle. Another disk cut diagonally into his shoulder and opened up his chest, so that one of his lungs blew out like a balloon. His groin was minced into bloody rags, and his legs were twisted in opposite directions.

The plow-blades stopped. Martin could see Terence's head wedged against one of the disks. His eyes were wide with exhilaration.

He tried to say something, but all that came out from between his lips was a large bubble of blood, which wetly burst. His eyes slowly lost their focus, and he died.

Although Terence's death was so grisly, Martin was strangely elated by it. It was the expression on his face, as if he had found at last what he had always been looking for – as if he would have laughed, if he had been able to.

*   *   *

The following Saturday, inside the garage, Tybalt slowly reversed a Mercedes saloon over Sticky's stomach. Martin stayed outside, but he heard Sticky sobbing in pain for almost twenty minutes, and a single runnel of blood crept out from underneath the closed garage doors, and soaked into the pea-shingle.

"Have you seen anything yet?" he asked Tybalt, as the two of them sat over supper the following evening.

Tybalt poured himself another glass of Fleurie. "Not yet," he said evasively. "But you will, won't you? It's your turn tomorrow."

Martin didn't sleep that night. He sat on the end of the bed staring at his reflection in the dressing-room mirror and wondering if he were mad. Yet somehow, it seemed the most perfect and logical way to go. Even if he didn't meet Sarah in the afterlife, at least he would have shared the same death.

At seven o'clock, Tybalt knocked discreetly on his bedroom door and asked him if he were ready.

It had been impossible to find a lake or a reservoir where they could moor two boats close together and stretch a steel line between them. So Tybalt had devised a substitute: a motorcycle, and a wire tied at neck-level between two substantial horse-chestnut trees.

It was a sharp, sunny morning. They walked together down to the paddock, with Martin pushing the motorcycle.

"I haven't been on a bike for years," he told Tybalt. What he was trying to say was: I hope I don't make a mess of this, and blind myself, or cut half my face off, instead of dying instantly.

Tybalt said, "You'll be fine. Just make sure you're going full-throttle."

He sat patiently in the saddle while Tybalt attached the electrodes. "It's funny," he said. "I feel really at peace."

"Yes," said Tybalt. "Death is a good place to go to, when you understand what life really is."

"So what *is* life, really?"

"Life is mostly imaginary. That's what I saw when I nearly died, coming off that motorbike. Our imagination always protects us from ugliness, and unhappiness, and fear. We have a gift for rationalizing our existence, to make it seem bearable. We're always looking on the bright side."

"It's human nature," said Martin.

"No, no. You don't realize what I'm talking about when I say 'imaginary.' I mean that our lives as we know them and recognize them are mostly in our minds. You'll see, believe me. Beauty is imaginary. Happiness is imaginary."

"I was happy with Sarah."

"You *imagined* you were happy with Sarah."

"I just don't follow."

Tybalt stuck on the last electrode. "I can't explain it any more clearly than that. You'll just have to experience it for yourself."

"No – tell me!"

Tybalt shook his head. "If I told you, Martin, you wouldn't believe me. This is something you have to witness for yourself. Now, start up your engine, and think of Sarah. Think how *she* felt."

Martin took a deep breath. It was plain that Tybalt wasn't going to explain himself any further. All the same, what he had said had given Martin a strange feeling of dread, as if there were something far worse beyond those horse-chestnut trees than instant oblivion.

He pressed the self-starter, and the motorcycle whined into life. Tybalt leaned close to him and said, "You're still sure about this? You can change your mind . . . go home, build a new life. I won't think any the less of you."

Go home to what? A silent flat, with Sarah's clothes still hanging in the closet? Years of grief, and loneliness?

"The recording wires will play out behind you," said Tybalt. "Don't worry about them. Go as fast as you can. And keep your chin up."

Martin revved the motorcycle again and again. The sun began to come out behind the trees, and the morning looked almost heavenly. At last he thought: this is the moment. This is it. The dew was glittering and a flight of starlings came bursting past. You couldn't leave the world at a better time.

The motorcycle sped across the paddock. Martin thought of Sarah, on her jet-ski. He could see the two horse-chestnuts but he couldn't even see the wire yet. It must have been the same for Sarah. Perhaps she didn't see it at all. He opened the throttle wider and the motorcycle bucked and jostled over the grass at more than fifty miles an hour. The breeze fluffed in his ears; the sun shone in his eyes. Chin up, remember.

He felt the blow. It was like a tremendous karate-chop to the adam's apple. He heard the motorcycle roaring off-key, and then suddenly everything was spinning out of control. His head hit the grass, and bounced, and he *saw*, he could actually *see*.

And he understood then what Tybalt had been trying to tell him, and why Tybalt had been trying so hard to see what only the dying can see.

He couldn't scream, because he was decapitated, and his brain was a split-second instant away from total death. But he could scream inside his mind. And that was how he died, screaming.

Tybalt sat alone in the house in front of his computer, running the recordings again and again. Martin's was one of the clearest. He could see him approaching the horse-chestnut trees. At the last second, he could see the wire.

Then – as Martin's head flew from his body – he saw what he himself had seen when he nearly died on the Kingston bypass.

He saw the polluted yellow sky, with tattered rooks circling everywhere. He saw gnarled and shriveled trees, and grass as slimy as seaweed. He saw a distant house with a sagging roof, and fires burning in the distance. He saw hideous, hunched creatures running along the lane. He even glimpsed a brief blurred image of himself, the way he really was.

A tall, white-faced figure, distant and sinister, with frightening deformities.

He switched off the computer and went downstairs. He opened the back door and stepped out into the garden. The sun was still shining – or, at least, it was still shining in his imagination. He lit a cigarette.

A cat came stalking through the grass. It stopped for a moment, and stared at him, almost as if it instinctively knew what he had discovered with technology: that it was not a tortoiseshell with gray eyes and gleaming fur, but something grotesque, like he was, and that both of them were living in a hell on earth.

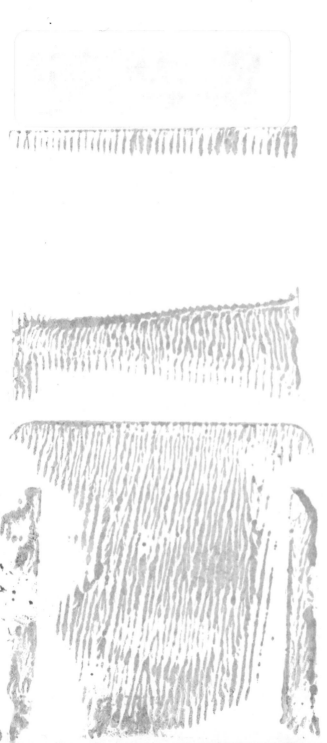